MURDER AT MORLAND MANOR

MARILYN CLAY

**A JULIETTE ABBOTT
REGENCY MYSTERY**

Book One

MURDER AT MORLAND MANOR
Book One of the Juliette Abbott Regency Mystery Series
A Regency Plume Press Publication

Copyright © July 2016 by Marilyn Jean Clay

All Rights Reserved.

Printed in the United States of America
ISBN-10: 1530422744
ISBN-13: 978-1530422746

The Primary Players – In Order of Appearance

Juliette Abbott – A seven and ten year-old girl who has come to stay with her cousin in the English countryside after the titled lady to whom she was employed as paid companion suddenly passed away, setting Juliette adrift.

Nancy Jane Abbott – Juliette's country cousin, who is employed as a chambermaid at Morland Manor.

Lady Morland – Wife of Sir Robert Morland, a wealthy English baronet. In the English title system, a baronet is addressed as Sir, but he is not a true peer of the realm. A baronet's title was either sold by the British Crown to fund something, such as a war, or could be granted to reward or recognize a gentleman for some service performed to the king, his political party, or country. Despite the new baronet being a wealthy man, his money was likely made in trade, as in the case of Sir Morland, therefore men of his ilk were not deemed of sufficient consequence to clutter up the House of Lords, so along with his title he was not granted a seat in Parliament.

Miss Caroline Featherstone – Seventeen year-old daughter of a baronet, and one of the five young ladies invited to the house party at Morland Manor. Daughters of a baronet are addressed as Miss, rather than Lady.

Mrs. Alice Collins – Miss Caroline Featherstone's older, married sister, of indeterminate age, who acts as Caroline's chaperone.

Lady Sedgwick – wife of the Earl of Sedgwick, mother and chaperone of her eighteen-year-old daughter, the Lady Sophia, who was also invited to the house party at Morland Manor. Being the wife of an earl makes Lady Sedgwick a countess and therefore the highest-ranking peer present at Morland Manor; higher ranking than her host, Lady Morland.

Lady Sophia – the eighteen-year-old daughter of the Earl and Countess of Sedgwick. To be entirely correct, Lady Sophia should be referred to as "the" Lady Sophia. Think of Carson when he referred to "the Lady Mary" in Downton Abbey. When reading a book this usage can often become cumbersome, therefore at times I have taken the liberty of deleting the "the" when referring to Lady Sophia. Lady Sophia's lady's maid is Lucy.

Miss Amelia Durham – daughter of the Right Honorable Baron Abernathy. A Baron occupies the bottom rung of the British Peerage system. Titled gentleman generally have both a title name and a family name; in this case Abernathy is the title name, Durham is the family name, which is the surname the Baron's children use. Miss Durham's chaperone is an elderly aunt Mrs. Throckmorton; her lady's maid is named Tilly.

Meg – Lady's maid to Miss Hester Grant.

Miss Hester Grant – daughter of the Right Honorable Baron Stanhope. Miss Grant's chaperone is her mother, Lady Stanhope. Although the bottom rank in the British title system, a Baron is a *bona fide* peer of the Realm, therefore his wife is addressed as Lady <title name> in this case Stanhope, while his children use the family surname. Miss Grant's lady's maid is Meg.

Miss Elizabeth Banes – daughter of the Viscount Wentworth, her mother is The Right Honorable Viscountess Wentworth, addressed as Lady Wentworth. A Viscount's daughter is addressed simply as Miss <family name>, in this case Banes. Miss Banes' lady's maid is Rosie.

Mr. Edward Morland – the two and twenty year-old second son of the wealthy baronet, Sir Morland and his wife, Lady Morland.

Mr. Philip Talbot – an unmarried gentleman friend of the aforementioned second son, Mr. Edward Morland. Both gentlemen reside in London.

Mr. William Morland – the unmarried five and twenty year-old eldest son of Sir and Lady Morland, often referred to in this story as "the heir". Being the eldest son, William is heir to the entire Morland estate, which includes all of Sir Robert Morland's business enterprises, all of his land and wealth. For the heir to choose a wife is the sole reason for the house party at Morland Manor.

Lesser Players

Temple Bradley – the elderly lady's maid to Lady Morland.

Reginald and Henry Morland – cousins of the Morland brothers.

Constable Wainwright – Constable in the nearby village of Thornbury.

Doctor Morgan – the village doctor, and Official Medical Examiner.

Griggs – the butler at Morland Manor.

Mrs. Fullerton – the Morland Manor housekeeper.

CHAPTER 1

A Fortnight In The Country? Oh, No . . .

Thornbury, England

Saturday, 14 October 1820

"It will only be for a fortnight, Juliette," declared my cousin Nancy Jane, a girl of six and ten, a year below the advanced age I have attained of seven and ten.

"But, I know nothing about being a lady's maid," I replied. The pair of us were seated on a rickety wooden bench just outside the door of the Abbott farmhouse on a sunny Autumn day in the year 1820. I'd only been here in the English countryside two full days and already Nancy Jane was trying to persuade me to come to work alongside her up at Morland Manor, the big fancy house on the hill.

"All ye' needs to know is how to bob a curtsy and say 'Yes m'lady' and 'No, m'lady' and 'As ye wish, m'lady.' The rest of the time, ye' jest keeps your eyes on the floor and don't speak out of turn." Nancy Jane paused, then added, "Of course, for you, that will likely prove the difficult part."

I gave her a look. As I said, I had only just come to stay with my aunt and uncle way out here in the countryside, far from any place truly civilized, even if you count the tiny hamlet of Thornbury, which we toured in less than a quarter hour the day before yesterday when I alighted from the mail coach. Journey here from London had taken two full days and nights, so my bones was pretty near shaken to bits when I climbed down from the coach and set foot upon solid earth again.

I had traveled all the way out here because the lady for whom I'd been employed as a paid companion up in London had suddenly stuck her spoon in the wall and I had no where else to go, both my parents having gone on to their rewards when I was a wee lass of ten. Before today, I'd always thought of Nancy Jane as my poor relation but now the tables had turned. She was the one with a home and a post and . . . me? I'd been cast adrift with only a few pennies in my pocket and nowhere to turn. Truth to say, I was having a bit of a time growing accustomed to this change in my circumstances and hadn't yet fully accepted this unexpected turn fate had dealt me.

But, being the resourceful sort I am, meaning I fancied I could get along on my wits alone if need be, I expected things would improve quite soon. When Lady What's-It passed on and her Last Will and Testament was read, her niece had kindly relayed to me that her aunt had stipulated that I was to receive ten pounds! *A veritable fortune!* I never expected to see that much money in the whole of my life. And, truth to tell, I hadn't yet seen it. But, Lady What's-It's niece said that when the funds were released, she'd send my share on to me. In the meantime, she kindly advanced me enough money to take the Mail Coach all the way out here to Thornbury.

Just as soon as I receive my inheritance, however, I have already decided to take myself off to Bath and enroll in the fine Academy for Young Ladies I've heard tell of there and get myself some decent book-learning and polish, then I'll hire myself out as a governess. Should be able to make a fine living teaching other folk's wee ones. Got all the Town Bronze I need whilst living up in London with Lady What's-It. (*Don't want to say her name aloud now she's gone, since that would likely rain more bad luck down on my head.*)

Truth is, I'd already had some schooling; way more'n Nancy Jane, make no mistake. I can read and write and even cipher. Not sure she can do either. When I lived up in London, her ladyship had often asked me to read aloud to her, mainly because she said the soothing sound of my voice lulled her to sleep. Still, I own I do need to know more about fine lit'rature; what Lady What's-It called the *classics*, and how to play the pianoforte a good deal better than I do now. It would also be nice to be able to perform the fancier dance steps that I remember seeing Lady What's-It's niece and her fine lady friends do whilst I was in Town. Therefore, in the very near future, I will, indeed, set off for Bath.

Because I sure couldn't stay here for long. Although my aunt and uncle's family do fit snugly within the four walls of their sturdy little farmhouse, adding another grown body (mine) to the mix is stretching the rafters a bit. To them I'm just another mouth to feed and truth to tell, I never wished to be a burden to anyone, least of all to my Aunt and Uncle Abbott. Which is why, right off, I insisted on paying for my keep whilst I'm here. Aunt Jane's eyes popped wide open when I handed her a whole shilling the day I arrived. Was very nearly all I had left after the coach trip here. I'd had no notion how costly travel could be these days, what with purchasing a bite to eat when the coach stopped and sleeping over; then, tipping this one and that one wherever you happen to be. Surprised me how everyone seemed to have a hand out and expected other folks to fill it.

In the two days I've been here, I've discovered another little-known fact, about myself. Turns out, clean, country air is just a little too *fresh*-smelling to my nose. Give me the foul odours and rackety sounds of bustling London-town any day. I far prefer the clatter of carriage wheels on cobblestones to that of birds chirping in the treetops. Far too peaceful out here for my blood. Fact is, I may have to stir things up myself a bit just to add some spice to m'life whilst I'm stuck here in the middle of nowhere.

"Well?" Nancy Jane prodded for an answer to her question. "Shall I tell Mrs. Fullerton, she's the housekeeper up at the Manor House, that you said you'd do it? I tol' her I 'spected you'd jump at the chance, seeing as how you was without a post and all."

I brought my thoughts back to the present. "Tell me again why Lady Morland is hosting a big to-do now? With wintertime just around the corner, who'd want to come all the way out here *now*? Won't be anything to do once snow covers the ground." *Not much to do now* without *snow on the ground.*

Nancy Jane huffed. "You wasn't listenin' to me, was you, Juliette? You was a'wool gatherin' agin, wasn't ya'?"

My lips firmed. "I was *not* wool gathering, Nancy Jane. I was thinking . . . deep thoughts." I thrust my chin up. "Such as the likes of you would never understand."

Of course, my cousin was a sweet and kind girl, but of the two of us, I'd always been the one with aspirations to better myself. Nancy Jane had been in service her whole life and thought the entire world revolved around the doings up at the big house on the hill. Every time I met up with her, it was Morland Manor this and Morland Manor that. Poor girl had worked as a chambermaid at Morland Manor since she was twelve, which is when my Mama passed on and when I went to live with my late employer, Lady What's-It.

Nancy Jane's mother, my Aunt Jane, had also worked up at the big house before she married Uncle George, who at the time was already a tenant farmer beholden to the almighty Sir Morland, who owns all the land around here as far as a body can see. Aunt Jane is about wore out now and quit her post to come back home to the farm. Fortunately, her eldest boy, my cousin Jack Abbott has recently married and he and his new wife Betsy now also live here. Jack and the younger boys help my uncle with the crops; Betsy helps Aunt Jane and the two youngest girls (who still live at home) tend to the kitchen garden and the indoor chores. Nancy Jane mostly stays up at Morland Manor. She was home today, due to it being her half-day off.

And despite what she thought, I had been listening to everything she said, but I let her tell me all of it again anyhow. To sum up, Nancy Jane revealed the following: that the talk below-stairs up at the Manor House was that Sir Robert Morland's eldest son William, the heir to his entire estate, seemed bent on gambling away the family fortune and was a wastrel besides. His mother, the baronet's wife, Lady Morland, was now fixing her hopes on the second son carrying on the family name since the heir was likely to get himself kilt afore long. (Nancy Jane's words, not mine.)

"There'd been rumors," she said, "of a duel or two being fought over the heir having spoilt more than one young lady's reputation."

I knew how servants liked to gossip about the families they worked for. Lady What's-It's servants were always gossiping about things they knew nothing of and which were none of their business.

"Well," Nancy Jane concluded. "Will you do it?"

"What I want to know is how much money I'll make."

"I don't know how much money Lady Morland will give you! But whatever it is, it's more than you got now!"

Nancy Jane shifted on the wobbly old bench where we sat just beyond the front door of the thatched-roof farmhouse. Bench had been painted so many times I feared there wasn't any wood left under all those layers of paint. If you tried to chip all the old paint away you'd probably just get down to air. Wood underneath had likely rotted away a century or more ago.

"Stop wiggling," I said, "you'll knock this old bench over. I'm wearing one of my good dresses, I don't want to land in the . . ." I cast a disdainful gaze down at the black earth where our feet rested, me wearing my almost-new, half boots, Nancy Jane in her scuffed-up brown brogues with the frayed laces. I grimaced. I had no idea what awful things were mixed up in the muck and mire down there, but the gaggle of chickens waddling around the yard, the old black dog asleep in the shade next to the pig sty, and the score or more of gray and orange stripped kittens romping around provided a few unsavory clues.

Nancy Jane stilled. "Since you're already a-wearin' your good frock, Juliette, why don't ye' come with me now? I tol' Mrs. Fullerton I'd bring ye' up to the house. We can talk more about it on the way up the hill."

"Oh, all right." I muttered. "I suppose taking a temporary post that won't last more than a fortnight won't hurt. But, make no mistake, I'll not be staying around here much longer than that."

After Griggs the Morland butler had shown me up to the drawing room that sleepy Saturday afternoon, Lady Morland politely greeted me. "I am so pleased to meet you, Miss Abbott, do sit down."

Nancy Jane and I had entered the grand manor home through the servant's entrance at the back of the huge house and the housekeeper, Mrs.

Fullerton had promptly awakened the butler to take me up to meet her ladyship, leaving Nancy Jane below-stairs, I assume to pace and fidget while she waited to hear the outcome of my interview. Why she was so anxious for me to go to work for Lady Morland I did not know.

Upon entering the drawing room, I was not given the leisure to so much as glance about the spacious chamber, although I did see there was another woman present. Near the age of Lady Morland, but not dressed as finely as she, the other lady was seated in a wing-back chair leafing through a lady's magazine. She didn't so much as look up when Griggs showed me in, or when Lady Morland politely acknowledged me.

"I understand you were recently in the employ of Lady Carstairs in London?"

Upon hearing *my* dearly departed ladyship's name said aloud I cringed, but nonetheless managed a tight nod. "That is correct, ma'am."

"I was so sorry to hear of her passing."

The sympathetic look on Lady Morland's face told me her sentiment was sincere and did cause a rush of warmth within me to rise towards her. I confess I still sorely missed Lady What's-It, and also my fine life with her up in London. But, as I'd been told, the past was over and done with and it was time now to move on.

Since I'd entered the elegant Morland drawing room, I'd been trying to keep my eyes downcast but every now and then I risked a peek upward at Lady Morland. For a woman in her middle years, she was quite handsome, even regal-looking. Despite her thick brown hair beginning to gray at the temples, I spotted nary a wrinkle upon her smooth forehead and cheeks. She was quite finely turned out this afternoon in a russet-colored gown, a rope of creamy pearls dangling around her neck, and even more pearls and diamonds gracing her wrists and fingers.

"Lady Carstairs' charitable work in London was legendary," the fine Lady Morland was saying, "even to those of us so far removed from the City."

Far removed from the City was putting it mildly.

"She was very kind to me, m'lady."

"I've no doubt she was." Her ladyship paused as if considering what sort of questions to ask me in order to determine if I was qualified to serve as a lady's maid or not. At length, she said, "I assume your cousin told you I am hosting a small house party, five or six young ladies and their chaperones. Most all the girls will be bringing along their own personal maids, of course, but it has come to my attention that one young lady does not have a maid, which is why I was hoping you would consider filling the post while my guests are here."

When she paused again, I wondered if I was supposed to say something, and if so, what? When I couldn't think of anything, I simply nodded and looked back down again. Because I'd been staring at the floor since I got here, I noticed now how very plush and fine the carpet was beneath my feet. The burgundy and blue flowers set against a creamy background reminded me of . . . of the fine carpet gracing the floor in Lady What's-It's drawing room. Feeling a rush of moisture well in my eyes, I quickly blinked it away. To reside here would certainly be a far sight better than resting my feet in the muck and mire surrounding the farmhouse. Or inside it, for all that.

"I suppose I should apprise you of the sort of duties that will be expected of you as a lady's maid. Mainly you will attend to your mistress's clothing, see that her outer and under garments are kept clean and fresh, and if necessary, mended. As I'm certain you know, the occasional rent or tear in a hem is quite a common occurrence. I trust you are clever with a needle and thread."

I nodded tightly. *'Clever' might be overstating it a bit, but I could mend something if the task didn't require much in the way of expertise.*

"You will of course assist with your mistress' toilette every morning, then once she has gone down to breakfast, you will be free to repair to the kitchen for your own morning meal, which is taken in the servant's quarters with the rest of the household staff. If your mistress has left word that she wishes to change her clothes for luncheon, you will return upstairs to lay out the fresh garments for her, or if there is a special outing planned for the afternoon, you will help her into whatever frock she chooses to don for the afternoon."

She paused, then added, "I do plan to keep my guests well-entertained while they are here so I expect there will be a good many afternoon activities which will require special costumes. Of course, you will also assist her to change her clothes again for dinner. And, you will, no doubt, also be called upon to dress her hair. I trust that will not pose a problem."

Because her ladyship's gaze on me had seemed quite intent, I rather nervously lowered my eyes again.

"You are a very pretty girl, Miss Abbott," she remarked. "Am I to assume that you dress your own hair?"

I looked up, but did not reply. People often noticed my hair, it being a rich, honey blonde color and inordinately thick and wavy. I attempted to keep it pinned up, but stray tendrils seemed to always be escaping the pins with the effect that my face was generally always framed with a good many wispy curls.

"Your coiffure is quite charming," she said.

A small smile wavered across my face.

"Your cousin tells me you recently spent half a year in Paris with Lady Carstairs, is that correct?"

My head jerked up. "*Oui, Madame.*"

Now, whatever possessed me to answer her question in French? Other than the fact that Lady What's-It often liked me to speak French when her friends came to call.

But I noted that my reply also caused Lady Morland's countenance to brighten.

"You are proficient in French, my dear?"

I gave a little shrug. "Um, how you say? A . . . bit."

Oh dear me, I really was doing it up, wasn't I? What mischief was I getting myself into now?

"Why, how simply marvelous!" Her ladyship sat up a good deal straighter. "I had no idea." She cast a gaze toward the other woman in the room. "Did you hear that, Temple? This young lady speaks French!" She turned back to me. "Your cousin said nothing of your education. How edifying for you that Lady Carstairs allowed you to accompany her to France! Since the war ended everyone has wished to travel on the continent. Including my eldest son," she murmured, more to herself than to me I thought, noting that for a fleeting second, her expression had hardened before she seemed to dismiss the thought altogether.

But as I was warming to the part I had inadvertently invented, I mustered my thickest French accent and said, "*Oui, et* was wonderful. I learn a great deal of the language while in *Pair-ee.* So much so I fear I forgot very much my *Anglais.*"

Lady Morland's eyes widened again. "Why, your cousin did not mention that you are . . . that is," she leaned forward, "do you have *French* relations, my dear?"

"My Mama was French." *Not a lie. She was. I had often heard my former employer proudly inform her uppity London friends that her companion,* moi, *was the daughter of a French actress.*

Lady Morland clasped her hands together. "Temple," again she addressed the other woman in the room. "We have found ourselves a French lady's maid! Why, I simply *must* have you here, Miss Abbott. I am prepared to double your wages if you agree to take the post at once!"

I smiled, quite sincerely this time. "*Merci, Madame.* When it is your guests to arrive?" For good measure, I purposely turned my words around a little. If Lady Morland wanted a French maid, I could play the part to perfection! I used to entertain Lady Carstairs (*Oh dear! now* I've *said her name; bad luck is sure to follow*) by play-acting; pretending to be the characters I read to her about in stories. Why, there were times I'd even mimic the other ladies who called upon my mistress, speaking as they did with their high-born manners. Her Ladyship would laugh 'til tears rolled down her cheeks.

And, my French-born mama *had* been an actress when she was young, even played minor parts on the London stage after she came to England. My father met and married my mama whilst he was in France fighting the war. I was born soon after he brought his pretty French bride home to England. She had thick honey blonde hair, too. And green eyes like mine. *Did having a French mama make* me *French? I had never considered that before.*

"The young ladies will begin arriving on Monday," Lady Morland was saying. "I will need you to take up residence here for the duration of the party. I trust that will be acceptable to you?"

"*Oui, Madame.* I shall come on Monday if that is *très bon*, I mean . . . all right?"

"It is *more* than all right, my dear. In fact, why don't you come bright and early Monday morning? It will give you a bit more time to settle in. It is possible one or two of the young ladies will be here by afternoon. I am *very* pleased to have you, Miss Abbott, *very* pleased, indeed. I expect you will be the *only* French lady's maid in attendance. All the young ladies will be quite envious of dear Miss Featherstone." Smiling from ear to ear, she rose to her feet; whereupon I could not help noticing that she was, indeed, quite a tall woman.

I too stood, and endeavoring to keep my countenance placid, murmured, "*Merci, Madame*," then for good measure, added, "*Au revoir . . . until Monday.*"

"I look forward to seeing you on Monday, as well, Miss Abbott."

"*Bonjour, Madame.*" I smiled shyly. *Surely I could keep up the ruse of being French for a mere fortnight. To do so would liven up my long days here, and if it meant Lady Morland would double my wages, then all the better.*

When Griggs the butler reappeared, seemingly out of nowhere, I silently followed him back down the long, carpeted corridor of the huge house, passing beneath portraits of previous Morland ancestors, who stared down upon me, none too kindly, I might add, judging from the grim looks upon their faces. Still despite their censoring looks, which seemed to be mocking me, I ignored them and turned my thoughts to what lay ahead. Quite clear to me now was that Morland Manor could, indeed, draw one in.

A few minutes later when I spotted Nancy Jane below-stairs in the kitchen, a half dozen or so kitchen maids now clanging pots and pans around as they began to prepare dinner for the Morland family and for themselves, I suppose, I motioned my cousin aside.

"Did ye' get the post?" she asked, her blue eyes wide.

My eyes were equally as wide as I nodded my reply. "But, her ladyship thinks I speak French," I whispered, "and I'm certain that's what sealed the deal."

My cousin drew back, her face scrunched up. "Do ya' speak French?"

"A bit and I will even better in a couple of days. Did I not spot a subscription library when we were in Thornbury?"

The scrunched up look on my cousin's face deepened. "They's books to let in the little room over the green-grocer if tha's wot ye' mean."

"Then I'm off to the village now." I put a finger to my lips. "Not a word to anyone, Nancy Jane. *À bientôt*."

"Wha---?"

Leaving my cousin standing there with her mouth hanging open, I turned to exit through the side door of the kitchen, then hurried off down the hill toward the village of Thornbury where I was counting upon finding myself a handy little pamphlet on French grammar. If not at the subscription library, then perhaps I'd purchase one from a bookseller's shop. Shouldn't take me too very long to brush up on my French nouns and verbs.

All things considered, I thought, as I fairly skipped along, this would indeed be a pleasant interval before I took myself off to Bath and the finishing school. To have a more thorough knowledge of the French language would serve me well there, too.

CHAPTER 2

A French Lady's Maid? Heaven Help Us!

Morland Manor

Monday, 16 October 1820

Upon arriving at the servant's entrance to Morland Manor bright and early on Monday morning, a tall footman, finely turned out in black livery with gold buttons on his coat, was quickly dispatched to carry my valise and hatbox up the back stairs to the wing of the house where the Morland houseguests would be staying. The housekeeper Mrs. Fullerton led the way, now and again motioning to one closed door or another and quietly telling James the footman which suite of rooms were to be occupied by which young lady and her chaperone and maid.

At length she paused to unlock the door at the end of a long hallway and stood aside for both James and myself to enter.

"Your mistress," she told me, "will be a Miss Featherstone, who will be accompanied by her chaperone, a married sister named Mrs. Collins. This outer room, of course, will serve as their bedchamber." Leading the way deeper into the suite of rooms, we passed through a smaller chamber, which I assumed to be a dressing room, or perhaps a private sitting room, then into a far smaller chamber containing a bed, a washstand, a small cupboard and chair. "This will be your room, Miss Abbott. You will keep the door open at all times so as to be able to hear your young mistress call if she should need you at those times when you are not in her bedchamber attending her."

"*Oui, Madame.*"

The footman's head whirled toward me, but he said nothing.

"You may go, James," Mrs. Fullerton said. "I understand you have been in service before, Miss Abbott, therefore I needn't remind you that any conversations you overhear between your mistress and her chaperone, or between any of the ladies in attendance during the entire fortnight, are to be held in the strictest confidence. Is that understood?"

I nodded.

"Very well, then; I shall leave you to get settled in. I am unsure when Miss Featherstone will be arriving, but once you have put away your things, you are welcome to join the rest of the staff midday in the servant's quarters for luncheon. A bell to this suite is fastened to the Bell Board below-stairs, so if Miss Featherstone should arrive and ring for you while you are below-stairs, you will be notified at once that your services are required. At such time, you must leave your tea, or dinner, and return to your duties without delay. Do you understand what I am saying, Miss Abbott?"

"*Oui. Merci, Madame.*"

This time, I couldn't help noticing Mrs. Fullerton's headshake and her eyes roll. "Heaven, help us," she murmured as she turned to exit the room.

No doubt she was thinking that me being *French* would pose some sort of problem but . . . I had taken on the role of a French maid and I was determined to play my part to the hilt. Therefore, play it I would no matter who I was talking to.

As expected my young mistress, Miss Caroline Featherstone and her older sister, Mrs. Collins, who looked to be about thirty or so, arrived late that afternoon as did another of the young ladies, a Miss Amelia Durham and her elderly aunt named Mrs. Throckmorton who was serving as her chaperone, along with Miss Durham's lady's maid, Tilly. This bit of information I overheard being discussed by my young charge, Miss Featherstone, who couldn't have been a great deal older than me, and her sister, Mrs. Collins, whose given name I had yet to learn. Miss Featherstone, although quite young, was a pretty girl with smooth pink cheeks and hazel eyes, albeit rather mousey brown hair that I couldn't help noticing was worn in quite an unbecoming fashion.

Although I was clearly right there in the same room with both ladies, Miss Featherstone and her sister talked freely amongst themselves as I silently helped them hang up their garments, and put their shoes and bonnets on the topmost shelves of the clothespress. To them, it seemed, I was not even present, which was fine with me. As I was more than a bit curious now about the goings-on in the manor house, for the nonce, I was content to merely listen and say nothing.

"Miss Durham looks to be a good deal older than me," mused Caroline Featherstone to her older sister, Mrs. Collins, who appeared to be getting a bit thick about the middle, which told me she might be increasing, or perhaps she was already going to fat.

"The other girl's ages are of no concern to you, Caroline," admonished her sister. "You are here to garner the notice of the elder Morland son, the heir. *He* is the prime reason you were invited and the *only* reason we are here. At the end of the fortnight, the young man will select a bride and if all goes well, the Morland heir will choose you!"

"But, I've never laid eyes on him and I heard Miss Durham say that he wasn't even here yet. Plus, she said there are *two* Morland sons."

"That may be the case, but the *heir* is the prize and you mustn't forget that *he* is the important one." Mrs. Collins handed me a cloth bag containing a delicate pair of pink satin slippers. I stood on tiptoe to place them on the top shelf of the cupboard alongside several other pairs. Apparently Miss Featherstone expected dancing to be among the festivities planned for the guests.

"I wonder how Lady Morland decided whom to invite?" Caroline asked. "Neither you nor I have ever met her, nor any member of the Morland family for all that."

Hmmm, now that she mentioned it; that seemed a bit odd to me, too. How did *Lady Morland decide whom to invite?*

Mrs. Collins, however, simply paused in her work and parked both hands on her hips. "You are a lovely girl, Caroline, and despite our father's . . . ahem, reduced circumstances, as a family we are very well-connected, which makes you quite eligible."

At that instant, Miss Featherstone seemed to take note of my presence, for following her older sister's remark upon their father's reduced circumstances, she shot a quick glance at me as if to determine if I were, indeed, listening, or if the delicate information had, or had not, registered with me.

"You needn't pay the maid any mind, Caroline," her sister said. "Lady Morland informed me that Miss Abbott is French and that the girl's English is woefully lacking." Mrs. Collins turned toward me. "Young lady . . . do you understand anything I am saying?"

I didn't even look up.

"Miss Abbott?" she said.

Again, I said nothing.

"Does she not understand her own name?" Miss Featherstone asked. "If that is the case, how am I to convey to her *my* needs?" She then attempted to garner my attention. "Miss Abbott?"

At that, I turned toward her. "*Oui, Mademoiselle?*"

Mrs. Collins' lips pursed. "Why did the girl not answer to *me*?" she demanded.

Caroline shrugged. "Perhaps because she is *my* lady's maid."

With a huff, Mrs. Collins turned back to her work.

I thought it best to let it be known at the outset that I had been hired to answer *only* to Miss Featherstone and that I was not obliged to do the bidding of all and sundry. I believe I accomplished that rather well, don't you?

After having discharged my duties for Miss Featherstone that evening and inquiring, in rather halting English, if she needed anything else, I repaired to my own little room for the night. But, as instructed by Mrs. Fullerton, I left the door standing open and as a consequence, was again made privy to the ladies' bedtime conversation.

"Lady Morland informed me that once all the guests had arrived tomorrow, she would address all you young ladies soon after luncheon, or perhaps before then, if everyone is here. I expect at that time you will be introduced to the heir and perhaps, also to the second son."

"What if I don't like him?"

"The Morland heir stands to inherit several hundred thousand pounds per annum, my dear," Mrs. Collins replied. "I have no doubt that you *will* like him. Now, go to sleep, little sister, you must look your very best tomorrow."

Tuesday, 17 October 1820

Over my breakfast the following morning, seated below-stairs around a long table situated in the largest room within the area designated as the servant's quarters, I heard a good deal more gossip about the houseguests from the household servants. Perhaps because I was the only lady's maid present thus far, or maybe because I was Nancy Jane's cousin, none of the footmen or chambermaids seemed loath to speak openly in front of me even though as a lady's maid, I outranked all of them save Griggs the butler and the housekeeper Mrs. Fullerton.

"All the girls who's been invited is from titled families," one of the maids observed. "They's a earl's daughter coming, a viscount's daughter, two baron's girls, and a baronet's daughter. She's the one what's already come, Miss Featherstone."

"One of the baron's daughter's is also here. Miss Amelia Durham, and her maid Tilly. I know 'cuz I brung trays to their suite this morning for breakfast. I'm guessin' the little London twit Tilly thinks herself too far above us to take her meals down here amongst the lower orders."

This brought a round of laugher.

"The heir ain't here yet," spoke up one of the footmen. "When's he gonna' git here?"

"Younger boy just now come," put in another footman. "Brung along his own valet, he did; and also a gentl'man friend named Mr. Talbot, nice-lookin' chap, up from Town."

"Lady Morland weren't pleased to see the friend, make no mistake. She's countin' on gittin' the heir wed off and don't want no competition lurin' away any of the fine young ladies."

Quietly eating the coddled eggs, chunks of ham, and buttered toast upon my plate, which all tasted delicious to me and was certainly far finer fare than I'd had in days, I was rather enjoying the tittle-tattle. I'd already decided that since I wasn't going to be at Morland Manor for too very long that I wouldn't attempt to learn the names of any of the footmen, or the housemaids. Especially since Nancy Jane told me that Lady Morland hadn't bothered to learn their names either. She called all the chambermaids Mary and all the footmen James. She recognized Nancy Jane because she'd been here the longest and also because my Aunt Jane had served as her lady's maid when Aunt Jane first came to the manor. Anyhow, I figured I'd be doing good to remember all the young ladies' names and perhaps the names of their chaperones and maybe their maids. As soon as I finished my meal, I smiled a goodbye at Nancy Jane, then hurried back upstairs to see what was happening up there.

As it turned out, plenty.

CHAPTER 3

There Are Hidey-holes In The Walls?

Above-stairs, I found the corridor of the wing where the houseguests were to reside a veritable jumble of valises, portmanteaus, hatboxes and trunks sitting here and there, some standing on end, which meant they'd been set down by a footman. In my experience, men didn't know the first thing about how to properly handle a lady's belongings.

A host of ladies, some young, some old and some of a middling age were to-ing and fro-ing up and down the corridor, everyone talking at once. At first glance, it was hard to tell which ladies were candidates for the heir's hand in marriage and which were the girl's chaperones and maids since so many seemed near the same age. I skirted past several excited young ladies on my way to the end of the hall and paused before my mistress' door only long enough to lightly rap upon it. Due to the noise and confusion in the corridor, I was unable to hear a response, if indeed there was one, so I took the liberty of entering the room anyways.

"Oh, there you are, Juliette . . . oh, my, should I address you as Juliette, or . . . Miss Abbott?" inquired Miss Caroline Featherstone. "I've never had my own lady's maid before so I am unsure how to . . . properly . . . which do you prefer?"

"*Je m'appelle . . . excusez-moi . . .*" I began, merely to further the ruse that I was, indeed, French; then with a smile began afresh. "My given name, it is Juliette."

My young mistress also smiled. "Very well, I shall call you Juliette. Which, to be sure, is a very pretty French name. Please, when we are alone, you may address me as Caroline. Miss Featherstone sounds far too formal."

At that point, Caroline's sister Mrs. Collins entered the room, seemingly in a rush to escape the crowded corridor. "I only just came from speaking with Lady Morland," she stated briskly. "Her ladyship wishes to address all the young ladies *and* their maids, although I cannot imagine why *they* should be included, in the drawing room in one hour, Caroline." She cast a glance my direction. "You will please inform Miss Abbott of the summons."

Caroline huffed. "Alice, I do believe Juliette understands a good bit of English. Juliette, you are to accompany us below-stairs in one hour."

"*Oui, Mademoiselle; merci.*" I nodded at Caroline; and smiled to myself as my innocent gaze slid to her thin-lipped older sister Alice. After a pause, I asked Caroline, "Will you wish to change your frock before going down, *Mademoiselle*?"

Caroline turned an alarmed gaze upon her sister.

"The morning gown you are wearing is satisfactory, my dear. I do not believe the heir has yet arrived. We must endeavor to . . . conserve your wardrobe for the more . . . important occasions. That will be all, Miss . . . er, Juliette."

With another nod, I repaired to my small chamber to sit and wait out the hour, during which time I again left the door standing open in case Caroline needed me. I had pinned up her baby fine brown hair as best I could this morning. To arrange it in a *becoming* fashion would be another matter. However, it still looked presentable so perhaps it would not require re-arranging before we adjourned to the drawing room to hear what Lady Morland had to say.

Like Mrs. Collins, I, too, wondered why we lady's maids were being included in the meeting since upon my arrival at the manor house, I assumed I had been given all the instruction I would need in order to perform my duties. At that time, I had also been presented with two crisp black cotton dresses, two white pinafores and two small frilly white caps, shaped rather like puffy handkerchiefs, which I was to pin atop my head. At that time I was told that the dress, pinafore and cap were my uniform for the fortnight, therefore as I was already thusly attired, I, as well, felt no need to freshen my appearance. I further assumed that once the other lady's maids had donned their uniforms, that alone would make it easy to tell apart the houseguests from their maids; and age would make the further distinction between the girls and their chaperones.

Sure enough, once everyone had assembled below-stairs in the cavernous withdrawing room, the young ladies and their respective chaperones, all perched precariously upon the edges of sofas and chairs, were easily distinguishable from their maids. We, all bunched together at the bottom of the room in a clump, looked rather like a cluster of small black crows wearing puffy white caps. Glancing to the right and left at my companions, I also noted the older woman I had seen here with Lady Morland the day I was hired. Today she was also wearing a black frock and white pinafore and cap, so I assumed she was Lady Morland's personal maid, the woman whom her ladyship had addressed as Temple.

Lady Morland, again looking tall and regal, and today wearing a lovely green morning gown, stood before a long mahogany table situated mid-way down the length of the beautifully appointed chamber. Flanking her on either side stood two gentlemen. Both men appeared to be of a similar age, possibly in their early twenties, and both handsome in their own way. The one with thick brown hair who bore a definite resemblance to Lady Morland, I assumed to be her youngest son, as no word of the heir having yet arrived had been bandied about.

The other one, I thought, must be the second son's gentleman friend Mr. Talbot, as the talk below-stairs this morning had confirmed that Mr. Edward Morland had, indeed, brought along a friend. Of the two men, I thought Mr. Talbot was far and away the better looking. Taller and leaner than the second son, he had dark wavy hair, fine brown eyes and possessed an easy, open countenance. At the moment, he was smiling at all the young ladies and their chaperones, seated opposite from where he and the second son stood.

When Lady Morland began to speak, I abandoned my ruminations in order to learn all I could from what she had to say. She first welcomed everyone to Morland Manor and briefly explained that her husband Sir Morland was presently away attending to estate business, but was expected back for dinner that evening, then she introduced the pair of gentlemen, turning to the shorter, brown-haired one first.

"This fine young man is my son, Mr. Edward Morland and this is his friend, Mr. Philip Talbot. Both my son and Mr. Talbot currently reside in London; therefore it is quite possible that some of you might already be acquainted with either gentleman. I had hoped that my . . . elder son, Mr. William Morland, the heir, would also be present this morning, but I only recently learned that his arrival has been . . . unfortunately delayed. However, I am certain he will grace us with his presence for dinner this evening."

I thought I detected a note of derision in her tone when she declared that her elder son, William, the all-important heir, would 'grace us with his presence for dinner.' I quickly thrust the thought aside as she had already launched into introducing the ladies. I had already noticed that of all the girls, only one of them was strikingly beautiful; that being the Earl of Sedgwick's daughter, the Lady Sophia, a delicate auburn-haired girl with large blue eyes. Her mother, the Countess, Lady Sedgwick, was apparently serving as her chaperone.

Lady Sophia's crowning glory was her mane of thick auburn hair that, even to my eyes, could have been dressed to far greater advantage than it currently was. Of the four other girls, only one stood out to me as also being remarkably pretty, and that was the Viscount's daughter, Miss Elizabeth Banes, who had coal black hair and very light, sky-blue eyes. The other three girls, including my Miss Featherstone, could have been cut from the same cloth. All had varying degrees of brown hair and not a one of them was any prettier than the last. I wondered again upon what basis Lady Morland had chosen her houseguests?

After the introductions had been made, she turned to address her son Edward in a whispered undertone. In seconds, both gentlemen excused themselves, turning polite smiles and nods upon the women as they hastily exited the room.

Lady Morland smiled. "I have asked the gentlemen to excuse us so that we ladies might speak openly." She moved to take a seat on one of the japanned chairs closer to the grouping of sofas and settees where the ladies were perched. "Now, then, shall we begin? As you all know, William Morland is the eldest of my two sons and it is he who will one day inherit Morland Manor, his father's mills, all the surrounding land, the hills, the woods, the farms, the farmhouses, the outbuildings, and indeed, the entire village of Thornbury."

This pronouncement elicited a good many oh's and ah's accompanied by wide-eyed looks of amazement, and a few astonished exclamations from those assembled in the room, young ladies, their chaperones, and maids alike.

"Some, or perhaps, all of you may be wondering why you have been invited to my home since, with only one or two exceptions, we are none of us well-acquainted." She paused and looked down, as if somehow reluctant to disclose everything, but at length, she looked back up and pressed on. "I wish each of you to know that I have not simply *invited* you here, I have carefully *chosen*, each and every one of you for the express purpose of presenting you to my sons, yes, to *both* of my sons, in the hope that by the end of the fortnight, *both* of my sons will have chosen . . . a bride."

This pronouncement elicited another round of tittered exclamations and even a smattering of excited giggles. The expressions on the faces of those of us wearing black frocks also revealed pleasure over the prospect of our mistresses being put on display for the express purpose of matrimonial bliss, to say nothing of the promise of security for most of us from the day of the wedding onward. I, of course, did not count myself amongst that number, as that did not concern me. Once the fortnight drew to a close, I would be off to Bath to pursue my own bright future. And, as a result of this sojourn with considerably fuller pockets. I did not yet fully believe that I would ever receive the ten pounds that my former employer had left to me, so I did not intend to cause myself sorrow by expecting something that might never come.

Amidst the girl's titters, Lady Morland held up a hand. "Please ladies, I am not yet finished. In order that my sons will have the opportunity, the *equal* opportunity, to become *equally* acquainted with each and every one of you, I have devised a . . . set of rules, if you will, that will ensure that not a single young lady is overlooked or neglected in the coming days. I have planned a lengthy list of afternoon activities, as well as, diverting entertainments for each and every evening. During every activity, such as a carriage ride to and from the village, or to a picnic on the grounds of the estate, each of you young ladies will have the opportunity to sit with the heir and also with his brother, accompanied by your lady's maid, of course, *alone*, in the gentleman's private carriage." She directed a gaze toward us, the covey of black-clad crows at the far end of the chamber. "Which is why I have included your maids in this meeting."

I had already noted two of the girl's chaperones thrust up a hand, obviously with an urgent desire to protest their charges being allowed to sit with a gentleman with only a maid as chaperone. Both women wore scowls of disapproval on their faces as they clamored for Lady Morland's attention.

She too had noticed the alarmed looks on the older women's faces for without yet asking them what they eagerly wished to say, she began, "Lady Sedgwick, Mrs. Collins, please believe me when I say there is no cause for alarm. Your young charges will be perfectly safe at all times when the girls are alone with my sons."

Nonetheless, the imperious Lady Sedgwick could not contain her outcry. "As you yourself said," her angry words spilled out, "we are most of us *un*acquainted with you, *or* your sons!"

By way of answer, Lady Morland merely tilted up her chin and smiled serenely as one bejeweled hand again indicated us, the cluster of crows. "Which is precisely why I included the girl's abigails in this meeting. I wish *them* to understand what is at stake, and also what is afoot. The reason why I wish *only* the lady's maids to be present while the girl's are alone with my sons is because I believe that on their own, the young ladies will be more apt to speak freely, to be open and honest in their discourse with the gentlemen, if you will. As you know, time is of the essence. I have only allowed a fortnight for the courtship and for a decision to be reached; therefore the ladies must dispense with all the usual *missish* behaviours and endeavor to present themselves in as forthright a manner as possible. I believe they will be more apt to do so without the censoring presence of their chaperones, no insult intended, of course. Still, I do not want the ladies to feel uncomfortable, so as to adhere as closely as possible to the rules of propriety, they will at all times be properly chaperoned by their maids. I trust that each of you will understand and accept my decision in the matter."

Both Lady Morland's expression and her words conveyed her belief in her authority to suggest and enforce such an outrageous rule. Consequently, for whatever reason, not a single one of the chaperones raised a further objection.

"Of an evening," Lady Morland continued, "each lady, by turns, will also be invited to sit with first the heir and then with my second son, in plain sight upon a sofa or settee right here in the drawing room. Perhaps, if the weather is fine, the couple might even take a quick turn about the terrace, once again accompanied by her maid. In the evenings, each of you young ladies will also have the opportunity to impress the gentlemen with your talents upon the pianoforte, and in song.

"I am also planning an elaborate ball to be held quite soon, as well as other pleasant diversions, such as a picnic on the grounds, and a sightseeing expedition. Because our time together is limited, I urge each of you to make the most of those precious moments in which you are alone with my sons."

She paused. "Do any of you have a question, or perhaps, a concern?"

Rather wide-eyed myself now, I waited with bated breath to see if anyone, other than the girl's chaperones who had already spoken up, had anything else to say, or ask.

One did. The girl who had been introduced as Miss Amelia Durham, her brown hair, I had earlier noted, rather severely pulled back into a tight wad at the nape of her neck, and who looked to be the oldest of the candidates. Older than the gentlemen, and perhaps even one or two of the chaperones.

"Lady Morland, I was unaware there was to be a ball. I . . . confess I did not bring along anything fine enough to wear. I wonder if there is sufficient time for me to send to London for one of my ball gowns to be brought up, or if perhaps there is a local *modiste* who I might commission to fashion something suitable to wear?"

"I will be glad to help you with that, Miss Durham. You may speak with me privately after luncheon."

"Thank you, my lady," Miss Durham replied demurely.

"Very well, then." Lady Morland rose. "Shall we all go into luncheon?"

We black crows hung back 'til our betters had quitted the room. Then, since thus far, I was the only one, besides Temple, who had ventured below-stairs, I took the lead and led the way from the drawing room to the end of the long corridor and through the inconspicuous doorway that led down a steep flight of stairs to the servant's quarters where we had all been instructed to take our meals. As yet, our luncheon had not been laid out as most of the footmen were now engaged hurrying up and down the steps carrying trays loaded with covered dishes to the dining hall above. Upon spotting our approach, Mrs. Fullerton ushered the lot of us into the servant's dining hall and bid us sit down until she could free up a kitchen maid to serve our meal.

That afternoon was spent quietly, I assume, with every guest in this wing of the huge house sequestered within her own suite of rooms, thinking on what lay ahead. Because Caroline and her sister spent the bulk of the afternoon napping, I was left to fend for myself. Because I longed for a book to read, I eventually slipped out and went in search of Lady Morland to ask if I might borrow a book from the Morland Manor library.

Despite there being a great deal of company in the house, and everyone now ensconced in their individual rooms, to me the huge house seemed eerily silent, as silent a tomb or a mausoleum actually. Though I searched first in the drawing room, then risked a peek into several other chambers whose doors stood open, I never once caught sight of anyone. Not even Lady Morland. Eventually, however, I did come upon a pair of fine gentlemen engaged in a round of billiards inside a chamber that I took to be a gentleman's study, or smoking room. Both gentlemen had shucked their coats and rolled up their shirtsleeves to the elbows and were joking and laughing with one another as they played their game. The gentleman, whom I recognized as the second son's friend Mr. Talbot, eventually glanced up; and noting me lurking near the doorway, alerted his companion.

"Eh, Morland, appears we've got an audience." A raised cue stick indicated my presence.

Mr. Edward Morland looked up. "I take it you have lost your way, miss. The ladies' wing is . . ."

"No, sir. I am not lost." I boldly took a step into the rather smoky chamber. "I was looking for Lady Morland, or rather actually, the library. My mistress and her companion are sleeping and . . ." I shrugged. "I've nothing to do this afternoon so I thought a book might help pass the time."

At that, Mr. Talbot laughed. "A bookish maid! Did you ever see the like, eh, Morland?"

A smile twitched about the corners of Edward Morland's lips. "We've no romances in the Morland Manor library, miss," he informed me roundly, which gave his friend Mr. Talbot another chuckle.

I, too, smiled. "I was thinking I'd like to read something a bit more *classical,* if you please."

"Oh, not only bookish, but a bluestocking, as well," exclaimed Mr. Talbot on another merry laugh.

"Very well, miss, we'll be glad to show you the way." Mr. Edward Morland put down his cue stick and the small cigarillo he'd been smoking. "Come along, Talbot. This might be fun."

Both gentlemen ushered me into the corridor and off we went, down another long hallway, up a flight of stairs and into an enormous picture gallery, the heels of our shoes tapping out a rhythm as we three walked across the polished floor of the enormous chamber.

"Might this be the ballroom?" I inquired, glancing right and left and upward at the dozen or more crystal chandeliers majestically gracing the ceiling overhead.

"One of them," Edward Morland replied, not pausing in his determined trek across the room.

"This the one with the hidey holes in the walls?" Mr. Talbot asked, the deep timbre of his voice echoing in the empty chamber.

His companion turned toward him. "There are hidey holes in *all* the walls, Talbot."

I turned a wide-eyed look up at him. "Might you be larking, sir?"

Edward Morland shrugged. "Not at all. Trick is to find 'em, lass."

"What's your name, miss?" Mr. Talbot asked.

I gazed up at him in a far more flirtatious manner than I should have. He was quite good looking, with very dark hair and twinkling brown eyes. Tilting up my chin, I smartly replied, "*Je m'appelle Julietta.*"

Both gentlemen fairly skidded to a halt and both starred down upon me as if I were a *bona fide* oddity.

"So, we've encountered the *French* maid mother mentioned."

"Very pleased to make your acquaintance, Mam'selle Julietta," said Mr. Talbot, with a very deep bow.

I tilted my chin up another notch. "Miss Abbott to you, sir."

Edward Morland laughed aloud. "French *and* saucy. A deadly combination, to be sure."

"My dear Miss Abbott," Mr. Talbot began solemnly. "You will please do me the very great honor of accepting my apology, and both our apologies for . . . staring."

Then, as if they'd previously planned their next move, both reached for one of my arms, draped them over the crooks of their elbows and off we went again, a threesome united in our search of the library.

Although I later realized that Edward Morland had quite possibly taken the long way around, with the effect of adding greatly to my confusion, we did, indeed, finally end up in the library where both gentlemen went to great lengths to see that I found several volumes to my liking for my afternoon reading pleasure. They then gallantly escorted me back to the flight of stairs that led to the wing of the house where the ladies' chambers were located, at the far end of which is my own suite. That they did not walk up the stairs with me led me to surmise that according to Lady Morland's rules, our particular wing of the house had been designated as off limits to the gentlemen. Still, the unexpected excursion made for a pleasant interlude for me and one, I suspect, every last young lady on the floor would be quite jealous of had they known of it.

Word did not filter up to the Featherstone suite that the heir had arrived until close on the dinner hour, at which time, pandemonium is the only word that can adequately describe the chaos that ensued in the otherwise quiet and secluded guest wing of Morland Manor.

CHAPTER 4

A Shadowy Figure Lurking In The Woods

Tuesday Evening, 17 October 1820

Just as I was finishing up with as elaborate a coiffure as I could manage given Miss Featherstone's thin brown locks, a rap sounded at the door and Mrs. Collins rose to answer it.

Without being invited, the elegant woman at the door swept in with the air of one accustomed to being catered to without question. "I am Lady Sedgwick." Her tone was imperious. "I would like a word with you."

"As you wish, my lady." Alice Collins, apparently aware that she was addressing a countess, a woman who most assuredly outranked her, as she possessed no title at all, stepped aside. "How may I be of assistance, madam?"

Lady Sedgwick cast a glance about Miss Featherstone's small bedchamber. "What a charming room," she murmured with little sincerity and even less enthusiasm. "I came to inquire if Miss Featherstone could spare her abigail for a moment this evening? My daughter Lady Sophia's maid is not . . . well, it has come to my attention that Miss Featherstone's maid is *French* and I would very much like her to dress my daughter's hair this evening. Might I prevail upon you for the loan of her, just this once?"

Mrs. Collins turned toward me. "Miss Abbott?"

Although I had clearly heard Lady Sedgwick's request, I, of course, chose not to acknowledge the summons.

To Lady Sedgwick I heard Mrs. Collins remark, "Miss Abbott does not always understand English. Caroline, dear?"

By then, I was a mere step away from quitting the room altogether, so Miss Featherstone rose to follow me. Touching my arm, she said, "Juliette, Lady Sedgwick has asked that you dress her daughter's hair this evening. If you would not mind too terribly much."

I turned to re-enter the bedchamber in time to hear Lady Sedgwick say with a disdainful sniff, "The French do often think themselves quite above us. I see this girl is no exception."

"Juliette," Mrs. Collins said as I drew nearer. "You will please accompany Lady Sedgwick to her suite."

I bobbed a curtsy. "*Bein sûr, madame.*"

Lady Sedgwick lips pursed. "This way, my dear."

I obediently followed the woman all the way to the opposite end of the corridor. Just before reaching the Sedgwick suite, I noticed the door of the adjacent chamber standing ajar and caught a glimpse of the viscount's black haired daughter, Miss Elizabeth Banes moving about within. It was then that it dawned upon me that the guests had been assigned their suites according to rank. My Miss Featherstone, being the daughter of a mere baronet had the last, and quite possibly smallest, bedchamber on the floor.

My suspicion was confirmed upon entering Lady Sophia's suite. Her father being an earl meant her mother Lady Sedgwick was, indeed, a countess and therefore, the highest-ranking lady present at Morland Manor, of greater consequence even than Lady Morland as Sir Morland, being a mere baronet, was not even a true peer of the realm.

Lady Sedgwick's daughter, the Lady Sophia, being the highest ranking of all the young ladies present had been given a bedchamber that was easily twice the size, and far more elaborately furnished, than my Miss Featherstone's suite. The draperies and bed hangings here were a deep wine color festooned with gold braid and tassels. The tall heavy wardrobe that reached from floor to ceiling was made of a rich burl wood and exactly matched the dressing table with its elaborate three-fold set of gleaming mirrors comprising the top half. There was both a sofa and a settee and even a pretty little writing desk in one corner. The carpet in this chamber was a thick, rich burgundy pile as compared to the threadbare rug gracing the floor in Caroline's room, and no rug at all in my room. A cheery fire burned in the grate; the fireplace surround an elaborately carved affair with a painted porcelain clock gracing the center of the mantelpiece.

"Sophia, dear, Miss Featherstone's *French* maid Juliette has consented to dress your hair this evening."

"Oh!" The pretty girl seated before the dressing table appeared delighted as she turned to face me.

Glancing about, I noted that her maid Lucy, to whom I had spoken at luncheon, was nowhere in sight.

"Might you do up my hair . . . like yours, please?" Lady Sophia asked a tad bit shyly.

I bobbed a curtsy. "*Oui, Mademoiselle.*" The Lady Sophia appeared to be far less impressed by her own elevated status than did her highborn mother, which at once caused me to like her daughter a good deal better.

Taking up the silver-backed brush which Lady Sophia handed me, I went to work brushing her thick auburn tresses 'til they shone; then carefully sectioned off and pinned up handfuls of long hair atop her head. I next pulled out several long tendrils, which created the effect of wispy curls to frame her lovely face. The girl's complexion was exquisite, smooth and creamy. With an upturned nose and full rosy lips, she was quite lovely, indeed. Her glittering eyes were a rich, deep blue and tonight she had on a beautiful blue silk gown with a darker, wide blue ribbon tied beneath her small breasts.

When I had completed the upswept coiffure, I stepped back. "You like, *non?*"

She preened before the mirrors, turning her head this way and that, then a sweet smile lit up both her face and eyes. "Mama, look! The heir will surely notice me tonight. What do you think?"

"You will be the loveliest young lady there," her mother said, reaching to affectionately clasp her daughter's shoulders. When the haughty woman turned toward me, her kind manner abruptly vanished. "You will come every morning and evening to dress my daughter's hair, do you understand?"

I hesitated before casting my eyes downward and bobbing a curtsy. "*Oui, Madame.*"

Leaving the fine suite, I hurried back down the corridor, Lady Sedgwick's stern command ringing in my ears. I would have to tell Caroline of my new duties, of course, but should I also alert Lady Morland to the countess' additional demand upon my time? What would she say, I wondered.

Later that evening, following my own dinner taken below-stairs with the household staff, I was again privy to all that was said between Caroline and her sister Alice regarding the doings in the drawing room on that first official evening of the festivities at Morland Manor.

"The heir is not at all what I expected," declared Caroline as I stood behind her unfastening the tiny buttons that marched down the back of her gown.

"True; he is not nearly so handsome as his younger brother Edward," Alice replied, straining to undo the pins holding her rather plain muslin gown in place. "Although he is quite tall and dashing. Were the young man to smile more often, I daresay he would be *quite* handsome, as it is, the scowl he wears does rather render him more like his father, Sir Morland. Unfortunately, *he* is *not* a handsome man at all, although he must be clever to have amassed such enormous wealth. It is quite clear the younger son takes his good looks from his mother."

"The heir is just so . . . sullen," Caroline fretted.

"Trust me, I kept a sharp eye on you whilst you stood near him before the mantlepiece," Alice told her younger sibling. "What, pray, were the pair of you speaking of?"

"Very little of substance, I regret to say. I found him quite difficult to converse with. It seems he does not really wish to be here. He never once looked directly at me. I wonder that he would recognize me again if he bumped into me in the hallway," Caroline lamented.

"It did not appear to me that he took a fancy to any one of the young ladies. I also noticed that you never had the opportunity to speak with the second son."

"I was not the only young lady who did not speak with him. I saw that he and his friend Mr. Talbot, to whom I have also not been introduced, abandoned the drawing room quite early this evening. The pair simply . . . vanished without a word."

"Quite odd, indeed," Alice replied, stepping from her dress. She carried it to the cupboard herself and hung it inside. "Surely you will have an opportunity to speak with both gentlemen tomorrow. You must remember, Caroline, if the heir is to settle on a bride inside a fortnight, you must endeavor to put yourself forward. Our futures depend upon it."

"Indeed, sister." Caroline emitted a long sigh. "With you to remind me at every turn, how can I possibly forget?"

Wednesday, 18 October 1820

The following morning after I had finished with my duties to my mistress, I hurried down the corridor to the Lady Sophia's suite to dress her hair. Her maid Lucy was only just gathering up both of the ladies' soiled small clothes from the day before. The black-clad girl brushed past me on her way to the laundry room as I entered the fine chamber.

"Ah, there you are, Juliette," said Lady Sedgwick. "Please make haste. Sophia is always quite hungry of a morning, so in future, you will come to dress her hair *before* you do Miss Featherstone's. It is imperative that my daughter have her breakfast quite soon after she awakens."

A saucy reply on the tip of my tongue nearly popped out. I worked to tamp it down, but in the end, it leaked out anyway. "Perhaps you could ring for a tray to be brought up, my lady."

The countess blinked at my effrontery. "You are far too impertinent for your own good, missy! You are in England now where lady's maids remember their station."

"Yes, my lady." *The woman's sharp tone scared the French right out of me.*

The Lady Sophia was again quietly seated before the dressing table. Looking at me in the mirror, she said, in a far less disagreeable tone than her mother, "Perhaps a less elaborate coiffure for today, if you please, Juliette."

"*Oui, mademoiselle*," I meekly replied, remembering both my French and my station.

I was quite hungry by the time I made my way below-stairs to break my fast that morning. Although most of the household staff had already eaten, the kitchen still seemed abuzz with activity, the cook and half a dozen helpers running thither and yon. Still seated at the table sipping her chocolate, however, was Miss Hester Grant's lady's maid, a friendly girl named Meg, who told me that a picnic luncheon was on tap to entertain the ladies that afternoon, which explained the noisy preparations currently underway in the kitchen.

"And we are to join them!" Meg exclaimed. "It will be the first time the ladies are to ride *alone* with the gentlemen in their carriages."

"I see." I dipped my spoon into the bowl of somewhat lumpy, and by now, rather cold, oatmeal before me. Caroline had said nothing about the picnic earlier, but then, perhaps the girls only learned of the plan at breakfast. "Is your Miss Grant looking forward to the outing?"

"To say truth," Meg confided, "she thinks the heir is a boor." A laugh escaped her. "Which quite displeases her mama, Lady Stanhope. They's pockets to let, you know." She wrinkled her nose. "'Spose I shouldn't have said that. But, 'tis true and it's precisely why Miss Grant's mum is demanding *she* be the one the heir chooses."

Just then a footman stepped to the doorway. "Which of ye' is Meg?" Not waiting for an answer, he said, "Your mistress has rung for ye'. Best go up now."

Meg popped up. "I shall see you this afternoon, Juliette."

Gulping down the remainder of my oatmeal, I nodded.

Moments later, as I made my way back up the steep stairs, I was still mulling over what I'd learned from Miss Hester Grant's maid, Meg, that the Baron Stanhope and his wife Lady Stanhope were also in the suds. Same as Miss Featherstone's family. The news did make me wonder about the circumstances of the rest of the ladies. Had Lady Morland purposely chosen the daughters of titled families who were in dire straits? And, if so, why?

Above-stairs, I found Mrs. Collins in a quandary as to what sort of garment her younger sister Caroline should don for the picnic that afternoon.

"You've nothing suitable!" Mrs. Collins cried. Then apparently an idea struck. "Juliette, go at once to the Sedgwick suite and ask if Lady Sophia needs you to freshen her hair."

"But, I just did up her . . ."

"Yes, yes, I know. What I really want is for you to notice what the girl is wearing. Go now, and come back straightaway!"

As I hurried to do as Alice Collins bid, I heard Caroline address her older sister. "But, Alice, no matter what Lady Sophia is wearing, I'll not have anything nearly as grand as she . . ."

There was no need for me to rap at the Sedgwick suite for as I approached, both Lady Sedgwick and her lovely daughter were just then emerging from their chamber into the corridor. Lady Sophia was wearing a slim, forest green walking dress edged with black braid at the hem and a matching green Spencer jacket featuring long fitted sleeves. Green gloves and a pretty ruffled green parasol completed her costume. They neither one took notice of me, so I spun around and retraced my steps back to my waiting mistress, Miss Featherstone.

Walking straight to the clothespress, I drew out a blue plaid walking dress and a tiny blue Spencer jacket, although it had short puffed sleeves as opposed to long ones. "This should do nicely," I said.

After helping Miss Featherstone into her outdoor costume, we three joined the other ladies already gathered at the foot of the stairs in the large marble tiled foyer of the house.

Lady Morland, accompanied by her personal maid the elderly Temple, again attired in her black uniform, white pinafore and white cap, was soon on hand to usher everyone out of doors and into a veritable parade of open-air carriages that each looked as if they could comfortably seat as many as four people. Almost all of the vehicles, I noted, had a sort of "hood" that could be pulled up if the weather turned nasty, or lay folded back flat if skies were clear, as they were today. All the carriages were now drawn up in a single line on the graveled drive in front of the mansion.

The Lady Sophia, I noted, and her maid Lucy, were the first chosen to ride with the heir in the lead landau. Directly behind them, in the second coach, sat the Viscount Wentworth's daughter, Miss Elizabeth Banes, next to Lady Morland's second son Edward and across from them, Miss Banes' maid, Rosie.

Once again, I noted, the ladies had been chosen according to rank. The rest of us were handed willy-nilly into the remaining vehicles while Lady Morland and Temple were put into the very front-most carriage seated across from Mr. Talbot. Bringing up the rear was a sort of dogcart, or wagon, with benches along either side of the outer railing, carrying a dozen or more maids and liveried footmen. The whole procession was followed by yet another wagon piled high with wicker baskets and supplies. At length, the caravan got underway, albeit slowly.

This afternoon was the first time I had caught a glimpse of the heir and from the looks of him, I daresay if it were left to me to choose, I would far prefer the second son. Yes, William Morland was quite a tall man . . . still, for a gentleman not yet thirty his mid-section seemed to already be going to paunch. Evidently he drank far too much ale and consumed far too much rich food than was considered prudent to maintain a trim physique. But, perhaps, being heir to such an immense fortune provided him with all the consequence needed by a young man in search of a wife, if indeed he was in search of one. Residing up in London as he did, you'd think he would have found a bride by now if he truly wanted one, great wealth generally being sufficient bait to lure a multitude of young ladies who longed for nothing more in life than to walk down the aisle of a church on the arm of a wealthy man.

Setting off on our sojourn, conversation within the carriage where I sat with Caroline Featherstone and her sister was noticeably thin. Apart from a few laudatory remarks about the pleasant weather and the lovely scenery, which was indeed quite lovely, given the clear blue sky overhead and the leaves on the trees displaying varying hues of red and gold; plus a bit of speculation as to where we might be headed that day, virtually nothing was said until Mrs. Collins ventured a speculative remark.

"Did you notice that last evening in the drawing room after dinner, that Lady Sophia was the first, and only, young lady invited to sit with the heir? And that she is also the first to sit with him today in his carriage?"

Ah, so I was not the only one who had noticed that rank seemed to be playing a part, thought I, but said nothing.

Caroline merely shrugged. "Well, she is the highest ranking amongst us. I suppose it is only natural she should go first."

"But it means that the heir will likely be exhausted by time he finally gets around to speaking with you, Caroline."

To me, Mrs. Collins' tone sounded more than a bit peeved over the fact that things were being done in order of precedence.

"Would be more fair and just if things were turned around on occasion," the older woman remarked irritably. "Do promise me, Caroline, that when you are granted the opportunity to sit with him, you will make every effort to be as pleasant as possible. You must ask the young man questions that require more than a simple 'yes' or 'no' reply. Gentlemen like to talk about themselves and they appreciate a woman who will listen to them talk, however boring and inconsequential their reply might seem to you." Mrs. Collins paused. "Caroline, are you listening to me?"

"Indeed, I am, sister. And I shall do precisely as you say."

"Papa will be most disappointed if you return home without a . . . and, with no . . ."

At that moment, our small coach drew to an abrupt halt. We three craned our necks to see around the driver perched atop the bench in an effort to determine what was causing the hold-up.

"Oh, apparently it is time for a switch-up," I blurted out. "Look just there, up ahead, Lady Sophia is being handed into Master Edward's carriage now and Miss Banes is climbing into the heir's landau."

"Indeed, it is a . . . switch-up," agreed Caroline. She and I exchanged a grin and then both giggled.

"At this rate, it will be long after luncheon before it is your turn to ride with either of the gentlemen," declared Mrs. Collins, her tone again sounding more than a trifle annoyed.

Sometime later, upon driving 'round a wide bend in the dusty road, we came upon a clearing that overlooked a pretty lake. On the opposite side of the road was a grassy meadow that I thought must have recently been mowed down by a herd of hungry cows or goats as the grass that lay further up the road was still very nearly knee high. The carriages all halted and the liveried footmen hurried forth to solemnly hand the ladies out. In the center of the cleared area a large, white, open-air tent had been erected with a number of small tables and chairs sitting here and there beneath it.

Everyone began to slowly troupe that direction while the virtual army of servants hurried past us carrying heavy baskets and other supplies toward the tent.

"Ladies! Ladies, if I may have your attention, please!" The male voice belonged to the Morland butler, Griggs, who after waiting for us all to catch up to where he stood, resumed speaking. "Lady Morland wishes me to inform you that luncheon will be served in a quarter hour and that, until then, you may walk a bit or . . . or do whatever suits your fancy." He cleared his throat, then after Lady Morland herself stepped up to quietly say something to him, he added, "The gong will sound, and once inside the pavilion, you are free to sit at the table of your choice."

"So, appears luncheon is not to be served according to rank," Alice Collins muttered to no one in particular.

Caroline did not reply to her sister's remark, but rather took my arm. "Shall we walk a bit, Juliette?"

"I would like that very much," I said. "Would your sister care to join . . ."

"Just you and me for now." Caroline attempted to pull me forward. "She is no doubt too tired to walk." Casting a glance back at her sister, she said a bit louder, "We shall return in plenty of time for luncheon, Alice. Choose a table and we will join you."

The other ladies, some with chaperones, some without, but every girl with her maid in tow, began to set off in all directions, most all heading across the road toward the shore of a sparkling lake visible through the trees. Caroline and I followed suit. Presently we became aware of the sound of footfalls a bit heavier than ours crunching the dry grass behind us. We both turned at the selfsame moment in time to see the person following us hurry forward.

"Good day, Miss Abbott," called the dark-haired Mr. Talbot, who was finely turned out this afternoon in a plum-colored waistcoat, a dark brown jacket and buff-colored breeches with the cuff of his top boots turned down. The pleasant smile on his face brought answering smiles from both Caroline and myself.

"*Bon jour,* Mr. Talbot." I smiled and waited for him to catch up to us.

"Might I prevail upon you to introduce me to your mistress, *s'il vous plait?*"

"I would be delighted, sir. Miss Featherstone, this gentleman is Mr. Philip Talbot, Mr. Edward Morland's friend come up from London."

The two exchanged polite greetings and I purposely fell back a few steps, allowing Mr. Talbot and my young mistress to walk alone together and converse with one another in private. In minutes, however, we all heard the gong summoning us back to the tent as apparently luncheon was even then awaiting us on the tables.

Nearing the tent, Mr. Talbot touched the brim of his hat and murmured something that sounded like, "My pleasure," before he disappeared leaving Caroline and myself to search out Alice. Once we three had taken seats around one of the small tables, Alice was atwitter to know what the gentleman had spoken to her sister about. I paid no attention to Caroline's reply as by now, considering that I'd had little to nothing to eat for breakfast that morning, I was fairly starved for something solid to put in my stomach.

Following the lengthy meal which consisted of a variety of cold meats, chicken, ham, roast beef, an asparagus salad, plus assorted stalks of crisp, cold vegetables and hard-boiled buttered eggs; all washed down with mugs of lemonade or ale and followed by a choice of sugary biscuits and fruit tarts, we all, or at least the young ladies and their maids, rose once again to leisurely walk along the road or across it towards the lake. Already the shadows were beginning to lengthen and the interior of the thicket of tall trees up ahead looked more than a bit dark and foreboding to me.

As Caroline and I strolled across the road, from the corner of my eye, I again spotted Mr. Talbot seemingly headed our way once again. I slowed my step to allow him to more easily catch up to us. Before he reached us, however, I also noticed Mr. Edward Morland hurrying toward his friend. Then, the pair of them did, indeed, walk straight toward Miss Featherstone and myself.

"*Bon jour,* Miss Abbott," Edward Morland called out in a friendly manner. "Do you ladies mind if we join you? There is a pretty little inlet just beyond that grove of trees . . ." he pointed up ahead, ". . . that you might enjoy seeing."

"That sounds delightful," I replied, then turned to introduce Mr. Edward Morland to Miss Featherstone and before I knew how it all came about, he and Caroline were walking side-by-side whilst Mr. Talbot and I, keeping step with one another, brought up the rear. That gentleman even took my arm! This time I couldn't help noticing the thin-lipped stares and glares that we four were garnering from the other twosomes, all ladies, who were walking a bit apart from us, and not a pair of them accompanied by a gentleman.

Mr. Talbot and I kept up an easy discussion, he asking me which of the books I'd borrowed from the Morland library I was reading and was I enjoying it? He told me the name of a volume he'd only just read and enjoyed, to which I replied conversationally. For a good quarter hour, we continued to speak of this and that in quite an easy manner. Once we had passed through the grove of tall trees and strolled a bit beyond it, we entered the secluded inlet that Edward Morland had spoken of.

The area was very still and quiet as the thicket of tall trees on three sides effectively absorbed the mingled sounds of talking and laughter drifting toward us on the air from others strolling along the grounds near the lake.

"My, it is, indeed, very private here," I said. "As if we are the only souls left in the world."

Mr. Talbot smiled. "I hardly think that to be the case."

Suddenly a quick movement and a sound coming from within the grove of trees to the right of us caught my attention and I turned towards the disturbance. "What was that?" I asked, genuinely alarmed.

Mr. Talbot also turned. "Probably just a woodland creature." His lips began to twitch as his voice rose. "I say Morland, are there bears in these woods?"

"What woods?"

"*Bears?*" exclaimed Caroline, her tone sounding quite frightened. "I've never seen a wild bear, Mr. Morland. Except among the animals in Mr. Astley's circus."

"Bears are also kept locked up in cages in The Tower of London, Miss Featherstone. Have you been there?" Mr. Morland asked of his now wide-eyed companion.

At that point, I ceased listening to their conversation as a rustling noise and another movement in the trees had again claimed my attention. Suddenly a narrow shaft of light penetrated the interior of the forest and I clearly saw the shadowy figure of a man stealthily step from behind the tree trunk where he'd been hiding and dash toward another tree, and then in a blur, he seemed to disappear.

"Look, just there, Mr. Talbot! I saw a man dashing from one tree to another!" I edged a bit closer to his side and wrapped my free arm about the one of his to which my other arm was already clinging.

He patted my bare hand with his gloved one. "I am certain there is nothing to fear, Miss Abbott. Was no doubt an estate worker, or perhaps a gardener. The Morland grounds are quite extensive, you know. I doubt Sir Morland even knows how many workers he employs. Especially if one takes into account his many mills, the manufactories, and all the shops in the village."

"He owns all the shops in the village?"

Mr. Talbot nodded. "That is my understanding."

"I wonder that the village is not called Morlandville, or Morlandthorpe."

Mr. Talbot smiled. "You have quite an imagination, Miss Abbott. I daresay you are unlike any lady's maid I have ever met."

"Well, truth to tell, this position is only a temporary post for me. You see, I . . . oh! There he is again!" The stranger's head had popped up from behind a tall tree and he appeared now to be staring directly at us.

Mr. Talbot's head spun around to look in the direction I indicated. "Quite shadowy in there. But, I confess I don't see anyone. Perhaps it was just a breeze lifting a bough or somesuch."

"I believe we should return to the tent now, please, sir."

"Certainly, Miss Abbott. Morland!" called Mr. Talbot to his friend, strolling alongside Caroline a few feet from us. "I am told it is time we return to the tent."

Mr. Talbot reached to squeeze my hand, which was still tightly clasping the crook of his elbow, then looking down into my somewhat frightened eyes, the tall gentleman actually winked at me! I confess I was quite taken aback. The unexpectedness of the . . . *over* familiar gesture made me wonder if he thought that because I was a mere lady's maid, or perhaps because I was a *French* lady's maid, that I might be possessed of . . . loose morals and that he was therefore free to trifle with me?

Still thinking on the odd occurrence as we headed back to the road, I said nothing further to my companion the entire way.

At length, Mr. Talbot leaned down to speak in a low tone to me. "If I have done, or said, anything to offend you, Miss Abbott, please accept my sincerest apologies."

Inhaling a sharp breath, I looked up. "I . . . could not help wondering, sir, why you . . . winked at me?"

"Why, because I like you, Miss Abbott." He paused. "I . . . was merely attempting to put your worries to rest, to assure you that you had nothing to fear from the stranger in the woods."

"So, you saw him, as well!"

By then, we had already crossed the road and were approaching the carriages into which a few footmen were already handing up the ladies and their maids.

Mr. Talbot did not reply, but instead favored me with another smile. "I quite enjoyed our walk, Miss Abbott, and our conversation. Good day." He turned and hurried toward the lead carriage where Lady Morland and her maid already sat within awaiting his arrival.

After being handed up into a carriage and taking a seat on the bench opposite Caroline and her sister, I had to admit that I also quite liked Mr. Talbot and that . . . for the most part, I, too, enjoyed conversing with him . . . still, the entire way back to Morland Manor, I could not shake the niggling fear that the man I had spotted hiding in the woods was not an innocent estate worker, but was instead an outsider who seemed intent upon some sort of mischief. But, what? Why would a stranger be lurking in the woods on the grounds of the Morland Estate? And why did Mr. Talbot not admit at the outset that he had also seen the man?

CHAPTER 5

In Which The Heir Argues With His Mother

Wednesday Evening, 18 October 1820

Much later that evening the unsettled feeling that had overtaken me in the woods that afternoon had not yet lifted.

I took my dinner as usual below-stairs with the rest of the household staff. It did not escape my notice that the other lady's maids suddenly seemed a bit stand-offish towards me. I surmised it was due to my having spent a few minutes in the company of Mr. Talbot. Still, I quietly listened to their hushed talk regarding the events of the long afternoon in which not everyone's mistress had been accorded the opportunity to sit with either of the Morland brothers. Everyone had also noticed that the heir did not so much as leave the pavilion after luncheon, therefore he had not walked with any one of the ladies before or after the meal, but had instead lingered over his ale. Then, on our way back to Morland Manor, the heir had declared himself far too fatigued to sit with anyone and had reportedly slept the entire way home!

Since the only one of the maids who seemed to want to talk to me was Miss Hester Grant's maid, Meg, it was she who confided to me that

Miss Grant had already expressed a wish to leave Morland Manor straightaway and return home to London.

"Why does she wish to do that?" I inquired.

"Miss Grant says she finds the heir repugnant. I heard her declare to her mum that she wouldn't marry him if he did ask, in fact, she said she wouldn't marry him if he was the last man on earth. However, she quite likes the second son, Mr. Edward, but her mum told her not to bother with him. 'Tis true he may also be a-lookin' for a bride, but Miss Grant's mum, Lady Stanhope, says he'll likely inherit only a pittance compared to what the heir can expect to receive."

"I rather like Mr. Talbot," I ventured to say.

"Sure and he's handsome enough, make no mistake." Meg grinned conspiratorially. "Looks as if he singled you out today. I saw you a-clingin' to his arm. You was a-lookin' up at him and smilin' like you quite fancied him. Perhaps I shouldn't tell you this, but," she leaned in close to my ear, "I heard Lady Sophia's mum say you was puttin' on airs and for a lady's maid you was quite oversteppin' the bounds. 'Course I don't think so," she added, with a grin. "No reason why we shouldn't also put ourselves forward if given the chance, right?"

My breath caught in my throat. Though I had suspected the others thought ill of me, still to hear the words spoken aloud stung to the quick. But, deciding that I didn't care a fig what Lady Sedgwick thought, I vowed then and there to not think on the haughty woman's words ever again. True, I was still bound to dress her daughter's hair each and every morning and again every evening, but I could easily avoid speaking to the girl's mother if I chose.

Of an evening, most of us maids, except Temple, who generally rushed back up to her ladyship right off, lingered awhile around the dining table in the servant's hall until one of the footmen, or even Griggs, the butler, summoned us to the drawing room for the remainder of the evening. However, when tonight the summons never came, we all eventually drifted back up the stairs to our respective suites.

Wasn't long before Caroline, accompanied by her sister Alice, appeared there, as well. As usual Alice Collins was complaining about one thing or another. Tonight it was that the heir had not even put in an appearance at dinner and beyond those few minutes Caroline had spent with him in the drawing room the previous evening, she had not yet been granted any additional time in his company at all. Mrs. Collins did, however, admit to being delighted that her younger sister had, in fact, garnered a few unexpected moments alone with the second son this afternoon.

"I suppose if the heir does not offer for you, then there would be no shame in having snagged the second son. After all, Sir Morland is surely possessed of enough wealth to go around."

"Of the pair of them, I daresay Edward Morland is the more desirable," Caroline replied. "On the other hand," she lamented, "he is warm and friendly to *all* the girls, so it is not as if he is singling me out."

"Make no mistake, my dear, it did not appear that way to others. Lady Sedgwick was quite incensed when she saw you and Juliette walk off arm-in-arm this afternoon with Mr. Edward Morland and his friend Mr. Talbot." Alice's lips twitched as she turned down the counterpane on the bed in preparation to retire. "She declares our Miss Abbott thinks herself quite above the other lady's maids and blames it on her being French. I confess I find the uppity woman's annoyance vastly amusing. If you ask me, she's the one who should be taken down a peg or two."

"Did I tell you she actually forbid Lady Sophia to speak to me?" Caroline asked, as she slid onto the bench before the dressing table and handed the brush to me in order to comb the tangles from her hair and braid it before bed. "Then following dinner, Lady Sedgwick made a point of reminding me to send Juliette to her suite first thing tomorrow morning to dress her daughter's hair. She insists Lady Sophia's hair *must* be done before mine!"

"Quite cheeky of her if you ask me," declared Alice.

"Well, she is a countess, so I suppose she is accustomed to having things her way."

When I had finished braiding Caroline's hair, I turned to hang up her gown and put away her shoes, aware that I still had to gather up both her, and her sister's, soiled undergarments and take them downstairs to be laundered. In addition, Caroline had somehow managed to tear the hem in her plaid frock whilst we were out walking this afternoon, so before I could crawl into bed tonight, I knew I must mend the dress and then also take it down to be pressed in case she wished to wear it again tomorrow. Truth to say, my Miss Featherstone did possess precious few frocks and it was my duty to keep every last one of them ship-shape.

After hurrying to pick up both sisters' discarded small clothes I asked Caroline if she required my assistance with anything else tonight, then told her I meant to quietly slip down to the laundry and come straight back up here, therefore she mustn't be alarmed if she heard the door open and shut behind me.

"I shall try not to disturb you," I assured her.

"Thank you, Juliette. You are very thoughtful." Caroline favored me with a sleepy smile as she turned back the bedcovers on her side of the bed. "I do not think the least bit ill of you for also doing Lady Sophia's hair. I am most grateful that you agreed to assist me while I am here."

Caroline's kind words made me warm toward her all the more. Miss Featherstone was a sweet-natured girl, and I fervently hoped the second son did offer for her.

Stifling a yawn, she climbed into bed beside her already dozing sister. Seconds later, I blew out the candles then tiptoed from the room and hurried off down the long corridor. Although dozens of candles still burned brightly in the wall sconces, no one but me was about and all seemed quiet.

When I reached the laundry room, I bumped into my cousin Nancy Jane, and was glad of it, as she assured me that she'd personally see that my mistress's underclothes were indeed washed and pressed. She, too, had heard the rumor that I thought myself superior to the other maids because I was French. But, kind soul that my cousin is, Nancy Jane did not point out to me that the ruse, or rather downright falsehood, that I was forwarding was my own doing.

A quarter hour later, I left the laundry room below-stairs now carrying a single candlestick in my hand to light my way back up the dark, narrow stairwell, which also emerged onto the ground floor of the house a bit apart from the wider flight of stairs used by footmen carrying tea up to the drawing room. The back stairs generally were used only when a maid or footman was headed to the laundry room, or early of a morn when one or another servant toted hot water up for a bath, or coal for m'lady's fire.

After pushing open the narrow, nearly invisible, door upon my return to the corridor on the ground floor, I was hurrying toward the wider stairs that led up to the guest wing, when I overheard hushed voices coming from within a chamber I had never before noticed. Although the door to the room was tightly closed, the raised voices coming from within were easily discernable. I recognized Lady Morland's well-modulated treble as she conversed with a gentleman. And, due to what was being said, I soon realized the gentleman was the heir, to whom I had not yet had the dubious pleasure of meeting face-to-face. I'd caught only a glimpse of him at the picnic earlier that day and must say I was not impressed with the chap in the least. Up until now, I'd never heard his grating voice.

"Where were you tonight at dinner, young man? We are two days into this venture and you have not yet spoken with all of the ladies! How is my plan to succeed if you refuse to cooperate?"

"I did not agree to this ridiculous scheme of yours, madam, it is all your contrivance. I doubt even father agreed to it. Though I have not yet spoken with him since I arrived."

"If you had been at dinner tonight, you would have met up with your father! For that matter, where were you all evening? Out wenching, I presume. I would have thought you had learned your lesson by now, young man. For your information, your father wishes you to settle down at once and dispatch your duty by the family the same as I do!"

"On the contrary, madam." The heir snorted. "Father is well aware that I have no intention of leg-shackling myself to a wife any time soon, therefore so far as I am concerned, you may send those eager little misses back to wherever you found them and leave me in peace! I want none of it!"

Although I was secreted just outside the door in the dimly-lit corridor, I clearly heard Lady Morland's huff of displeasure. A few seconds later, she tried another tact with her wayward son.

"Your father is a busy man, William, and not entirely well. When you do speak with him, you will find that we are of the same mind in believing it imperative that you abandon your reckless ways at once and marry and produce an heir. Should your father suffer another one of his debilitating attacks, and does not survive the next one, where will we be? *I cannot run the mills.*"

"The mills and manufactories run themselves. Father has a competent land agent and a dozen or more knowledgeable overseers. Things will continue on as they always have with no interruption."

Staying as silent as possible from where I stood, I soon surmised that there was no plush carpet in this chamber, for at this juncture I heard the heir's footfalls as he angrily paced up and down.

Said Lady Morland, "Nonetheless, it is your duty, William, to learn all you can about managing the Morland estate and to understand the ins and outs of your father's extensive holdings. Thus far, you have only succeeded in learning how to waste your time, and spend your father's money! He indeed expects you to take over for him once he is gone."

"Despite your fears regarding my father's health, madam, rest assured, *you* will quite possibly be the first to meet your maker and if not, you will never be left penniless!"

"My being left penniless is the least of my concerns! The fact is, your *duty* is to marry and beget an heir. And do not attempt to tell me your father is not in complete accord with that!"

"I've no interest in marriage or children," the heir hotly declared again. "And I will thank you to leave off badgering me about it." He snorted. "Tell the little misses they have wasted their time in coming here, that I will have none of it! Truth is I mean to return to London as soon as I've procured additional funds from father. If you must know, I'm down to my last farthing."

"Why does that not surprise me? You are a wasteful, ungrateful wretch, William Morland. For your information, I have instructed your father to not advance you another pound until you take a wife."

"How dare you . . .?"

The next sound I heard was scuffling and then something breaking. I very nearly bolted, but before I could set my feet in motion, Lady Morland started up again.

"I have chosen these ladies carefully, William! I have no doubt that every last one of them will agree to marry you without delay."

"Hmmp. It has been my experience that a young lady must be courted and wooed *ad nauseam*, and then there's no certainty the girl's father will agree to the match. As you well know, I've nothing to recommend me but father's money and you have stupidly included the daughter of an earl amongst your bevy of candidates. Why would the Earl of Sedgwick allow his precious daughter to marry the son of a lowly baronet?"

"He would agree to it because the earl's daughter, as well as every last one of the young ladies present, will *not* be bringing a dowry to the marriage! For your information, every family represented here is destitute. Why else do you think they are so eager to spend time with you? Certainly not due to your fine manners, or civility!"

Once again, I heard the gentleman's snort of derision. "You have wasted everyone's time, madam. Father *will* give me the money I need; I've only to ask him."

Because I now feared the heir might be about to burst forth into the corridor, I took off running towards the stairwell, shielding the flame of the single candle I carried with one hand as best I could.

I had heard plenty. The question now burning like a candle flame in my mind was: *what should I do with my newfound knowledge?*

CHAPTER 6

A Dead Body On The Estate Grounds

For the nonce, I decided to say nothing to anyone about what I'd learnt, although I now knew that Lady Morland was essentially setting a trap to lure an unsuspecting young lady into what could quite possibly be a loveless marriage with her disagreeable son William. However, just knowing that the uppity Lady Sedgwick was as penniless as my Miss Featherstone's family, did render me less fearful of that woman's wrath or condemnation.

Thursday Morning, 19 October 1820
After breakfast the next morning, Caroline and her sister returned to their suite both excitedly discussing the new plans Lady Morland had laid out at breakfast for her houseguests that day.

"Just think, Alice!" Miss Featherstone cried. "A ball! A grand *affaire* at a grand estate!" She twirled about the room before hurrying to the clothespress to fling it wide open. "What shall I wear?" She pulled out one frock after another, then dismissed each in turn. "Oh dear, I fear the only fancy-dress gown I own is far too plain. Cannot we do something to . . . brighten it up?"

Drawing forth the dress, she held it up before herself. Her eyes wide, she whirled towards me. "While you were in Paris, Juliette, you must have seen a good many fashionable gowns! Do tell me how we might . . .?"

"Oh, my," I began, not wanting to admit that on that score, I was completely at a loss. I had, indeed, beheld fashionable gowns in both Paris and London but I had no notion how to *make* one.

"Your gown is quite suitable as it is, Caroline," her sister declared, snatching the frock from the younger girl and returning it to the clothespress.

For once, I quite agreed with the older woman's assessment. And, rushed to say so. "The gown is quite lovely as it is, *Mademoiselle.* You will look beautiful."

Still, Caroline's face fell. "I will not look half so fine as Lady Sophia," she whined.

"Never mind that. If the heir runs true to form, he may not even attend the ball." Alice's tone was as disagreeable as ever. "Let us think instead about the theatrical production that Lady Morland mentioned to us this morning."

Theatrical production? My ears perked up.

"Very well," Caroline said, her plain ball gown all but forgotten. She turned again to me. "The ball is two nights hence and Lady Morland told us she has invited a goodly number of additional guests to come to Morland Manor for the occasion. But because most of those guests will be staying the night, on the following afternoon after church services, all of us are to act out a little play for the guest's entertainment before they depart." Her countenance began to brighten. "It should be amusing; I've never taken part in a real play before either!"

"We are all to gather in the drawing room right after luncheon this very afternoon," Alice added, taking a seat on the bench before the dressing table and attempting to smooth her own gray-streaked locks. "At that time, I assume we will all be assigned our various roles in the play. You and the other maids are also invited to participate, Juliette."

"Oh-h-h," I breathed, my eyes widening with pleasure. Would Nancy Jane or perhaps, others of the chambermaids, also be included in the theatrical production, I wondered, but, of course, refrained from inquiring.

"Now then, my dears," began Lady Morland, once everyone had taken seats in the drawing room directly after luncheon that very afternoon. "I have here several copies of our little play, one of which I will keep as I will be directing our production." She directed a smile of satisfaction all around.

"And these," she reached to pat a stack of pages to the right of her on the table near where she sat, "are copies of each of your individual parts. Unfortunately, I've not enough copies to go around, so you ladies will have to team up with one another in order to learn your lines and to practice repeating them from memory. This evening, after dinner, we will hold our first rehearsal right here in the drawing room."

She glanced up as both her sons, William and Edward, and Mr. Talbot quietly entered the room and settled into comfortable chairs just inside the doorway.

"I am grateful that all three of you gentlemen are here," she said, nodding their way, "as you each also have roles to play in our theatrical production."

I glanced over in time to see the scowl that at once appeared on the heir's face. When he made as if to rise, his younger brother grabbed his arm to pull him back down, but the heir jerked from his grasp as if his brother had accosted him and was also causing him a great deal of pain. He at once began to rub the place on his arm where his brother had grasped it.

"If Talbot and I have to play a part, then you do, as well," Edward said aloud.

"Well, you needn't manhandle me!" The heir commenced to hold his injured arm close to his chest as he sullenly scooted onto his tailbone, cradling his injured arm upon the swell of his fine silk waistcoat, which appeared to be stretched to the limit over his swollen midsection.

During this exchange, Lady Morland had been sifting through the pages of the script; now she said, "Here are your scripts, gentlemen. You can decide amongst yourselves which part you will each play."

Because Edward was still keeping a watchful eye on his older brother, Mr. Talbot stepped forward to retrieve the sheaf of papers.

"Now then, ladies, you will please divide yourselves up into groups of three or four. Yes, go ahead and do so now, please. But, only the younger girls. We elder ones," she said on a laugh, "will be needed to make up part of the audience."

A bit of shuffling ensued and when we had rearranged ourselves into groups, she rose to pass out the pages of the script. As instructed the chaperones had moved to a pair of sofas at the opposite end of the spacious room.

"Do keep in mind that during the grand finale everyone will be on stage to sing the final song together as a chorus. We shall practice the song this evening, as well, to ensure that on the day of the performance, it will be perfect! Let us all have fun now, shall we?"

A good bit of tittering and exclaiming ensued, then after the members of the three groups drew together, we all began to discuss the storyline. Eventually we each claimed the part we wished to play and everyone settled down to quietly study his or her lines.

A mere quarter-hour into our work, however, our concentration was interrupted by the appearance of the Morland butler Griggs advancing swiftly into the room, if a gentleman of his age and bearing can be said to do anything swiftly.

"Do forgive me, your ladyship," he began, "but there is a gentleman here to see . . ."

At that instant, a rather rough-looking, rotund chap wearing a dark blue coat with an official-looking insignia on the breast pocket barged into the room, skirting clean past the stolid Griggs. "I was told Sir Morland is not at home, your ladyship. Where might I find the gentleman, ma'am?"

"Why," Lady Morland rose, her countenance clearly revealing both her confusion and indignation over the intrusion. "You are Constable Wainwright, are you not? Has some trouble arisen, my good man?"

"A dead body was found on the grounds, ma'am, quite near where your party was assembled yesterday afternoon. I assume the man to be one of Sir Morland's estate workers which is why I need him to properly identify the corpse, if you please."

At the word 'corpse' every single young lady in the room, as well as the chaperones, I expect, gasped aloud. I even heard a few shrieks coming from the more sheltered amongst us.

"You are oversetting my guests, sir. Please step this way." Lady Morland hurriedly ushered the ruddy-faced man from the room, an impassive Griggs following close on her heels.

It was the younger son Edward, rather than the heir as one might expect, who rose to take charge of the proceedings in the drawing room.

"Ladies, I assure you there is no cause for alarm. Pay the constable's words no mind. He and my father will no doubt have this sorted out in no time. Do carry on as before." He smiled all around.

When not a one of us appeared the least bit mollified, he added, "Rest assured, ladies, you are every one safe. M'brother and Mr. Talbot and I will stay right here with you the remainder of the afternoon."

"Hmph," grumbled the heir. "You can count me out of this nonsense." Popping up from his chair, he flung open a small side door nearly hidden in the far wall of the drawing room and let it bang shut behind him as he retreated from the premises.

Exchanging apprehensive glances amongst ourselves, one by one, we ladies turned hesitantly back to our work. As several of the chaperones had also quitted the room soon after the scripts had been handed out, the few who remained now also rose to leave, each wearing anxious looks on their faces.

Hmm, thought I, a dead body found on the grounds . . . and quite near where we picnicked yesterday. Naturally, I could not help wondering if the stranger I spotted lurking in the woods had anything to say to this new turn.

I cast a glance toward Mr. Talbot to ascertain what he might be thinking. Would he tell the constable what I had seen, or perhaps, should I?

As it turned out, we were all given a chance to tell the constable if we had spotted anything out of the ordinary whilst picnicking the previous afternoon. A half hour before tea was brought in that very afternoon, Constable Wainwright sent word via Lady Morland that he wished to speak with each and every one of us in turn.

The interviews with the constable proceeded soon afterward, the ladies again taken in by rank and precedence, along with their maids and chaperones, but, by all accounts, each interview took only a few moments and were over and done with quickly.

After everyone else had been interviewed, Griggs finally ushered Mrs. Collins and Caroline and myself into the small anteroom into which the heir had earlier disappeared, and which appeared to be used as a reading room as it contained only a square desk with a chair sitting behind it and two overstuffed chairs placed at angles before a built-in bookcase lining one wall. Today, Constable Wainwright sat behind the desk, which contained only an inkpot, a scattering of quill pens, and a sheaf of papers he had spread out before him.

Not waiting for Griggs to properly state our names, the constable muttered, "I suppose none of you ladies saw anything unusual yesterday afternoon either." The man hadn't even bothered to look up when we filed in.

"I did, sir."

The constable's head jerked up the same moment as both Mrs. Collins' and Caroline's swiveled toward me.

"That so?" The constable sat up a bit straighter. "And what did you see, Miss . . .?"

"Abbott, sir. Juliette Abbott."

He appeared to take note of my black frock and white frilled pinafore and cap. "You from around here, Miss Abbott?"

"No, sir. Although I was staying with my cousin Nancy Jane Abbott before I . . ."

"Any kin to George, or, Jack Abbott?"

"Yessir, George Abbott is my uncle. Jack is my cousin."

"I see. And I take it you are employed here at the Manor, that correct?"

"I am employed here *temporarily,* sir."

"Meaning?" The man was now intently studying me.

"I am employed as lady's maid to Miss Featherstone . . ." a hand indicated Caroline, ". . . but only for the duration of the house party. After that I . . ."

He glanced at Caroline. "I take it you are Miss Featherstone?"

"Yessir," Caroline and I both replied in unison.

The constable looked towards Alice. "And you are?"

"Miss Featherstone's elder sister, Mrs. Collins. We both reside in London, sir."

The constable scribbled a notation on his pad, then looked back up at me. "So, what exactly did you see yesterday afternoon, Miss Abbott, that you deem . . . out of the ordinary?"

"I saw a man in the woods."

"Oh!" Caroline exclaimed. "But you never said a word, Juliette!"

I glanced at her. "I told Mr. Talbot what I had seen and very soon afterward, we all went back across the road."

The constable glared at me. "Mr. Talbot did not mention seeing a man in the woods, Miss Abbott. Are you certain that you saw a . . .?"

"Of course, I am certain! I saw a man hiding behind a tree, and then he dashed to another tree and stood there watching us. I am not mistaken, sir. I know what I saw."

"Very well, then. Can you describe the man for me? Tall, short, thin? What was he wearing?"

"Well, I . . . only just caught a glimpse of him. It happened right after Mr. Edward Morland and his friend, Mr. Talbot, took Miss Featherstone and me for a walk following luncheon, and then when we were all down by the lake, I spotted a man in the woods who appeared to be watching us."

"Would you recognize this . . . er, man, if you were to see him again?"

"I daresay I would not, sir. As you know, the woods are quite thick from that aspect, and already the shadows were lengthening. I fear I can tell you nothing at all about him." I shrugged. "I did not see what he wore, his clothing appeared . . . dark, but not the least bit fashionable. He was wearing a cap, a sort of flat cap . . ." I paused to consider a moment. "And, he wore a kerchief tied around his neck."

The constable fairly lurched up from his chair. "A kerchief tied around his neck, ye' say?"

"Yes, sir. It was red; I do recall that. The sunlight had caught it; in fact, it was his red kerchief that initially alerted me to him. At first I thought it was a redbird's wing, then when the man dashed off, I could see that it was not a bird at all, it was a man wearing a red kerchief tied about his neck."

The constable said nothing for a long moment, then exhaling the breath he'd been holding, he said, "The dead man wore a red kerchief tied around his neck."

"Oh-h!" All three of us sucked in our breath.

"You saw the dead man, Juliette!" Caroline exclaimed.

"Appears I did," I murmured. Although I tried, I could not refrain from asking a question of the constable myself. "W-When do you think the man might have . . . passed on, sir?"

"Difficult to say. The body was discovered late this morning. Skull bashed in."

"Oh-h!" We three gasped once again.

"That will be quite enough, sir." Griggs moved to usher the three of us from the room.

Hmmm, thought I, a man murdered on the Morland Manor grounds. And here I thought life in the country would be as dull as dishwater.

CHAPTER 7

An Accusation from an Unexpected Quarter

Thursday Evening, 19 October 1820

Before going down to dinner that evening, the Lady Sophia's maid Lucy rapped at Miss Featherstone's bedchamber door to deliver a message for me from Lady Sedgwick in which the countess said that she and her daughter had requested a tray be sent up to their room, therefore I was not needed to dress Lady Sophia's hair as they would not be going down to dinner.

Lucy confided to Miss Featherstone that both ladies were quite overset due to the afternoon's disclosure that a dead body had been found on the estate grounds. "'Spect they's neither one been so close to that sort of happenin' afore," she added.

When Lucy departed, Alice voiced her thoughts on the subject. "I expect we'll soon hear that Lady Sedgwick and her daughter have returned to London, which, now that I think on it, is precisely what we should do, Caroline. . ."

"No!" Caroline cried. "I don't want to leave. Unless you think Lady Morland will cancel the ball. I do *so* wish to attend a real ball in a grand ballroom. I fear I shall never have another opportunity to do so. It's not as if I will ever have a proper London Season," she pouted. "Please say we can stay, Alice, at least until the ball is over."

Poor Caroline looked quite forlorn perched on the little bench before the dressing table, absently twisting the thin gold ring she wore on her finger. Alice sat on the edge of the bed, her lips pursed with annoyance. Across the small room, I was busy picking up bits and pieces of discarded garments and replacing them in the clothespress. When my task was completed, I asked, "Would you ladies like me to ring for a tray to be sent up for you this evening?"

"That will not be necessary, Juliette." Alice rose. "I would like to be on hand to see what, if anything, Sir Morland has to say on the matter. The older gentleman was present at dinner last evening, but had very little to say to anyone."

"I can certainly see where the heir comes by his dour demeanor," Caroline chimed in. "Sir Morland may be clever enough to have amassed a great fortune but he is a veritable curmudgeon."

"Which . . ." I ventured to say (*although I probably shouldn't have freely blurted out my thoughts on the subject*) ". . . should give you a good notion of what the heir will be like once he's attained his father's age." Standing on tiptoe before the clothespress, I reached to take down Miss Featherstone's nightrail. Crossing the room to lay the garment on the end of the bed, I asked, "Will you be wanting to change into another frock before going down to dinner, Caroline?"

"Miss Abbott," the girl's sister addressed me angrily, "I have noticed of late that your manner has become a good deal *too* familiar with your mistress. First of all, you should *not* be addressing Caroline by her . . ."

"Alice, *I* granted Juliette permission to address me by my given name. Miss Featherstone sounds far too formal when we are alone together." Caroline thrust up her chin. "Besides, in the short time I have known Juliette, I feel that she and I have become friends. If you wish to go down to dinner tonight Alice, you are free to do so." She turned toward me. "Juliette, you will please ring for a tray to be brought up. A tray for *two.* I would like *you* to dine with me tonight, if you please."

"Very well," I murmured and moved to the bell pull to do as my mistress bid.

"Well, then. I suppose that while I am gone, you two girls can study your lines for the play." Her lips forming a thin, straight line, Alice Collins emitted one final huff of displeasure before exiting the room, her graying head held high.

Upon returning from dinner later that evening, however, Alice rather gleefully brought back some interesting news. It seemed that Lady Sedgwick and her daughter Lady Sophia were not the only guests overly disturbed by a dead body having been found on the estate grounds, especially since Constable Wainwright's decision to question everyone seemed to suggest that the man had not died of natural causes but was, in fact, *murdered*. A number of other guests, specifically Miss Amelia Durham and her aunt were quite annoyed.

"Miss Durham possesses a somewhat spinsterish attitude," Alice Collins said. "I daresay I have never once seen the young woman smile. However, that has nothing to say to anything. What I meant to say was that Sir Morland himself is of the same mind regarding the murder. In fact, after dinner in the drawing room, he came quite close to actually accusing his elder son, William, of committing the crime!"

"Sir Morland accused his own son?" Caroline cried. I had never seen her eyes quite so wide. "What did Lady Morland say?"

"She appeared quite enraged by her husband's accusations and hastily ushered both her husband and the heir from the room. Not a one of the three of them bothered to excuse themselves," Alice declared in a somewhat offended tone.

The murder and the fact that Sir Morland suspected his own son of having committed the crime all seemed rather havey-cavey to me, but because I had earlier decided that henceforth when I was in Mrs. Collins' presence, I would keep my personal thoughts to myself, I said nothing. Still, I longed to discuss the matter with *someone*.

Therefore, soon after I helped my mistress change into her nightclothes and had gathered up the ladies' soiled undergarments, I hurried below-stairs in the hope of coming upon my cousin Nancy Jane. With so many guests in the house, I knew the chambermaids were now kept over-busy each and every day, as well as up overlong each and every night. Nancy Jane told me the last time I spoke with her that since the house had filled up with guests she rarely crawled into bed before midnight. It was close on that now.

Sure enough, I found my cousin seated alone before a long table in a cluttered closet polishing a pair of muddy boots. She looked near to falling asleep when I stuck my head in the door.

"Are you going to be here a spell, Nancy Jane?"

At the sound of my voice, her mob-capped head jerked up.

"I ain't free to go no where 'til I get the heir's boots clean."

I walked on in. "I've brought some small clothes to be laundered. Shall I leave them with you, or take them into the . . .?"

"I'll carry 'em in for you. More likely to get done if'n the others don't see it was you what brung 'em."

"Then I'll help you shine these boots." I drew up a stool and picked up a wire brush. "I wanted to ask you if you had heard anything about the murder? Did Uncle George, or Jack, know the dead man?"

Nancy Jane's head cocked. "Jack knowed him all right."

I kept my voice low. "Do you mean they were friends?"

"No, not that." She shook her head. "I mean most ever'one in the village knows who Kenneth Grimes is. And, they knows his sister, too."

"What do you mean? What does his sister have to say to anything?"

She shrugged. "Girl ain't no better'n she has to be. Rumor is, the Morland heir got a babe on her the last time he was here. Girl is shoddy goods now, an' that's a fact, but her mite is the spittin' image of the heir."

"No-o-o." My jaw dropped. "Well, that still doesn't explain why Sir Morland would accuse his own son of killing the girl's brother."

Nancy grinned. "I heard about that, too. Footman serving coffee in the drawin' room afterward said the master all but grabbed his boy by the ear and dragged him outta' there." She paused, then, shrugged again. "Don't matter none, though. Won't nothing happen even if William Morland did kill him."

"Why do you say that? Evidently the constable is trying to get to the bottom of it. Are you saying if the heir murdered a man he wouldn't hang for the crime?"

Nancy Jane stopped what she doing to look squarely at me. "What do you think, Juliette? Ever'one hereabouts is beholden to Sir Morland for their livelihoods, includin' my own mama and papa. I don't know a single soul around here who'd say a harsh word against any of the Morlands, no matter what they done."

I digested that as I swiped at the layer of dried mud clinging to the sole of the brown leather boot in my hands. "So why would Constable Wainwright bother to question anyone about it?"

Nancy Jane returned to her work on the other boot. "Constable might not know what the rest of us knows, about Kenneth Grimes' sister, I mean. Country folk don't keep secrets from one another, but we do our best to keep 'em from the 'thorities. Besides, maybe the Morland heir didn't do it. Lotsa' guests at the Manor house now. Some of the fine ladies brought along their own groomsmen. Lady Sedgwick brought along her own footman. Lady Morland put on extra stable hands, some from the next village over. Good many of 'em been seen a-drinkin' and carousin' at the Cock and Crow in Thornbury ever' night this week. All them extra hands ain't from this county."

I inhaled a long breath. "Well, to determine who might, and might not, have had a deadly run-in with the late Kenneth Grimes will probably take a heap of questions and a good bit of time."

"I 'spect the killer is a-thinkin' the same thing. If you ask me, Kenneth Grimes' murderer is likely to go free and unpunished."

Making my way back upstairs later that night, I continued to ponder what I'd learned from Nancy Jane. That Sir Morland would come so close to openly accusing his own son of murder, in front of houseguests, and the majority of them being women, did not make me think too terribly highly of him. On the other hand, that the baronet would be outraged over such an immoral act even if his own son was the guilty party told me he did expect his family to adhere to certain moral standards, even if those

standards did fall a good deal lower than that which was considered
entirely proper.

However, Sir Morland's actions in this particular case also told me
that quite possibly he was aware that his wayward son had sired a child by
a local trollop, the dead man's sister. Which made me wonder if Lady
Morland also knew, and was she, or her husband, contributing to the
child's welfare? Thinking further in that vein, I speculated it was quite
possible that the dead man, Kenneth Grimes, having heard that William
Morland was now back at Morland Manor, was in fact, seeking revenge for
the heir having dishonored his sister. But instead of just confronting him,
or stopping at a round of fisticuffs, the two had fought to the death and the
heir had killed him. Perhaps, unintentionally, but nonetheless the man was
dead.

Oh! Suddenly I recalled how this very afternoon, the heir had
clasped his arm to his middle as if it were paining him. His brother had
certainly not grasped William Morland's arm tightly enough to injure it.
From what I saw, he had barely touched him. Did that mean that the heir
had been in a fight with someone . . . Kenneth Grimes, perhaps?

But, if the heir did not *intend* to kill Grimes, would his death still
be considered murder? Or, merely an accident? Something told me that if
William Morland were, indeed, the guilty party, the ruling would likely
come down as . . . accidental death, even if he *had* intended to kill the man.

Before crawling into bed that night, I wondered if the whole truth
about the murder at Morland Manor would ever be brought to light?

CHAPTER 8

How Did His Boots Get So Muddy?

Friday, 20 October 1820

While dressing Lady Sophia's hair the following morning, I learned that Lady Sedgwick wished to leave Morland Manor at once and intended to approach Lady Morland first thing regarding her plans.

"We will likely be able to leave before luncheon," the countess declared to her daughter with me standing right there brush in hand.

"But, the ball, mama," Lady Sophia protested. "I should like to attend the ball. We could leave first thing the morning after."

From her position before the tall wardrobe, Lady Sedgwick whirled to face her daughter. "A man has been murdered on the estate grounds, Sophia! It is both unsafe and unwise to linger in the country another day! I have always been of the opinion that country folk are uncivilized; this heinous crime merely proves my point."

Gazing at me in the mirror as I stood behind her, Lady Sophia and I exchanged longsuffering looks. Still, I dared not voice my thoughts aloud for fear of censure from the girl's high-ranking mother.

"I will send word to my groomsmen to get our carriage ready post haste and we shall leave for London just as soon as our belongings are packed," declared the Countess in a tone that brooked no objection.

Neither her daughter nor I offered one.

A bit later, while eating my own breakfast in the servant's hall, I overheard additional talk on the same subject amongst the lady's maids.

"My mistress says the heir being accused of murder by his own father puts a different complexion on things," said Tilly, maid to Miss Amelia Durham, the daughter of a baron.

"Sir Morland accused his own son of the crime?" exclaimed Lucy, Lady Sophia's maid.

I smothered a grin as I recalled that Lady Sedgwick and Lady Sophia had both taken dinner in their room last evening, which meant that Lady Sedgwick had not witnessed, nor yet heard about, what had occurred in the drawing room after dinner. Had she known that the heir had been accused of the crime, no doubt she would have hustled her daughter off to London last night!

" . . . didn't accuse him outright," Miss Elizabeth Banes' maid Rosie was saying, "he merely asked him what he knew of it."

"But his tone told everyone that he *expected* his son knew plenty!" insisted Tilly.

"What about your mistress?" Miss Hester Grant's maid, Meg asked me.

"Miss Featherstone does not want to leave Morland Manor at all, but her sister Mrs. Collins wishes to. They have decided to stay at least for the ball, but beyond that, I haven't a clue what their plans are."

As I rose to leave the servant's dining hall, I caught a glimpse of Nancy Jane hurrying back down the stairs from her morning duties of changing the bed linens and airing out the bedchambers. Her brown curls were tousled and her cap askew. In her arms, she carried a bundle of dirty bed linens.

"Have 'ye heard what 'ye'll be a-doin' today?" she asked, pausing briefly before she hurried on her way.

"No. Have things changed again?"

My cousin nodded. "You're all to go sightseeing up to the old Castle ruins. Place is haunted, but legend says there's buried treasure, although no one's ever found it." She giggled. "Take a shovel and if'n ye' finds the treasure, ye' can share it with me!" Laughing, she hurried on her way.

Minutes later, in Miss Featherstone's bedchamber, Caroline and her sister were also talking about the altered plans for the day.

"No one wanted to stay indoors and study their lines for a silly old play," Caroline told me, "so suddenly Lady Morland ups and cancels the play altogether. "We're to go sightseeing today. Someplace called The Old Warwick Castle Ruins. Legend has it, the castle is haunted!" she added, a sparkle of delight in her hazel eyes.

"Well, I don't mind saying I was glad enough when the *heir* said he didn't want to go," Mrs. Collins interjected.

Caroline turned to me again. "William Morland said he'd seen all the sights around here and that he intended to go angling in the river today instead."

"What of Edward and Mr. Talbot," I asked. "Are they to go with us, or will they also go angling?"

"All the gentlemen are to go with us today," Caroline replied. "Lady Morland told the heir, 'you *will* accompany us today, sir, and *every* day, young man.' At times, she rather treats him as if he were still in the nursery," she declared.

"Well, as large a woman as she is," I said, although I probably shouldn't have, "I suppose she could still turn her eldest son over her knees and paddle him if necessary." Which brought a laugh from Caroline and surprisingly, also a chuckle from Alice.

In a mere half hour's time, all the ladies and their chaperones and maids were once again assembled below-stairs in the foyer. This time, I observed that Lady Morland was making the seating arrangements in the opposite manner from the usual order of precedence. Therefore, since Miss Featherstone occupied the bottom rung of the ranking ladder, she and I soon found ourselves seated in the same vehicle alongside the heir; Caroline beside Mr. William Morland, me on the bench opposite, our fancy landau picked out with red stripes on either side, at the front of the pack.

Miss Amelia Durham, I noted, was in the carriage directly behind us seated primly beside Mr. Edward Morland. Her chin was hitched up as tightly as her bun of brown hair was drawn back from her face. I wondered what, if anything, the pair of them would find to talk about? Sill, when we all traded places, Caroline would be the next young lady allowed to spend time in *his* company so that was something pleasant to look forward to.

Then, in a surprising twist, or perhaps in an effort to liven things up, I noticed Lady Morland paired Miss Hester Grant and her maid Meg with Mr. Talbot inside the third open-air landau. The rest of the ladies, except for Lady Sedgwick and her daughter, who were seated side-by-side in a small tidy curricle at the end of the parade, were all handed into a much larger barouche, though it was still a rather tight squeeze to fit everyone in. That I was also greatly looking forward to *our* turn to sit with Mr. Talbot brought a pleased smile to my face.

The brisk October day was especially warm and sunny, the blue sky overhead dotted with puffy white clouds, although on the horizon, I spotted a few dark ones lurking. Still, it felt good to be leaving the manor house altogether, if only for the day. The disclosure of the dead body found on the estate grounds and the resulting interrogation by the constable last evening had managed to transform the festive atmosphere in the house to one of anxiety and gloom and in some cases, even, suspicion.

Although I had not yet heard anything said on the subject, before everyone had been handed into a carriage, I spotted Lady Morland and Lady Sedgwick conversing together in the foyer, and suspected that Lady Morland had somehow persuaded Lady Sedgwick to postpone her plans to leave for London today. Although, now that I thought on it, the conversation could have been about Lady Sedgwick refusing to allow her daughter to ride with the heir in his carriage and that was what had precipitated the change in order. But, whatever the reason, I was glad of it, and settled back to enjoy the drive and whatever the day brought in the way of new adventure.

What it brought in the way of conversation with the heir was precious little. That surly gentleman was dressed as if he still fully intended to go angling today; wearing a tattered-looking pair of tweed breeches tucked into his boots, (*clean* boots, by the by) and a dark jacket hanging open over a plain cream-colored shirt. Thus far into our drive, he had spent the entire time with his arms folded across his middle, his eyes glued to the trees and open fields the tidy open landau was tooling past.

Since there hadn't yet been a scrap of talk amongst the three of us, I began to speculate upon the boots the gentleman wore, which looked to be the very boots I had scraped clean the night before. Suddenly, I wondered *how* the gentleman's boots had become so very muddy? The day of the picnic, which was merely the day before yesterday, he had not got out of the carriage to walk down by the lake as had the rest of us, then that night he wasn't at dinner, and had only arrived home much later when I overheard he and his mother arguing. The constable claimed the murdered man's body was discovered yesterday near where we had picnicked the day before. Although it had not rained a single day this week, I had noticed that the ground closer to the little lake where we ventured was indeed quite muddy, so if the man I spotted hiding in the woods had somehow come upon William Morland *there* and the two had fought, that could explain *where* the heir's boots had become so very muddy. And, they had, indeed, been *quite* muddy.

The heir was sitting right here, so close our knees were nearly knocking, so since no one was saying anything, I decided to ask him a question, or two. After all, I might never have another opportunity and I confess I would breathe easier if the identity of the killer were made known and the guilty party removed from the premises, even if it did turn out to be the Morland heir.

"I understand you wished to go angling today, sir," I began.

His eyes cut toward me. I watched his lips firm as if considering whether or not to answer my query. "Indeed," he finally muttered and promptly looked away.

"Do you often go angling?"

His dark eyes again shifted toward me, this time the scowl upon his face deepening, the look clearly saying: now why would a silly, no-account lady's maid want to know *that*?

So as not to anger him, or horrors! arouse *his* suspicions in any way, I smiled. "I merely wondered if you go angling in the little lake where we picnicked the other day? I'm certain I saw a fish jump clean out of the water as we walked near the shore."

The rude man sniffed but with his lips again pressed tightly together, he deigned to reply.

I smiled again. "Perhaps that very fish, and more like it, will be there another day; and you can catch them then."

As if to dismiss my foolish prattle altogether, the heir cast a disdainful eye-roll skyward and shook his uncovered head.

William Morland was, indeed, a disagreeable, foul-tempered man who lacked refinement and possessed not a shred of decent manners. I vowed then and there to never honor him again with a single word from my lips.

Neither Caroline nor I were one bit sorry when it was time to change places with Miss Durham and her maid. Once we were settled in Mr. Edward Morland's carriage, it was as if suddenly, the warm sun was, indeed, shining down upon us and filling every corner of the countryside with joy and cheer.

"Hello, again, Miss Featherstone; how nice to see you Miss Abbott. Lovely day for a drive, is it not?"

Caroline came instantly alive, a pretty smile lighting up her face, her hazel eyes sparkling. "It is quite a lovely day, sir. Might you tell us about the old castle ruins, please? I've never seen a ruin before."

"My cousin says there is also buried treasure there," I added, feeling inordinately at ease in this gentleman's company. It was as if the two gentlemen sprang from a completely different litter of pups.

"Your cousin?" the second son inquired.

"Nancy Jane Abbott. She's a chambermaid at the manor house. It was she who told Lady Morland about me, and . . . that's how I came to be here, as a lady's maid, I mean." I paused. "Forgive me, I should not be talking. You and Caroline carry on, please."

Looking away, I chastised myself for taking time away from Caroline's precious few moments with Mr. Edward Morland. *She* was keen on him, and *why* I was employed as a lady's maid at Morland Manor was truly a thoughtless thing to say. Suddenly, I realized that since the murder and the interrogation that followed, I'd clean forgot that I was pretending to be a *French* lady's maid. Couldn't even recall when was the last time I'd said, "*Oui, mademoiselle.*"

"Tell me, Miss Featherstone," I heard Edward ask Caroline, "where in London do you reside?"

I ceased to listen as Caroline and Edward Morland animatedly conversed with one another. For her sake, I was happy that the second son seemed to be taking a keen interest in her. And for my part, I was vastly looking forward to speaking with Mr. Talbot again very soon.

Unfortunately, we reached the Old Warwick Castle Ruins before another switch-up within the carriages was made. And, rather than begin to tramp through the picturesque ruins at once; ruins, which consisted mainly of bits and pieces of toppled towers and chards of old stone railings, Lady Morland declared that we should all eat a quick bite of lunch before we set out on foot. She directed us toward the four or five blankets that a brace of servants were even then spreading upon the ground.

With regret, I noticed that the three gentlemen grouped themselves together on one blanket forcing the ladies to seek out one another's company upon additional pallets spread upon the ground. Luncheon today was obviously a hastily prepared affair as it consisted only of bread, three kinds of cheese, boiled eggs and apples. However, I noted that the men also had cold meats along with their bread and cheese. I assumed that men, being of a hardier constitution than we ladies, did, indeed, require hardier fare.

At any rate, as soon as we'd all eaten our fill, the servants began to gather up the remains of the food and the blankets, while Lady Morland and the three gentlemen led us towards the ruins. To tour the dilapidated structure took less time than to tell about it and soon we were all once again herded back into the carriages. And, none too soon, for almost at once the heavens opened up and a pelting rain began to shower down upon us. This, of course, necessitated a quick halt as drivers and footmen hopped down to hurriedly haul up the leather hoods on those landaus possessed of such a contraption. Fortunately, ours was. But, unfortunately, Lady Sedgwick's was not. Therefore, both she and her daughter, Lady Sophia, were already quite rain-soaked by the time they climbed up and squeezed into our small carriage.

Conversation was also noticeably thin on the return trip to Morland Manor. Except for numerous huffs and loud complaints coming from the incensed and now quite wet Lady Sedgwick, nary a pleasant word was said or heard. Whether or not this occurrence would cause the soggy countess to renew her decision to leave Morland Manor before the day was out was anyone's guess.

CHAPTER 9

Juliette Finds A Hidey-Hole

Friday Evening, 20 October 1820

That I was called upon that evening to dress the Lady Sophia's hair, which was still a bit damp at the time, told me that her mother had, indeed, decided to hold off on their return trip to Town. Lady Sophia confided to me that she was quite looking forward to the ball the following evening so I supposed that meant mother and daughter, and all of Lady Sedgwick's groomsmen, her personal footman and maids, would be staying. At least, until after the ball.

While the ladies were at dinner, I once again took my place for the evening meal at the long table in the servant's hall with the other lady's maids. Meg, Miss Hester Grant's maid, was still the only one friendly enough to draw me into conversation.

"I noticed your Miss Featherstone was the first to ride with the heir today," Meg said. "How did she like him?"

I emitted a rather haughty "hmmp" sound. "I don't believe she liked him one bit. I know I don't care a fig for the man. A more disagreeable, discourteous, boorish gentleman I have never met."

"Come now, Miss Abbott," said Rosie, Miss Elizabeth Banes' maid, "tell us what you *really* think of him."

"What I really think is . . . if that gentleman can persuade even *one* of our mistresses to wed him it will be a miracle! I daresay we would all be a good deal better off if he would take himself out of the running. Why, if the second son were the heir instead of William Morland, everyone of our ladies would have their caps set for him." I was warming to my subject now. "I daresay, it's too bad *he* wasn't the one found dead on the estate grounds yesterday instead of that other bloke!"

A few titters followed my brash pronouncement. But, I also noticed there was also a few nods of agreement.

Meg said, "Mr. Edward Morland does seem to find your Miss Featherstone agreeable."

"Indeed, he does," I replied. "If a gentleman can be called a diamond of the first water, to be sure, he is that. Edward Morland is a thoughtful, kind, gentleman; and he is also charming and charitable. He even listens when *I* speak." I paused, then added, "Unlike his boor of a brother."

The talk amongst the maids turned to other things and I was soon climbing the stairs back up to Miss Featherstone's suite. I did feel a bit guilty for unburdening myself so roundly in front of everyone tonight, but I meant every single word I said, and more. I truly did wish Kenneth Grimes had killed William Morland instead of the other way around. Had that happened, it would instantly elevate Edward to the role of Morland heir and place my Miss Featherstone in good stead to become his wife. Not that I thought for an instant that that would ever come about. The heir being killed, I mean; not that Edward would wed my Miss Featherstone.

Saturday, 21 October 1820

The next morning, the entire manor house was a flurry of activity as a host of additional guests arrived especially for the ball that night. Since most of the new arrivals had come from a long way off, they would be staying the night and return home the following day. Though new guests had been expected, still the influx threw the footmen, the chambermaids and the entire kitchen staff and scullery into an anxious frenzy as everyone's backbreaking duties increased at least ten-fold and their stamina did not.

"Half of us ain't slept in two days," Nancy Jane declared to me as I hurried past her into the laundry room, me for the third or fourth time that day.

I had already spent a good deal of time traipsing up and down the back stairs in a rush to have ball gowns pressed, to wash out a special petticoat (and hope it would dry in time to wear that night), to iron a ribbon for my mistresses hair, to attempt to remove a spot on the finger of a glove and to see if I could find someone to help me repair the tattered toe of a dancing slipper. Today, we maids had been instructed to use the back stairs exclusively as the wide, front stairs were reserved especially for new guests and their maids and footmen carrying up valises and other baggage, therefore to bump into another lady's maid hurrying either up or down the narrow back stairs had become commonplace.

"Don't forget that Lady Sophia wishes you to dress her hair *before* tea, Miss Abbott," Lucy said to me in passing.

"Tell her I'll be there as quickly as I can!"

As the day wore on, the excitement in the manor house grew. I saw armloads of flowers and greenery being carted into the house, and later, a score or more of musicians carrying in instruments and thick packets of music. Giving in to my innate curiosity at that point, I decided to furtively follow them and soon learned that the ballroom was on the backside of the huge house overlooking an enormous knot garden, which I did not know was there, and certainly had not had an opportunity to explore. Perhaps another time.

Now, all I wished was that Lady Morland had included we lady's maids in tonight's festivities! My longing to attend a fancy-dress ball was every bit as fervent as that of Miss Featherstone. To be sure, tonight's "do" was as close as I would ever come to a real ball. If only I could figure out a way to, at least, *watch* the proceedings.

From Nancy Jane, I learned that there was to be a lavish supper served that night following the ball, which meant that tea this afternoon was essentially the main meal of the day. Therefore, right after I dressed Lady Sophia's hair and then, while my mistress and everyone else were ensconced in the drawing room for tea, I skipped my own tea in the servant's hall and instead boldly betook myself up the front stairs. Earlier, when I had peeked into the ballroom, I had looked up and noticed a decorative expanse of grillwork encompassing the top third of the ballroom just beneath the arched ceiling.

Thought I, that fancy grillwork, which was gilt in color and featured an intricate design composed of scrolls and curly-ques with open spaces in-between, would provide an excellent vantage point from which to view the proceedings below; while at the same time being unobserved by those within the ballroom, of course. And, I expected, at the bottom of it was a ledge wide enough to accommodate a person. Thinking further in that vein, I decided to turn my mind to figuring exactly *how* to go about getting up there.

Upon reaching the second floor of the manor house, which I calculated would put me on the same level as the ceiling of the ballroom, I slowly headed down the long corridor searching for something I fully expected to find if I looked carefully enough. It took three trips up and down the long hallway before I found what I was looking for. A jib door. Lady Carstairs had several within her home; a small, narrow door cut into a wall but covered over in the same wall covering as the rest of the wall in order to render the small door that was cut in virtually invisible.

And, here it was.

I reached for the tiny latch handle, it obscured within the elaborate carved chair rail that marched mid-way down the entire corridor. With only a gentle tug the door opened and I slithered into the narrow passageway inside. It was quite dark in the tight enclosure which, sure enough, ran parallel with the backside of the grill-work, and on this side was black . . . but, just as I thought, as I slowly made my way along, the ceiling of the cavernous ballroom was clearly visible to me.

Moving closer to the backside of the grillwork, I peeked through the first opening I came to and carefully looked down, down, down. Directly below me inside the ballroom, I spotted four housemaids on their knees rubbing polish onto one section of the floor. Five footmen nearby were busy lining three walls of the huge chamber with straight-backed Japanned chairs and a few matching settees; resting places, I surmised, for elderly matrons, who would rather sit than cavort about on the dance floor.

Smiling to myself, I grew bolder and quickly and easily traversed the entire narrow passageway that ran parallel to the ballroom ceiling on three sides, the entire fourth wall of the chamber being composed of tall narrow windows and wide double doors that gave onto the garden. The fancy grillwork also marched along the wall on that side, as well, but with no passageway on the backside.

My, my. I paused to look down again. From this lofty aspect, I could, indeed, clearly see everything that was going on below. Pleased with my discovery, the excitement within me grew. That I had not been invited to the ball did not mean that I would not be in attendance. Why, I executed a careful twirl within the narrow enclosure, I could even dance up here if I wanted to! And, tonight, I probably would.

For now, however, I had best return to my duties.

It did not occur to me then that tonight I might encounter another curious, or perhaps, even dangerous, soul also lurking up here on the hidden passageway high above the ballroom floor.

CHAPTER 10

Juliette Goes To The Ball. Sort of.

Caroline and her chaperone Alice Collins were very nearly ready to go downstairs to the ballroom when Caroline turned to ask me what I planned to do all evening.

"Oh," my mistress's unexpected question caught me off-guard. "I will, no doubt, spend the evening up here in my room. Reading," I fabricated. "It's . . . been an exceptionally busy day with everyone below-stairs running thither and yon and whatnot."

"Indeed, it has," Caroline agreed. "Thank you for all your help, Juliette." Her sweet smile was sincere. She reached up to pat her freshly coiffed hair. "I love the way you dressed my hair for tonight. It looks very pretty. Thank you, indeed."

For half a second, I thought she was about to embrace me, or perhaps plant a small kiss upon my cheek. But just as she leaned forward to do one or the other, her tight-lipped sister Alice jerked her away. "There is no need to *thank* servants, Caroline," she declared through gritted teeth. "They are merely doing what they ought. One is to take no more notice of a servant than one does of . . . an empty chair. Servants are not . . . people."

"Do have a wonderful time at the ball, Caroline," I murmured. "I'll be anxious to hear all about it tomorrow."

"Indeed, I shall tell you everything!" She sang as they both swept from the room into the corridor, leaving the door standing slightly ajar. From the hallway, I could hear excited voices as other ladies left their suites and adjourned to the ballroom. I had earlier dressed the Lady Sophia's hair and knew she was as excited about the ball tonight as was my mistress. The entire house, it seemed was a-tremor with excitement. Even me. But, for a slightly different reason. I crossed the room to close the door; then stood with my backside pressed against it, my heart beginning to hammer in my chest. As soon as everything grew still in this wing of the house . . . I would also leave for the ball.

Growing impatient, I began to pace up and down, my heart beginning to pound in my ears as I was unable to contain my excitement over what might lie ahead. Walking to the opposite side of the small room, I slid onto the bench before my mistress's dressing table. Gazing at myself in the mirror, I saw that my cheeks were already flushed a becoming pink. On impulse, I yanked the frilly white cap from my head, and unpinned the untidy knot of curls at the nape of my neck. Then I snatched up the hairbrush and began to drag it through my honey-blonde hair. While listening with half an ear to the tittering noise coming from the corridor, I brushed and brushed.

Eventually when all grew quiet in this wing of the manor house, my long hair lay in soft waves nearly to my waist. Lifting a few curly strands up from either side of my face, I secured them atop my head, which created a cascade of curls dangling down to mingle with the remainder of my hair hanging loose down my back. Turning this way and that, I noticed that the curls bunched up at the back of my head bounced as I turned my head from side to side. A giggle escaped me as I thought about how charming that would look if I were executing a hand-over-hand on the dance floor. If I were *really* going to the ball tonight, this is exactly how I would dress my hair. And since, no one would see me tonight, this is exactly how I *would* dress my hair.

Laying aside the brush, I crept to the door of our suite once more and slowly turned the handle to cautiously peek out. I saw no one moving about in the corridor. I heard no one. Just then, a door at the top of the corridor sprang open and out stepped Lucy, Lady Sophia's maid. Of course, the girl didn't turn my way, but all the same, I eased the door shut again. From within, I could hear her footfalls as they echoed on the bare wooden floor, the sound receding as she headed towards the back stairs, on her way down to the servant's hall, I presumed. Late that afternoon when I'd finally joined the others for tea, I had overheard those few of the maids who still lingered at the table say they all meant to gather there tonight to pass the long hours of the evening in one another's company. Since no one had included me in the plans, I hadn't ventured to say whether or not I'd join them.

Once I felt it was safe to leave our suite, in no time at all, I gained the wide sweep of front stairs. On my way up, I cringed when a busy footman skirted past me also on his way up, but he appeared to not notice me, and said nothing; therefore I also remained silent. Minutes later, I pushed open the nearly invisible jib door, and carefully walked along the narrow passageway high up above the ballroom, it now aglitter with a mélange of color blended with the twinkling lights coming from the low-hanging chandeliers and the multitude of gilt sconces on the walls, each ablaze with flickering candle flames. The ballroom itself was a blur of noise and color as hundreds of people, it seemed, milled about within the spacious chamber below; although in truth, I knew there were no more than forty or fifty guests expected tonight, at least according to my cousin's calculation.

I noted that on a raised platform at the top of the room, the musicians were already in position to play and even as I watched, they struck up a chord and suddenly, the elegant Morland Manor ball was underway.

Gentlemen, resplendent in black evening clothes began to claim their partners and together they glided onto the floor to take up their positions for the first set of the night. I held my breath as I watched Mr. Edward Morland at once claim Miss Featherstone's hand. She was smiling up into his eyes as they hurried together onto the polished wooden floor, and took their places opposite one another in a long line of other twosomes also standing there in readiness for the first dance of the evening.

Because the chairs and settees, upon which those who were not dancing could sit, were located directly beneath me, I would have had to poke my head through one of the open spaces in the grill-work and strain to look down just to see who might be seated there, so that maneuver, of course, I did not attempt. Instead I satisfied myself just to watch all that I beheld taking place on the gleaming dance floor below.

Inside, I was grinning from ear to ear.

A *real* ball!

A *real* ball at a grand manor home in the country! And, I was *almost* there!

As everyone moved about the shiny floor, I picked out those faces I recognized. I spotted Lady Wentworth, Miss Elizabeth Banes' mother in animated conversation with Mrs. Throckmorton, who was Miss Amelia Durham's aunt, talking to several other women whom I did not recognize.

Quite possibly locals, I thought, or some of the other guests that had come from afar to attend Sir and Lady Morland's fine ball. And just there, next to a potted palm, stood the haughty Lady Sedgwick furtively claiming a fluted glass of champagne from a liveried footman who passed by carrying a tray of the same. When that woman had gulped down the liquid refreshment and seconds later, claimed yet another glass of the sparkling brew, I stifled a laugh. The highborn Lady Sedgwick was a tippler! Who'd have thought?

I soon spotted Lady Morland, looking tall and elegant in a flowing midnight blue ball gown, a stunning diamond necklace glittering at her throat and another glistening on her arm. She, too, was lifting a long-stemmed glass of champagne to her lips. Clustered about her were a group of ladies and gentleman, all with fluted goblets of champagne in their hands, all seeming to talk at once. Because I'd only ever caught but a glimpse of Sir Morland, this was the first time I'd seen him standing near his lady wife, and the first time I noticed that she was a good head taller than he. Lady Morland was, indeed, quite a tall woman, which I assumed explained the height of her first-born son, the heir.

And there *he* was! Surprisingly, on the dance floor partnering the prim-faced Miss Amelia Durham, who was wearing a rather unbecoming pea-green gown that I knew she had borrowed from Lady Morland because Nancy Jane told me so. One of the chamber maids had been called upon to alter it a bit in order to make it properly fit Miss Durham's long, lean frame. At the moment, neither the heir nor Miss Durham were saying a word to one another as they moved stiffly though the patterns of the dance. Perhaps they would make a good match after all, I thought. She seemed as pinched-faced and sullen as he.

And then I saw *him*. Mr. Talbot. Looking elegant in his black tailcoat and trousers, a gleaming white shirt with a starched white cravat wound around his neck. But, with whom was he dancing? In an attempt to better see, I leaned closer to the open space through which I was peeking. I didn't recognize the girl. Which meant that she was either a local miss, or one of the guests who had only arrived today. Perhaps she was the daughter of a neighboring squire. I'd heard the lady's maids, and even Nancy Jane, speculating on who amongst the locals might be coming to the ball. Bandied about were the names of two or three associates of Sir Morland, highly regarded and highly-paid gentlemen in whom he placed a great deal of trust as it was they who managed his many business concerns.

Glancing further across the room, I even spotted the ruddy-faced Constable Wainwright standing with a knot of other men, none as finely turned-out as Sir Morland or those of his ilk, but all the same, looking clean and freshly shaven as they helped themselves to the costly amber-colored champagne, which by all accounts was flowing freely tonight.

All agog with the proceedings going on below me, I closely watched everything for a good long while. A bit further along, I began to notice one or another of the guests commence to drift from the ballroom and out onto the wide terrace and perhaps even down into the knot garden, a place I longed to explore. Because it was becoming quite warm up here where I stood, I could only imagine how warm it must be in the ballroom with hundreds of candles burning and dozens of guests moving about. To me it looked as if they were packed in so close that they were obliged to elbow their way through the crush, while those who were dancing did so with such vigor they appeared very near to dropping from exhaustion. Until tonight I had had no idea how very long-lasting a single dance could be. Near to half an hour I calculated. Earlier I had noticed one of the footmen flinging open the long, casement windows. Now the double doors also stood wide open, allowing whatever cool breeze might be wafting about the terrace to find its way into the now overheated ballroom.

When the third dance finally ended, my attention turned again to those dancers milling about on the dance floor, most likely all now winded and seeking refreshment. Soon, however, flushed-faced couples began to position themselves for yet another set. All three of the gentlemen I had previously watched dancing chose partners once again, this time the heir with the Lady Sophia, who looked stunning tonight in a rose-colored gown with flounces about the hem; Edward Morland with Miss Hester Grant, and Mr. Talbot with the lovely Miss Elizabeth Banes, who also looked lovely in a soft blue silk gown and filmy overdress, several strings of pearls encircling her slim neck.

This time, it appeared that the dance they were about to perform was one that required everyone to form a circle. When the circle seemed to grow too big, half of the dancers pulled away and re-positioned themselves into another circle. Then, the music started up. I watched closely, in the hope of being able to pick out some of the steps and perhaps move through the pattern myself right here where I stood. But, it was no use. The wooden platform between the wall and the backside of the grillwork was, indeed, quite narrow and also a bit uneven.

My attention drifted away from the dancers. Sometime later following the completion of the circle dance, I noticed the heir, standing to the far side of the room, both hands stuffed into his pockets, his shoulders seemingly hunched over. In seconds, Miss Durham approached him and the two fell into conversation. I could not help noticing that she did not seem particularly pleased regarding whatever it was they were talking about, and of a sudden, lifted her chin and departed in a huff.

Suddenly, the heir cast a quick glance about, then turned and strode purposefully through the double doors and onto the terrace. Perhaps he was quite winded and needed a breath of fresh air. However, a scant second later, I also spotted Edward Morland carrying a silver candlestick upon which one lone candle burned, also hurriedly leave the ballroom, seemingly in the wake of his older brother. A bit odd, I thought. Then decided that perhaps the brothers had something they wished to discuss in private and had chosen to do so in the garden, as far away from their parents, and everyone else, as possible.

Inhaling a long breath, I turned back to watching the dancers on the dance floor. My heart plunged to my feet for the second time that night when I saw *him* again, Mr. Talbot, once again his arm encircling the trim waist of the beautiful, black-haired Miss Elizabeth Banes. Oh! She was so much prettier than me! And unless I had miscounted, this was the *second* time he had stood up with her.

I continued to watch that elegant gentleman, who without a doubt in my mind, was the kindest and most handsome of all the gentlemen present at the ball and the very one I truly wished to partner *me* for a dance. The longer I watched him dancing with the beautiful Miss Banes, the larger the lump in my throat grew. It wasn't long before I felt a tight knot form in my stomach and soon felt it inch its way up to my throat. This was not the way I wanted to feel tonight. Why was it so *very* disturbing to see *my* Mr. Talbot with another young lady on his arm? Plus, appearing to *enjoy* himself immensely!

It was then I realized that my head had dropped forward and my forehead was now resting against the backside of the scrolled design of the grillwork through which I had been looking. I jerked myself upright and stepped back with alarm. How dreadful if someone in the ballroom were to catch sight of me secreted up here, *spying* on them. For, in truth, that is *exactly* what I was doing. *Spying!*

Because my breath was now coming in fits and starts, I made a valiant effort to calm myself. I mustn't be seen and I also mustn't be heard, although I doubted anyone could hear me even if I were to scream aloud! Which, of course, I would not do. Although a part of me wanted to.

Suddenly, I realized I hadn't heard the strains of music in a while. That round dance must be over. Perhaps that meant Mr. Talbot would now be . . . suddenly a cool hand gripped my bare arm and scream is exactly what I did do at that very moment!

"Miss Abbott, it is only me!"

Before I could scream again, a hand clapped over my mouth from behind and I felt my body pressed up against the hard, muscular from of . . . of . . . I twisted my head around as the man's hand fell away.

"M-Mr. Talbot? Wh-what are you doing here?"

"I might ask you the same thing, Miss Abbott." The handsome man's lips twitched.

My hand flew to my breast as I stood gazing up at him in wonderment, a part of me attempting valiantly to calm myself. "I-I only wished to attend the ball, sir. I-I wasn't spying, truly I wasn't, sir."

"I truly believe you, Miss Abbott." The tall gentleman laughed softly. "But, how did you find this place?"

"How did *you* find this place?" I countered. Parking both hands on my hips, I glared up at him, although truth to tell, I was *delighted* to see him and wished only to fling myself into his arms! "And how did you know I was up here?"

"When Edward and I were boys and should have been fast asleep in the nursery, we used to come up here and watch the proceedings the same as you are doing now."

"So, why did you come up here tonight? You were obviously allowed to attend *this* ball."

He took a small step forward which brought him closer to my side. We both stood there, looking down, him leaning over to rest his elbows upon the narrow strip of wood at the base of the grill-work. The railing reached as far down as his waist while the bottom of it was only slightly lower than my shoulders.

"I came up here for one reason only, Miss Abbott," he said, turning his head to gaze intently at me, "because *you* are not down *there*."

I grinned in spite of the alarm still coursing through me. "I daresay you are larking with me, Mr. Talbot." Then, I cried, "Does that mean you *saw* me up here?"

Eyes twinkling afresh, he nodded assent. "Near the close of that last dance I happened to glance up and suddenly, I spotted your face. Quite in the shadows, I own, but I recognized your golden hair. I recalled how you seemed enthralled by the notion of hidey-holes in the walls that day Edward and I escorted you to the library and I thought, by Jove! She's found one!" He grinned. "Generally the servants are the only ones who come up here when they decorate the ballroom with evergreen and holly boughs for Christmastide. Now, here *you* are."

"And . . . here you are," I breathed, still staring up at him as if I could not believe he was actually secreted up here with me. The two of us, alone, high up above the others enjoying themselves down below in the ballroom. *This* delightful possibility had *never* occurred to me, although now that it had come about, I was pleased beyond measure!

To my surprise, he reached to finger a strand of curling blonde hair that lay over my shoulder. "You look very pretty tonight, Miss Abbott," he said softly.

"Thank you, sir. And you look very handsome."

At that instant, we both heard the orchestra start up again.

I glanced down toward the ballroom floor as he asked, "Shall we watch the proceedings together?"

"Indeed."

For a good quarter hour we pointed out one or another of the young ladies we both knew; and if he were acquainted with their gentleman partners in the dance, he told me their names and a bit about them, none of which I could later recall, so distracted was I to be standing so very near him to share this covert experience together. However, I do recall him telling me that several of the young gentlemen present were Morland cousins and that part of the reason Lady Morland had resorted to inviting young ladies here as possible marriage candidates for the boys was because there were no female Morland cousins to whom the heir, or Edward, could be affianced, a fact I found most interesting.

When that dance ended, Mr. Talbot and I continued to stand side-by-side quietly watching. We both noticed when his good friend Edward Morland returned to the ballroom from the terrace.

"But he's not carrying the candlestick," I said.

"Why would he be carrying a candlestick?"

Without looking up, I told him that earlier I had watched William Morland leave the ballroom, and seconds later, as if perhaps planning to meet up with his brother in the garden, I had also seen Edward leave the ballroom, but he was carrying a tall, silver candlestick with a lone candle flickering atop it.

"Now, as you can clearly see," I pointed out, "Edward has returned to the ballroom, but *without* the candlestick. I wonder what he did with it?"

"Hmm." My companion appeared to ponder the oddity. "Quite curious, indeed," he murmured.

We fell silent, then I said, "Also curious was the news of the dead body found so very near where we picnicked the other day. Has the constable made a determination regarding who he thinks the murderer might be?"

Without turning around, Mr. Talbot casually replied, "It's my understanding that in the end, he and Sir Morland declared the foul deed was not murder at all, but merely an unfortunate accident. Appeared the chap had hoisted too many pints at the Cock and Crow; then as he stumbled home, he simply fell and hit his head on a rock. Was evidently stumbling near the water's edge as both his trousers and boots were muddy."

At the mention of mud, my head jerked up. "So, it was an accident. I see." Although, I didn't, and in my mind, doubts lingered.

"And what of William?" Mr. Talbot asked, returning to our former conversation. "Has he also returned from the garden?"

"I-I've not yet seen him," I replied, my thoughts still mulling over Mr. Talbot's disclosure regarding the demise of the hapless Kenneth Grimes, whose death it now appeared William Morland had had nothing to do with. Which was good news all around, I suppose; and with a shrug, thrust the distasteful topic from mind.

Several seconds later, the music started up again.

Smiling, Mr. Talbot turned toward me and sketched a bow with his head, there being insufficient room in which to sketch one from his waist. "Would you be so kind as to honor me with this dance, Miss Abbott?"

I sucked in my breath. *Was my dream about to come true?*

"You do dance do you not?"

I nodded tightly. "A bit."

He looked around. "I daresay a *bit* is all we shall be able to do up here. Shall we give it a go, then?"

Gazing breathlessly up at him, for a certainty the eager smile on my face also brought a sparkle to my eyes.

He cocked an ear as the strains of the music, rising and falling in a precise rhythm, reached us. "This one appears to be a waltz. Were we at Almack's in London, I would be obliged to ask, 'Do you waltz, Miss Abbott?' To which you would reply, 'Yessir' only if . . ."

"The esteemed patronesses at Almack's had granted me permission to do so," I finished for him.

"Ah, so you are not unfamiliar with the silly rules of the *ton*. Therefore, what is your answer, Miss Abbott? Do you, or do you not, waltz?"

Without awaiting my reply, he held up both arms and I, after inhaling a very, *very* deep breath, placed one bare hand in his palm and felt his other hand at my waist as he drew me into the circle of his arms. I had never before stood so very near a gentleman. Therefore I could now clearly see how the waltz was considered quite beyond the bounds of propriety; but given the narrowness of the enclosure where we stood, standing close to one another was the only option open to us within the extremely small space of this very narrow platform.

In perfect concert with one another, the pair of us managed to execute several steps in time to the intoxicating one-two-three rhythm of the music. I breathed a small prayer of gratitude to Lady Carstairs' niece, who had managed to teach me this particular pattern. I recall I had begged it of her many times but it was only when her aunt, my employer, had left the room that she agreed to show me the steps.

"Ah. So, you *do* dance, Miss Abbott. And very well, I see. What a pity you are not at the ball tonight. If you were, I would make it a point to claim every dance."

Feeling as if I were dancing in the clouds rather than merely on a narrow platform high above the polished ballroom floor of Morland Manor, I smiled dreamily up into his eyes. "But, Mr. Talbot, if you were to claim *every* dance, I would have no choice but to decline, since, as you must know, a young lady is allowed only *two* dances with the same partner."

Again his lips twitched. "Those pesky rules again."

"Actually, sir," I began, suddenly realizing that even now I was breaking a rule simply by being up here alone with a gentleman. "I must ask, sir, that you please tell no one that we danced tonight. I really should not be here at all. And certainly not alone with you."

"Nor should I for all that," he confessed. "You may rest assured, my dear, I would never betray you. My friends have a habit of trusting me with all their secrets since I have proven to be so very good at keeping them."

I smiled up into his dark eyes, wishing, hoping the music and this delightful interlude would go on forever. I was standing close enough to the gentleman that I could feel the rise and fall of his strong chest against my far smaller body. Because the quickened rhythm of his breath exactly matched my own, I was not the least surprised when in one gentle, but deliberate motion, he released my hand and bent to encircle my waist with both of his arms and draw me closer still. Then, he lowered his head and settled his warm, moist lips upon mine.

As I wound both arms up around his neck, his tightened about my body. I felt the pressure of his hand against my back, and his fingers intertwine with soft strands of my hair. When the kiss ended, he continued to hold me tightly against him, both of us relishing the tingly feel of the delicious, stolen moment.

As we stood thusly together in the dim shadows high up above the glittering ballroom, I felt his warm breath pulsing against my head as a hand moved slowly up and down my back, gently caressing me.

"You are an enigma, Miss Abbott," he breathed at length.

Although I did not want to shatter this wondrous moment with talk, I knew I could not linger forever in his arms, so reluctantly I drew away. But I did not speak at once.

His breath still labored, he continued to gaze deeply into my eyes. "I confess, you are the prettiest girl I have every met, Julietta Abbot. Is that your real name?"

A small smile upon my lips, I nodded assent. "Yes. *Julietta* is my real name, although the English insist upon pronouncing it Juliette. My mama was French, my father . . . was not." A trifle sadly, I looked down.

"Of late, you seem to speak less French than you did . . . when we first met. Have you . . .?"

I shrugged. "When it appeared that Lady Morland wanted a French maid, I . . . complied. Truth is, I remember very little of the French language beyond the few words you, and the others, have heard from me." I sighed. "It was quite silly of me. I suspect I have fooled no one. It's just that when I arrived here, I . . . really did not wish to spend an entire fortnight in the country. I wanted only to return to London where life seems . . . livelier. And so, I . . . manufactured a bit of excitement. That is the whole truth, I swear it."

"You needn't swear anything to me, Julietta. Am I allowed now to address you by your given name?"

Again, I laughed softly.

Suddenly, our sweet *tête-à-tête* was interrupted by a bloodcurdling scream delivered at a pitch that would jangle the nerves of anyone who heard it. We both whirled around to press our faces into an opening to see what was happening below us on the ballroom floor.

A crowd had already gathered around a young lady and a gentleman who had evidently just burst in from the terrace.

"It's the heir!" the girl screamed. "He's dead! In the garden! There's blood everywh . . . ! Oh-h!" She screamed again.

Instantly all was pandemonium. The music ceased as Sir Morland rushed forward, thrusting aside all who stood in his way.

"Stand aside! Make way!"

He disappeared through the double doors leading to the terrace, his second son Edward close on his heels. Several other gentlemen followed suit.

"I must be going," Mr. Talbot said in a rush. He leaned down and gave me a quick peck on the check. "I shall never forget our dance, Miss Abbott. Perhaps we shall dance again, if not, thank you for a delightful memory."

Then he was gone.

I stood there wide-eyed; my lips parted. Then my eyes squeezed shut.

Thank you for a delightful memory, he had said.

A memory?

To him, I was no more than . . . *a memory?* When to me, the handsome Mr. Talbot meant far, *far* more!

My chest felt tight, my knees weak.

Hot tears of pain rolled down my cheeks. My breath lodged in my throat.

I slumped to the floor . . . and with no one to see me, or chastise me for being a silly, simpering miss, I wept. Both hands covering my face, I sobbed into the palms of my hands as my heart shattered into a million pieces.

A memory. To him, I was naught but a memory.

At length, the noise and commotion coming from the ballroom penetrated my consciousness.

Dragging myself to my feet, I no longer wanted to look down. What did I care if the heir was dead? I didn't like the man; no one liked the man. Alone in the shadows, I endeavored to squeeze back the tears that threatened still to seep from my eyes. I wanted only to return to my room. Pulling myself hand-over-hand along the narrow wooden railing, I made my way to the invisible door and giving a hard push, slipped from it.

Once outside in the brightly lit corridor of the manor home, I hurried toward where I *hoped* to find the back stairs that surely also rose to this floor, although I had not thought to use them either time I had come up here. Thankfully, I soon found the narrow stairwell, and as quickly as possible, made my way back up to our suite of rooms. I was grateful I saw no one on the way for I had not yet managed to completely staunch the flow of tears that still trickled down my cheeks.

But the instant I flung open the door to Miss Featherstone's suite, I came face-to-face with Mrs. Collins.

"Where have you been?" she demanded. "I sent for you above half an hour ago. You were not below-stairs with the other maids. Where were you?"

Caught unawares, there was no ready reply upon my lips. I stood stock still, staring at the woman as if I did not know her. Or, what to say.

"Well, where have you been?" she demanded again.

I could hardly confess to having spent the evening spying on everyone at the ball . . . nor could I lie and say that yes, I had been below-stairs with the other maids, so I blurted out, "I-I took a walk."

The woman glared at me. "You took a walk? *Where?*"

"Just . . . out . . . outdoors," I limped my reply, then asked, "Did . . . did you require something?"

"I did, but it doesn't matter now." She took one last look at herself in the dressing table mirror. "I repaired it myself."

Saying that, she skirted past me and quitted the room whereupon I all but ran toward my tiny room beyond the larger bedchamber and through the dressing room. Flinging myself across my narrow bed, I dissolved once more into tears. Nothing this evening had gone as planned.

And nothing in my life would *ever* be the same again! *Ever!*

CHAPTER 11

In which Juliette is Interrogated

In no time at all, it seemed, there came a rap-rap-rap upon the outer door to our suite. Still sniffling, I lay still. If Mrs. Collins had returned, she would answer it. I listened, but heard nothing beyond additional raps. Apparently Mrs. Collins had not returned, for in moments Mrs. Fullerton, the housekeeper, barged into my room.

"Juliette, you are to come with me at once!"

I obediently pulled myself to my feet and followed the stern-faced woman from the room and down the back stairwell to the servant's quarters. From most of the small chambers we walked past, even through closed doors, I could hear hushed voices coming from within. Evidently news of the heir's death had already reached most everyone in the manor house, including the household staff.

Mrs. Fullerton led me straight to the servant's dining hall where I saw that every last one of the lady's maids, including Lady Morland's maid Temple, were seated around the table, their hands folded primly before them, every one looking, or attempting to look, innocent and angelic, all properly attired in black with their tidy white caps pinned in place upon their heads.

"Sit down," Mrs. Fullerton said. "The constable has requested that all you lady's maids stay together. He will be here shortly." She turned to re-enter the corridor, flinging over her shoulder, "There's fresh coffee on the sideboard, if you like."

All the way here, I'd been wiping my tear-stained face on the sleeve of my wrinkled black frock. Nonetheless, I feared I looked a shambles with my flushed cheeks, tear-smudged face, and tangled hair hanging loose down my back. I was also not wearing my white cap as I had removed it before I went up to watch the guests at the ball.

Before sitting down, I managed to pour myself a cup of steaming black coffee, then aware that all eyes were fixed upon me, I slipped into an empty chair next to Meg, my only friend in the room. The only other available chair was next to Lady Morland's maid, Temple, a woman to whom I had never spoken.

"So, Miss Frenchie-wench, where have you been hidin' all night?" demanded the outspoken Rosie from across the table.

"Yeah, where have you been?" Lucy chimed in. "We've all been a-sittin' right here, pretty as you please."

"You mistress was a-lookin' for ya'," Rosie said.

"You look as if you've been tossed about in the wind. Have you been out a-walkin'?" Tilly asked. "In the garden, perhaps?" Her tone seemed to imply . . . *something*.

Following that pointed remark, I fairly choked. Had they all decided *I* was guilty of something? Nothing was going right tonight. My eyes squeezed shut and another rush of unbidden tears spilled forth. In search of a bit of warmth and comfort, I wrapped my cold hands around the warm cup before me and squeezed 'til my knuckles turned white.

"Don't expect no sympathy from us, cuz you won't be a-getting' it!" declared Rosie.

Meg reached to put an arm about my shoulders. "Leave off, ladies. Can't you see she's as overset as we are?"

"Sure, we can see. Wee-wee, Miss Frenchie-liar. We's all noticed that all of a sudden you talk 'jes like us," Rosie accused. "When we first come here, you was all wee-wee this and wee-wee that, and bone juice, and mercy madam-sell. Now, suddenly you's as English as the rest of us."

"What else you been lying about, you . . . *imposter*!"

"Ladies!" bellowed an authoritative male voice. "I'll be askin' the questions here."

Everyone's heads whirled around as Constable Wainwright advanced into the room. He sat down heavily upon the chair usually reserved for Griggs the butler at the top of the table.

Silence fell as he cleared his throat. "As you all know, they's been another murder at Morland Manor. Clearly, they's a mad-man runnin' loose; and this time, make no mistake, I *will* get to the bottom of it."

"We think we already knows who done it!" Rosie blurted out.

"And what makes you say that, Miss . . . uh . . ."

"Rosie, sir. My name's Rosie. I'm lady's maid to Miss Banes."

"Very well, Rosie. But, keep in mind that I will only entertain facts. Despite how promising your theory might be, without solid evidence to back it up, a theory is only a theory and is worthless in a court of law. Depend upon it, I mean to run the mad-man to ground afore this night is over." He directed an expectant look at her. "Now, if'n ye's anything *factual* to say, young lady, speak up. They's havin' their supper up in the ballroom at present, so I've got plenty o' time to ask questions of the rest of you down here. You'll all get a turn to talk," he promised.

"Well, we was jes' sayin', sir," Rosie went on, "as how all of us, except Miss Abbott, has spent the entire evenin' a-sittin' right here. All of us together. Not a one of us has left this room."

"Temple left," Lucy piped up. "Lady Morland sent for her, but she weren't gone long."

"And what have you young ladies been a-doin' here all this time, together?"

"We played charades," Tilly said. "Then we drank coffee and ate cake. And talked."

The constable's lips moved as he scribbled in his occurrence book. "Coffee, cake, played charades." He glanced back up. "Anything else?"

"Well," Rosie began afresh. "As I was saying, we was all right here this evenin' *except* for Miss Abbott. Mrs. Fullerton only 'jes now brung her down."

"You might be interested to know, sir, that yesterday," Tilly interjected, "Miss Frenchie-wench here said she wished it was the heir what got kilt instead of that other bloke. Those was her very words, sir, an' that's a fact."

"I see." The constable turned toward me. "You're the French maid the others been referrin' to. Miss Abbott, is that correct?"

"She ain't French!" Tilly cried. "She talks English as good as we do, an' that's a fact, too."

"Is this true, Miss Abbott?"

Inhaling a deep breath of courage, I nodded. "Yessir, it is true." Suddenly, my mind woke up, perhaps due to the influx of coffee. "Since I've been here at Morland Manor, sir, around all these . . . nice ladies, and my mistress, my English has improved considerably. Before coming here, I had only just returned from living in Paris, and . . . whilst there, I spoke

French, of course. If you recall, sir, my mama is . . . was French. My father was English but he was away from home a good deal when I was a wee one. Therefore, I learned French first from my mama, and then later, English from my father, before he passed on." I looked down as once again, I felt unbidden moisture well in my eyes. "My mama is . . . she is also no longer with us." I sniffed.

"My sympathies, Miss Abbott," the constable muttered, his head lowered as he scribbled notes on a page of his book. "Now then." He looked back up at me. "The ladies say you wasn't here with them all evenin', is that correct? Might I inquire where you passed the time, Miss Abbott?"

I paused before saying, "In my room, sir. I have been . . . reading."

"A French book?" Rosie inquired saucily.

A few titters followed.

"Ladies! Go on, Miss Abbott. Do you have anything further to add to your statement?"

"N-No, sir."

"Best make a clean breast of it, Miss Abbott," the constable admonished.

Chewing anxiously on my lower lip, I felt heat suffuse my cheeks and my heart to pound afresh. *Did I dare tell him everything? Had he already spoken with Mr. Talbot? What had he said? What about Mrs. Collins? I told her I'd . . . taken a walk.*

"Sir, I . . . I do have something more to say, but I-I prefer to . . . that is, I wonder if I might . . . speak privately with you, sir?"

The legs of his chair were already scraping against the floor. "Right this way, Miss Abbott."

I followed the constable from the room. In the hallway, we encountered Mrs. Fullerton and he asked her if there was a private place where we could talk. She offered the use of her own parlor and led the way there. Inside, both of us took seats opposite one another on straight-back chairs next to Mrs. Fullerton's small tea table. Opening his notepad on the unadorned surface of the table beside him, the constable gazed at me expectantly.

"What is it you want to say, Miss Abbott? And keep in mind, that I will entertain only facts. The *true* facts."

As carefully as I could, given my agitation, I considered what to say. Had Mrs. Collins already told Mrs. Fullerton that I said I had taken a walk tonight? Or had she returned to the ballroom to partake of supper along with the rest of the guests? If I told him the truth now about where I'd been this evening, and then Mrs. Collins told him something else later, would he believe me, or her?

Shifting uncomfortably on the straight-backed chair, I worked to keep my anxiety in check. "Earlier this evening, sir, I-I told Mrs. Collins, my mistress' chaperone, that I had . . . taken a walk, . . . outdoors, this evening."

His eyes widened. "You took a walk outdoors this evening, Miss Abbott? I was unaware of that." He head bent over his book as he furiously scribbled what I had just said. "Precisely where did you walk? Anywhere near the garden at the rear of the house?"

"No! No, sir!" Shaking my head vigorously, I cried, "I did *not* take a walk this evening, sir."

"But you just said you did. You said you told this Mrs. Collins that you took a walk. Which is it? The *truth*, Miss Abbott!"

"That *is* the truth. I did *not* take a walk, sir. I only *told* Mrs. Collins that I took a walk, but I didn't. And I . . . I wanted to set the record straight by telling you the truth, sir."

The constable sat back. "You seem to have little regard for the truth, Miss Abbott. First, you lead everyone here, including Lady Morland, to believe that you're a *bona fide* French lady's maid, and now you freely confess that you are not, and here's yet another lie. How many more lies are you forwardin'? Why should I believe anything you say now, Miss Abbott, if that be your *real* name?"

"Of course, it is my real name, sir. The truth about my whereabouts this evening, sir, is, that . . . I-I was somewhere tonight that I-I . . . should not have been. I did not want anyone to know. Most especially not the other lady's maids."

"Do you make a habit of concealing your whereabouts from others, Miss Abbott? To what purpose, if I may be so bold?"

The man's rapid-fire questions were confusing me. "To *no* purpose, sir. It's just that . . ."

"And what were the maids referring to when they said you'd declared you wished it was the heir what got hisself kilt instead of that other bloke? What was the meaning behind *that* statement, Miss Abbott?"

"I meant *nothing* by it, sir. The heir is . . . *was*, not a terribly *kind* person. Although I have only known him a short while, in all honesty, I find I cannot speak . . . charitably of him, sir. Still, I meant the gentleman no ill will, sir, truly, I do . . . *did* not; and I most certainly never wished him dead."

"And yet you do admit to makin' that threatenin' warnin', and now the heir *is* dead." He slapped his little book shut and rose to his feet. "Until I can find evidence to the contrary, Miss Abbott, I am forthwith addin' *your* name to my list of suspects." He reached for the door handle. "And, just so you know, I *will* alert Sir Morland to that fact. I advise you to return to your room at once, and stay there. But be forewarned, I *will* be a-wantin' to speak with you again, and quite possibly before this night is over. I am determined to solve this case as quickly as possible. I've still a goodly number of persons to question, so until I can turn up concrete evidence against you, Miss Abbott, you are not to leave the house again. Do you understand?"

My heart thudding in my ears, I nodded mutely, then slowly rose and obediently left the room in the constable's wake.

The man had not given me the chance to tell the whole truth. And I was prepared to do just that! Instead, he now suspected I had something to do with killing the heir! I had to clear myself; I had to! But, how?

CHAPTER 12

In Which Juliette Appeals to Mr. Talbot

On the way back upstairs to my room, I continued to mull over the tangled coil I'd fallen into. The first avenue of escape I entertained was to pack up my belongings at once and run from Morland Manor as fast as I could, but to do so would be the same as admitting I had committed the crime. Plus, I would, no doubt, be caught and hanged before the sun rose tomorrow!

And yet, to stay here was to run the risk that everyone, including my mistress, if she didn't already, would believe that I was the guilty party.

Juliette Abbott, a murderess!

I shuddered at the thought.

But, of course, it was not true. The truth was, I had *not* left the house all evening. And, there was only *one* way to prove that! I *must* find Mr. Talbot. He was the *only* person who could vouch for my whereabouts tonight and thereby prove my innocence to the constable and to anyone else who believed otherwise.

The constable had said that the guests were still in the ballroom having supper. Perhaps if I returned to the hidden enclosure high up in the ceiling there, Mr. Talbot might look up and see me once again. Perhaps I could even motion for him to join me.

Although he had promised to not betray my whereabouts to anyone, I *had* to speak with him as soon as possible and beg him to tell the truth *now*. And, of course, if given the opportunity, I would also freely admit the truth. No, I should *not* have spent the evening spying on everyone at the ball tonight, but that small crime was not tantamount to *murder!* I would gladly admit to the former indiscretion; I would fight tooth and nail before admitting to the latter. Or, hanging for it.

Dear God in Heaven, please help me!

Making my way back up the dimly-lit servant's stairs, I became aware of the sound of footfalls hurrying downward and looking up, was vastly relieved to see Nancy Jane hurrying down the stairs towards me.

"Nancy Jane!" I nearly burst into tears at the sight of a friendly face. "They all think I did it! Killed the heir, I mean!"

"Wh-Wha-? You can't mean . . . but, wh-hy?"

"I'm in a terrible fix, Nancy Jane! I need to talk to Mr. Talbot straightaway. He's the only one who can vouch for me. I was . . . I was with him tonight and I made him promise not to tell anyone, but now I *need* him to tell the constable that he and I were together."

"They's all in to supper now. I 'spect he's in there with 'em. All the guests is in there. Manor is in an uproar; make no mistake. Ever'one is scared there's a killer loose in the house. We's all afraid what's goin' to happen next. Tomorrow's supposed to be my half day, but Griggs already tol' us no one's gettin' off tomorrow. Looks like I'm stuck here 'til the murder's solved and all the guests is free to go. Even they's been tol' they can't leave. Ever'one's got to stay right here. Constable said no one's to leave the house. Gor! And, the killer right here with us!"

"Where have you been just now?" I asked. "I thought all the servants were supposed to stay below-stairs so the constable could question everyone down there while the guests are having supper."

"I been layin' out fires in some o' the guest's rooms. The footmen was all busy servin' and carrying' in more and more red wine, so most of us chambermaids was directed to lay out the fires tonight. House is almost full. At any rate, I just got done with that hateful task. I don't mind sayin' them coal shuttles is far too heavy for a girl as slight as me. "

"What's that you're carrying?" I only just noticed what appeared to be an item of clothing draped over my cousin's arm.

"It's Lady Morland's ball gown." She held it up for me to see. Of course, I'd already seen it, from afar. "Ain't it pretty?"

"It's lovely." I reached to finger the fine blue silk. "Poor woman. She has already changed into mourning. I'm just glad it wasn't the second son who was killed." Once more, the thought of the murder brought another rush of fear to my breast. "I'd best be on my way, Nancy Jane. I simply *must* speak with Mr. Talbot."

"Oh, I heard the constable tell Griggs a bit ago that once they's all done with their supper he wants folks separated into groups so's he can question 'em separate. Family . . . they's some aunts and uncles and cousins here . . . in the drawin' room, locals in the library, and so on. They might put Mr. Talbot in the drawing room with Mr. Edward since he's been like one o' the family. Him and Edward was boon companions as boys, went to school together, and all. He's been comin' 'round here since. . ."

"I must go, Nancy Jane. The constable told me to go to my room and stay there, but I *have to* speak with Mr. Talbot. I'm heading for the drawing room now. Don't tell anyone you saw me, please."

My heart once again pounding in my ears, I hurried on up the stairs to the ground floor. It was the long way around, of course, the fastest being the wide sweep of stairs in front, but I didn't dare risk being seen by the constable again. Or anyone, for all that. I didn't mind running into Nancy Jane; because she now knew what a pickle I was in and *I* was the one who told her, rather than her hearing it from someone else. Someone who was prejudiced against me.

I could always count on Nancy Jane to be on my side especially now that all the lady's maids were united in their conviction of my guilt. I just hoped Temple didn't pass on that erroneous assumption to Lady Morland. She'd sack me for sure without a character and I was counting on getting a good character from her to use when I hired myself out as a governess. Lady What's-It had been carried aloft so suddenly I didn't get one from her, and forgot to ask her niece if she'd give me one, although I suppose she'd be kind enough to provide one now if I asked.

Having reached the ground floor and was now edging my way carefully toward the double doors that gave onto the drawing room, I paused, not knowing precisely what to do at this juncture. I couldn't very well fling open the doors and yell for Mr. Talbot to please step into the corridor because I needed to speak with him. Plus, I didn't really know if the family was yet gathered there.

Suddenly I heard noises coming from the hallway that led to the ballroom and wondered if perhaps supper was now over and the family and guests were being directed to the various chambers where the constable meant to question them. I ducked behind one of a pair of tall porcelain vases that flanked the doorway to the solarium, located on the opposite side of the corridor and down a bit from the drawing room. The vase was a good six feet high, which made it over half a foot taller than me at a mere five feet, three inches.

Peeking around it at intervals, at last I caught sight of Mr. Talbot, talking and nodding with Edward Morland as they and the rest of the large Morland family slowly poured into the drawing room. When I saw Mr. Talbot hang back to allow a group of ladies to precede him into the room, I seized the moment and hurried from my hiding place toward him.

Coming up behind him, I bravely spoke up. "Mr. Talbot, might I have a word with you, sir? Please, it's important."

His dark head jerked around and thankfully he smiled. "Miss Abbott!"

His friendly smile rekindled the sweet memory of his kiss and I don't mind saying that memory nearly unleashed a fresh burst of tears from me all over again.

But, I successfully blinked back the moisture pooling in my eyes and the very second the last of the women advanced into the room, was vastly relieved to see Mr. Talbot turn back toward me.

"Is something the trouble, Juliette? Apart from the heir being found dead in the garden, I mean."

"Please, sir! Might we . . . " I cast a frantic gaze about, "I *must* speak with you at once, sir! Might we step into the solarium, *please*," I begged. "It's important."

"Certainly." He abandoned his post at the drawing room door and fell into step beside me. "I understand the constable intends to solve the murder tonight," he began conversationally. "Is refusing to let a single one of the guests leave the premises until he's questioned every last one and can personally attest to their innocence. Very thorough of him, I daresay.

But, also exhausting as it looks as if none of us will get a wink of sleep tonight." He grinned down upon me.

I gave him a pained look.

Upon reaching the solarium, I hurriedly reached for the gilt door handles, but was vastly disappointed to find the room locked up tight. "*Oh!*"

Mr. Talbot smiled. "Not to worry." He reached to wrap his arms about one of the huge vases and tilted it up a smidge. A nod of his head and a hushed, "Just there," directed my gaze downward.

"Oh! How clever of you!" I knelt to pick up the key that lay on the floor beneath the vase and upon handing it to him, watched eagerly as he made short work of unlocking the door and we both hurried into the darkened room.

"Wait here," Mr. Talbot said as he picked his way toward the opposite side of the chamber and flung back the draperies, which allowed long shafts of moonlight to pour into the expansive chamber. "Shall we sit?" A hand indicated one of several wicker settees made more comfortable by the addition of plush, damask cushions in cheerful colors.

By now, I was fairly wringing my hands together.

He approached me with both of his outstretched. "Come now, whatever the trouble is can't be all that bad." His tone was gentle. "Tell me what it is, sweet Juliette. Here. . ." Taking my hand he led me to one of the settees that faced the glassed-in wall of windows. "Let us sit here and you can tell me what is afoot."

I obediently perched on the edge of the cozy settee, my knees turned toward him. "The constable thinks I killed the heir!" I blurted out.

Mr. Talbot's jaw dropped. "Why, that's absurd! Whatever gave the man such a notion?"

When a wrenching sob racked my small body, I covered my face with both hands. I felt my companion's weight shift on the settee as he scooted forward from where he sat leant back against the squabs. I felt his hand touch my shoulder and for a split-second thought he meant to draw me into his arms. When he didn't, I bravely sniffed back my tears and lifted my chin.

"H-He drew that conclusion because when I returned to my room, after you and I . . . d-danced, I f-foolishly told Mrs. Collins that I had taken a walk tonight. Outdoors."

"Did you take a walk?" In the dim light, I could see that his face, made all the more handsome by moonlight, was now a question.

"No! I never left the house all evening. I was with *you*! High above the ballroom. I just didn't want anyone to know. I asked you not to tell anyone, remember, and you promised . . ."

"Indeed, I told you I was very good at keeping secrets and I am. I've told no one about our . . . clandestine rendezvous."

"But, you *must*! You must tell Constable Wainwright. You are the *only* person who can vouch for me. He will believe you, especially if he does not know that . . . that I have spoken with you since . . . then. Since we were together, I mean." I paused. "I fear I am not making a great deal of sense. The constable must not know that I *asked* you to tell him the truth. He has not yet questioned you, has he?"

"No." He shook his head. "Fear not, of course, I will tell him the truth, the whole truth." He did draw me into his arms then, and my head fell forward with relief onto his strong shoulder. "You needn't worry, sweeting. I'll not let anything happen to you. I promise."

As much as I dearly wanted to linger there beside him, I knew I mustn't. Raising my head, my lips were so very close to his that *I* could have kissed him! Instead, I said, "I must go up to my room now. I'm certain that as soon as the constable questions you and hears what you have to say, he'll send for me again. For a certainty, he'll want to hear my side of the story, and will quite possibly declare that I am lying to him again. He's already asked me how he can believe anything I say."

I made as if to rise but he gently pulled me back down beside him once more.

His voice was husky when he said, "You don't think I can let you go without another kiss, do you?"

I smiled through my anxiety, and blinked back the tears of relief that were now flooding my eyes. By then, his lips were already on mine, a deeper kiss this time. In an instant, both my breath and his had grown fitful. With difficulty, I managed to pull away.

"Please, I must go." I jerked myself up, my hands busily smoothing the wrinkles that I knew must now be marring my appearance; if I could be more marred than I already was.

"Forgive me, Juliette." Mr. Talbot rose also to his feet. "When I am near you, I seem unable to restrain myself."

"Please, sir; just tell the constable the truth." I paused, then amended my request. "Perhaps, not the *whole* truth. Perhaps it would be best if we neither one owned up to having kisse . . ."

He grasped my meaning. "You and I merely *talked* tonight. I spotted you on the walkway, joined you up there and we . . . talked. Seconds later, Miss Henderson burst into the ballroom, screaming that the heir was dead. Correct?"

I exhaled the breath I'd been holding. "Correct."

Near the doorway, I said, "If anyone in the drawing room wonders where you have been just now, what will you tell them?"

He shrugged. "The necessary? I drank a good bit of champagne at the ball, and then, at supper, the servants brought in dozens of bottles of red wine. I drank several goblets of that, as well. I daresay a trip to the necessary would be quite believable, surely you agree?"

Grinning, I nodded. "Thank you ever so, Mr. Talbot. I knew I could count on you."

"I doubt I could refuse you anything, sweet Juliette." He reached to lightly touch my cheek, then the dark-haired gentleman turned and rushed from the solarium a few seconds before I did.

Peeking out, I watched his backside disappear into the drawing room. Believing it now safe to do so, I emerged and headed the opposite direction to the back stairs and hurried up to my room, confident that before the night was over, I would once again be summoned to speak with the constable. This time, I hoped with a different outcome.

CHAPTER 13

In The Garden With The Candlestick

The hours crawled by before the summons came. When it did, I had to be roused from a deep slumber. Mrs. Fullerton seemed none too pleased that I had been allowed to rest while every other member of the household staff had had to remain alert and ready to cheerfully do the bidding of their betters.

"Get up, you lazy girl!" She slapped me on the cheek, which I'll allow is not the most pleasant manner in which to be awakened.

I sat up, one hand reaching to touch the stinging place on my cheek while my groggy gaze sought to focus upon the scowling face glaring down upon me.

"The constable wants to speak to you again. You are to repair to the drawing room at once!"

I worked to blink myself awake.

"Get up, you lyin' little Frenchie! You think yourself so far above the rest of us but you'll not get away with this, missy!" Standing with both fists planted on her hips, she watched me struggle to pull myself to my feet.

"Straighten your frock and put on your cap. You look a fright! I'll not have Lady Morland or her guests think I run a slip-shod household!"

Mrs. Fullerton, who weighed several stones more than me shoved me ahead of her. "I said put on your cap, girl!"

"I am getting it," I murmured, heading toward my mistress' dressing table where I'd earlier left it lying when I brushed out my hair. Reaching the little table, my hand groped here and there in search of the frilly white cap. "I am certain I left it right here." I glanced to the right and left. "I can scarcely see in the dark," I said.

Mrs. Fullerton snatched up a candle and held it aloft.

When I still didn't see the small scrap of white cloth edged with frilly lace, I turned palms up. "I left it right here," I said again.

The woman's head shook with exasperation as she reached to give me another shove. "Get along with ye'."

Attempting to pat my disheveled hair into some semblance of order, I hurried across the suite and through the door that she had left standing ajar when she stormed in to fetch me.

By the time we reached the drawing room, my heart was pounding so loudly in my ears, I could scarcely think for the deafening noise in my head. I feared I'd not be able to formulate a sensible reply to anything the constable might ask of me. However, recalling the conversation I'd had earlier with Mr. Talbot in which he promised to tell the truth regarding my whereabouts this evening, my fright lessened a mite.

Following Mrs. Fullerton into the drawing room, I felt all eyes fastened on me. At once I spotted Mr. Talbot, but the expression on his face was anything but reassuring, instead his frown sent a tremor of fear through me. Standing beside him Edward Morland looked none too collected either. Fact is, he looked . . . guilty of . . . something. Amongst the crowd of faces scattered about the room, most of whom I did not recognize, I also spotted Lady Morland, her chin elevated, her elegant features composed and serene. She looked as lovely now as she had at the ball, seated erect on the corner of a red velvet sofa, attired in a simple black gown, no diamond necklace glittering at her throat now. How brave she was following the sudden unexpected loss of her eldest son. Despite the fear trembling within me, my heart went out to Lady Morland.

Near her stood Sir Morland, his puffy face a veritable thundercloud, both arms folded across his middle as if it were taking all the control he could muster to remain calm in the face of all that had happened. That he was quietly holding in his grief while being forced to listen to the tedious monotony of the constable's interrogation of the houseguests was evident. How exceedingly difficult this must be for him. The question was, would he be able to contain his rage once the guilty party was revealed?

The constable was seated before the carved mahogany table upon which tea had been brought into the family on far pleasanter occasions than this. He did not deign to rise when I approached. I was a mere maid, after all. Before him on the fine tabletop I saw a handful of loose pages upon which he had scribbled his findings, along with a fresh inkpot and container full of quill pens.

"Take a seat, Miss Abbott," the constable instructed, still not rising as one hand indicated the vacant chair at the opposite end of the table. "I've a few more questions to put to ye'." He cast a glance toward Sir Morland, who acknowledged the question on the lawman's face with a grunt. "As do several of us gathered here," he added.

My heart lurched to my throat as I prayed that Sir Morland was also not already blaming *me* for his son's death.

"Firstly," the constable began, "may I remind ya', Miss Abbot, that a man has lost his life tonight at the hands of another, and the charges about to be brought to the guilty party are severe. Perhaps ye' are not aware that the penalty in this country for murder is death by hangin'." He paused. "In the interests of bringin' this investigation to a close as quickly as possible, ye' are to look on this as an official inquiry, or inquest, if ye' will." He looked again toward Sir Morland as if for confirmation. "Do you understand what I've just said, Miss Abbott?"

"O-Of course I do, sir." Even to me, my voice sounded frightened. I cast a quick glance at Mr. Talbot, who I thought now looked quite worried. The man was actually chewing on his lower lip. Which, I could not take as a good sign.

The constable cleared his throat. "Miss Abbott, you are obliged to answer *every* question I put to you in a truthful manner. On your oath, do ye' promise to do so?"

"I-I will, indeed, sir," I said softly.

The room fell silent as a tomb.

"If ye' recall, Miss Abbott, I asked ye' earlier where you had passed the long hours of this evening while the ball was in progress, and I recall . . ." At this point, he snatched up a piece of paper before him on the table. "Ah, yes, here it is. You said you told Mrs. Collins that you took a walk. Outdoors."

Audible gasps arose from the assembled onlookers.

"But, sir, that is *not* true!"

"What's that ye say, Miss Abbott?" The constable leaned forward. "Speak up, young lady! Did you not say those very words to Mrs. Collins?"

"Yes, sir," I nodded. "I-I did say that, but it's not true! And you gave me no opportunity to tell the truth!" I blurted out.

"And what *is* the truth, Miss Abbott?" Silence again reigned in the room. "Where *did* you spend the bulk of the evening, most specifically between the hours of nine and eleven of the clock?"

I looked down. No matter how much I did *not* want to do so, I had to reveal the truth. "I . . . I was . . . hiding, sir."

"*Hiding?*" my interrogator fairly shouted. "Where were you hiding, Miss Abbott? *Where?*"

My hand lifted to cover my trembling mouth as I looked straight at Mr. Talbot. "Please, sir; help me!"

"No one can help you now, Miss Abbott!" the constable barked. "*Where were you hiding, Miss Abbott?*"

Why did not Mr. Talbot step forward to save me?

"I-I was hiding . . . on the n-narrow ledge . . . behind the grill-work in the ceiling of the ballroom."

Glaring at me, the constable's bushy brows pulled together.

I listened for the sound of a pin to drop in the drawing room, but heard nothing. Not a word, not a breath. I hastened to fill the void with additional information, which I hoped would serve to strengthen my truthful disclosure.

"I watched as the ball guests spilled into the room. I watched the orchestra begin to play and the guests take their places for the first dance. I saw Mr. Edward Morland choose Miss Featherstone for the first set and also Mr. William Morland stand up with Miss Durham. And . . ."

Suddenly the constable sprang to his feet and shouted. "All of which could have been seen from a *hiding* place *outside* the ballroom! *Am I not right, Miss Abbott?*"

Once more, the man's clever way of turning my answers around served only to confuse me.

"But, I wasn't *outside* the ballroom, sir! I just told you I was high up on the ledge . . . looking *down* into the . . ."

The constable lurched 'round the table and leaned over me, his face now on a level with mine. "Then how do you explain *this*?" He reached into his pocket and withdrew a scrap of white linen edged with frilled lace. "I see you are not wearing your cap this evening, Miss Abbott. Is this not your cap?" He waved the cloth beneath my nose. "The one that *fell* from your head when you stole into the garden tonight and *murdered* the Morland heir!"

I drew back, both arms lifted as if to fend off my attacker. "W-where did you find it?"

The constable turned to gaze with satisfaction upon his now transfixed audience. "Right where you lost it, Miss Abbott. Near where William Morland's bloodied body lay, may his Soul Rest in Peace."

Such audible gasps arose from those assembled in the room that the noise could only be quelled by Sir Morland himself. "Let the man continue!"

The constable whirled back around to face me. "Death seems to follow you wherever you go, does it not, Miss Abbott?" Without awaiting my response, he rushed on. "Is it not true that your former employer, Lady Carstairs, a fine upstanding citizen of London, was found dead in her bed, and that the cause of her untimely death remains, to this day, unexplained? And, that *you* stand to inherit a good deal of money from that dearly departed woman's estate? It that not *true*, Miss Abbott?"

"I did not *kill* Lady Carstairs; nor did I murder the Morland heir! I do not even know *how* the gentleman was slain!"

"Another lie, Miss Abbott! For whatever reason, you, yourself, hastened this fine young man's departure from this earth, in the prime of his life, his entire future ahead of him, and all of it now gone because of *you*, Miss Abbott!" He rounded on me again. "*Why did you do it, Miss Abbott? Why did you kill Mr. William Morland?*"

"I did not kill him, sir! I did *not* kill the heir! *I did not!*"

"And, yet, you declared to the other lady's maids just last evening that you *wished* it had been the heir who had got himself kilt *instead* of Kenneth Grimes!"

Astonished gasps and a few cries arose from the Morland family who sat transfixed taking in every word of the drama unfolding before them.

"*Do you deny voicing that sentiment, Miss Abbott?*"

My head dropped forward. "No sir, I do not deny saying that. But . . ." I lifted my head. "I did not *mean* it. I never wished the heir dead . . . and I did *not* kill him. I do not even know *how* he was killed," I said again. "How *was* he killed, sir? With a candlestick?"

The constable paused. "Why would you ask such a thing?"

"Because," I found my voice at last, "from where I stood high up above the ballroom floor, I watched Mr. Edward Morland leave the ballroom carrying a silver candlestick and when he later returned, he was *not* carrying it. Moments later, a young lady whose identity I do not know, came bursting into the ballroom screaming that the heir was dead! I saw it all from my lofty perch high atop the ballroom floor! I swear that is the truth!"

I knew very well that by openly accusing an esteemed member of the Morland family of the horrible crime, I was overstepping the bounds, but it felt as if the last threads of my own life were fast slipping away from me. I saw nothing for it but to fight as hard as I could with the only weapon left to me . . . the *truth*!

"I was not the *only* witness to that occurrence, sir," I added. "Mr. Talbot *also* saw Edward Morland return to the ballroom *without* the candlestick!"

"Pray, what does Mr. Talbot have to say to this? You have not mentioned that gentleman before now. How does *he* fit into your fabrication of lies, young lady?"

"Sir, if I might?" My head jerked toward the direction of the calm male voice at last speaking up.

A sigh of relief escaped me. *Finally, Mr. Talbot was coming to my rescue!*

"Am I to assume that you, sir, are the aforementioned Mr. Talbot that Miss Abbott is referring to?"

"Indeed, sir," Mr. Talbot declared as he strode forward. "I am he. Miss Abbott is speaking the truth, sir."

"And how is it you are possessed of this knowledge, my good man?"

"Because, sir, I . . . I was also standing upon that ledge, alongside her, high up in the ceiling of the ballroom tonight. We both stood there together, watching the proceedings below us."

As Morland family members began to exchange curious glances, I watched the constable's satisfied expression dissolve.

"So . . . you are saying that you were . . . *with* her?"

"Yessir." Mr. Talbot lifted his chin. "That is precisely what I am saying, sir. And, not to put too fine a point on it, but had you questioned me *before* summoning Miss Abbott to the drawing room, I would have admitted as much to you, then. But . . . as you have not asked me where I spent the . . .uh . . . evening, I have not been given the opportunity to say anything on my behalf, or on the behalf of . . . anyone else." He directed an apologetic look at me. "I am sorry to have caused you such a great deal of anguish, Miss Abbott. But, apparently one is obliged to follow the letter of the law . . . and . . . speak only when directed to do so by the authorities. Thus far in these proceedings, no one has asked any questions at all of me."

"You . . . I . . ." the constable faltered as he fell back into his chair. "I-It was deemed unnecessary to question you, Mr. Talbot. What possible reason might *you* have to . . .?"

"What possible reason might *I* have?" I demanded of the now defeated lawman. Ratcheting up my own chin, I rose to my feet and glared down upon the man who seconds earlier was so very eager to fasten a noose around my neck. Now that I'd found my voice, I rushed on. "Mr. Talbot and I were indeed *together* on the ledge. I own that in so doing we were both overstepping the bounds of propriety, but there it is. We were there, *together*. We stood side-by-side and *watched* the proceedings on the ballroom floor below us. We saw Mr. Edward Morland return to the ballroom *without* the candlestick, which I had seen him leave the room with mere moments *after* the heir had also exited the ballroom in favor of the terrace. I did not see where the heir went, because at that point, his whereabouts were well beyond that which I *could* see."

Standing quite near me now, Mr. Talbot was nodding in agreement. "Everything Miss Abbott is saying is true, sir."

"Might I say something, Constable Wainwright?" The sound of Lady Morland's voice startled us, as well as caused everyone's heads to swivel her direction. All eyes were now fixed upon the tall woman as she rose to her full height, her chin elevated, affording her a vantage point rivaling that of the ledge from which I had watched the Morland Manor ball in progress.

Popping to his feet, the constable at once demurred to Lady Morland. "Indeed, you may speak, your ladyship. Please do."

Lady Morland increased the dramatic effect of her testimony by slowly looking about the crowded room before uttering a single solitary word. "*I* gave the candlestick to my son Edward. At the time, all of our footmen were engaged serving our guests liquid refreshment. Because it had come to my attention that not all of the torches in the garden were lit, that in fact, two of them had been extinguished by gusts of brisk wind, I prevailed upon Edward to go into the garden and relight those torches that were no longer burning. I did not want anyone of my guests, most especially the ladies, to lose their footing upon a slippery path should they venture into the garden." She paused to direct a long questioning look at her second son. "Precisely *why* Edward did not return to the ballroom carrying the candlestick after having completed his task, I cannot say. Edward," she looked a question at him, "perhaps you can enlighten us?"

"Madam, are you accusing *me* of killing my own brother?" Edward demanded in an affronted tone.

Lady Morland smiled at her youngest son. "No one is accusing you of killing anyone, my darling. At this point in the inquest, the constable is merely asking questions. Of each of us. However," she added, "it is patently clear that you *are* the person who stands to gain the most from your elder brother's demise. I need hardly remind you that *you*, my dear, are now your father's sole heir."

"*I did not kill my brother!*" Edward exclaimed, an expression of both disbelief and outrage marring his handsome face, it now being quite red.

Sir Morland as well as everyone in the room turned curious gazes upon the new Morland heir. "Perhaps you can explain to us why you did not return to the ballroom with the candlestick, son; which *two* witnesses claim to have seen you leave the ballroom with?"

Edward appeared to make a valiant attempt to regain his composure before he spoke. Inhaling several long breaths, he glanced toward both his father and his regal lady mother. "Upon completing the errand you requested of me, mother, I did, indeed, return, in the *direction* of the ballroom with the candlestick in my possession. I got as far as the terrace. Once there, I paused to speak with a gentleman, Mr. Macintosh, to be precise, who had repaired to the terrace in order to smoke. I recall that during our conversation, I laid the candlestick aside and evidently, neglected to pick it up again before I reentered the ballroom. I swear upon my honor, I am telling the whole truth."

When neither his father nor the constable probed for anything more, Edward pressed on. "I expect you will find the candlestick lying right where I left it; on the stone railing of the terrace, to the left of the double doors. Unless, perchance, a footman has already retrieved it."

No one said anything for several long seconds, during which time the constable returned to the desk upon which his papers lay scattered about. Lowering his head, he scribbled something, or perhaps, made a show of scribbling something, upon one of them. To me, it appeared that following this enlightening revelation, the so-called inquest had become as mired in mud as sticky as that which had soiled the boots of the heir following the unfortunate demise of the hapless Kenneth Grimes. Perhaps the only avenue left now was for the constable and Sir Morland to also declare the heir's death an accident and leave off any further attempts to solve this case. Least ways tonight.

Quite possibly Mr. Talbot agreed with my assessment. "I take it, sir, that Miss Abbott is free to go?"

The constable glanced up. "For now; but, she is *not* free to leave the premises, nor or you, Mr. Talbot. Nor is anyone, for all that." His mouth a straight line, he turned to address Sir Morland, who was now crossing the room toward the official man of law.

"I vowed to you earlier, sir," the constable said in an apologetic tone, "that I would bring the guilty party to bear before this night is over. Despite what has occurred here, I hereby renew my vow to do precisely that. With your permission, sir."

"Very well, Wainwright. Carry on. For now, I daresay, we could all use a bit of rest. The house is at your disposal, although I beg of you to refrain from disturbing my lady wife. Poor woman has suffered a severe blow. In the meantime, you are welcome to continue to scour the house and grounds for additional clues. We shall reconvene the investigation in the morning."

Not addressing me, or Mr. Talbot, Sir Morland re-crossed the room to offer his arm to his distressed, but stoic, wife. "My dear." With a nod to the other family members in the room, he added, "Good night, all. I trust you can find your own way to your beds."

Amid hushed whispers, everyone began to file from the drawing room into the corridor. Noticing that the constable had already gathered up his scattered papers and turned away from the elegant table he'd used as a desk, I reached to snatch up my white cap and stuff it into my apron pocket before I, too, quitted the room. Although Mr. Talbot was close on my heels, we neither one spoke a word to the other on our way out. Which to my mind was a horrid way to spoil the sweet moments we had shared together earlier in the evening.

CHAPTER 14

Re-enacting the Gruesome Crime

On the way to my room, I could not help wondering how the constable had come to be in possession of my white cap? Obviously someone had entered the Featherstone suite in search of . . . *what*? Something to incriminate me? Upon spying my cap laying on the dressing table the intruder must have seized upon *it,* and planted it near the scene of the crime as a way of making *me* appear guilty of murdering the heir. I knew that the lady's maids would all testify that not a one of them had left the house all evening, even if one of them had. Sill, *someone* must have left the house in order to plant my white cap in the knot garden. Or perhaps the guilty party did not bother taking my cap outdoors at all, maybe he or she just *told* the constable they'd *found* it there. But who, other than one of the maids, would do such a reprehensible thing? Who, besides *them* had it in for me and why?

Would do no good now to seek out Nancy Jane to ask if she had any knowledge regarding which of the lady's maids might have left the house in order to purposely take my white cap outdoors. More than likely, Nancy Jane and the other chambermaids were either already busy preparing a hearty breakfast for a houseful of guests, or if my cousin were very lucky, she had been granted a few hours in which to rest her own weary body before starting in on her chores for another long day.

It was now close on three of the clock in the morning and in only a few hours time, the entire household would be awake again and all of us hustled off to the pretty little stone church in Thornbury for Sabbath services.

Sunday, 22 October 1820

It was a somber gathering the following morning in the foyer as we all waited to be handed into the dozen or more coaches lined up on the gravel drive in front of the huge manor house. Once the carriages were full of family members and houseguests, the closed coaches all wheeled off towards the village. The late October day felt blustery and cold and not a one of us had had more than a few hours sleep the night before, therefore conversation within the crowded coaches was as thin as it had been earlier in the servant's hall when we lady's maids gathered for a quick bite of breakfast.

Of course, no one spoke to me during the meal, and I made no attempt to strike up a conversation with any one of them. Beyond murmuring a quiet greeting to Meg, who did cast a guarded smile my way, I said nothing to anyone. If the lady's maids had not yet heard of the events that transpired the previous evening in the drawing room and did not yet know that I had been exonerated of any and all involvement in the deadly crime, I was not going to be the one to tell them.

I also *thought* that because I had been exonerated of the crime, that no hard feelings remained between myself and any member of the Morland family. Evidently I was mistaken, for mere moments after everyone alighted from the coaches before the church house door and were solemnly filing into the vestibule of the little stone building, I felt a tug at my elbow and looked up to find Lady Morland glaring down upon me.

The tall, regal woman, who the previous evening appeared to have fallen into a state of shocked grief, all but jerked me back outdoors to stand beside her as the other family members passed ahead of us into the cramped little building. Then, before a footman had time to swing shut the heavy oaken doors, she turned to unleash a diatribe of anger upon me, although her heated words were spoken in a tone barely above a whisper.

"How dare you accuse my son of murder, you ungrateful little wench! And how dare you spy upon my family! If Morland Manor were not filled to the brim with guests, I would turn you out without a character and be glad of it. For now, you will carry on with your duties, but make no mistake, I have instructed Mrs. Fullerton to keep a close eye on you and to report to me your slightest misstep!"

I was so shocked by her ladyship's bitter charges that I could think of nothing to say in return. She sailed into the church so quickly that I was very nearly left standing alone on the doorstep. If the weather had not appeared so very close on to rain, I would have turned around and run all the way back to Morland Manor. After all, I had covered on foot the exact same distance the day I came into the village in search of a book on French grammar. That venture had turned out to be as useless an excursion as this entire fortnight was proving to be. I never found a book on French grammar and even if I had, I would not have had the leisure time in which to study it.

The atmosphere inside the church house was one of subdued grief. Not even the angelic figures, picked out in colored glass upon the windows and gazing peacefully down upon the congregation, could instill comfort within our tortured souls. The only shred of information I gleaned from services that day was when the curate sorrowfully informed the congregation that the medical examiner had indeed declared the Morland heir dead and his body had been borne to a private chapel within this very edifice and respectfully laid out. The date in which the funeral services would be conducted had not yet been determined, the reverend added; but since women did not attend funeral services anyway, even if the date had been set, I would not have taken note of it.

My thoughts continued to churn over what had transpired between Lady Morland and myself before services began. By the time we all arrived back at the manor house and I changed from my Sunday dress back into my black frock and white pinafore and cap and hurried down to luncheon, I had charitably come around to deciding that poor overset Lady Morland was simply distraught over the death of her eldest son and felt the need to lash out at someone and for whatever reason had chosen me as the recipient of her anger. Therefore since forgiveness on the Sabbath was the order of the day, it was clearly my Christian duty to forgive and forget; even if at this moment forgiveness was not the uppermost feeling in my heart.

At luncheon, talk around the table amongst the maids centered on what would happen now that the heir was gone. Were all the young ladies and their chaperones expected to return home to London now, or what? Was the party over, or would we all carry on as before, despite the fact that there was now only one unattached bachelor to vie for? The new heir.

Tilly, lady's maid to Miss Durham, the young lady I had seen William Morland dancing with the night before, said, "I believe my mistress had genuine feelin's for the heir. Quite shaken up, she is. I rather expect she'll be a-wantin' to leave the manor house straightaway."

"Not Miss Banes," Rosie put in, "she's hoping one of the Morland cousins decides to stay a bit longer. Miss Elizabeth quite liked the tall one, Mr. Reginald Morland. She believes he fancies her, as well. Said he stood up with her twice last night at the ball."

"I'll wager the Lady Sophia won't be stayin' on," Lucy put in, not glancing up as she dipped a fork into the creamed asparagus on her plate. "Her mum Lady Sedgwick keeps remindin' her she's the daughter of an earl, and even without a dowry she has sufficient consequence that she don't need to settle for the leavin's here. Now that the heir is dead and gone, that only leaves Mr. Edward; and my Lady don't care a fig for him."

"What do you mean, *leavin's*?" Rosie cried, her tone scornful. "I daresay to snag the second son would be a boon to anyone of our ladies, and for *us*, seeing's as how we'd be taking up residence here. I don't mind sayin' to live at Morland Manor would suit me quite well!"

"I'd be pleased to live here," Tilly chimed in, "that is, if'n the second son was to declare hisself to *my* lady!"

"So, what about Miss Featherstone?" Meg directed a question at me. "Second son seems to single her out a good bit."

It was the first time today any one of the maids had noted my presence. A shaky smile wavered across my face as I cast a glance at Meg. "I haven't a clue what Miss Featherstone intends to do. She and her sister have not discussed their plans with me." I continued to eat my meal in silence and soon thereafter excused myself from the table and returned above-stairs to our suite.

Despite my belly now being filled with a hot meal, my head was still pounding with pain following the distressing events of the previous evening plus a lack of sufficient sleep and Lady Morland's verbal lashing this morning at services. For my part, I wished only to have a nice lie-down before my mistress and her older sister returned from their luncheon. I assumed that a good many of the houseguests would be leaving this afternoon and that nothing particular in the way of entertainment had been planned for today, especially now that drizzling rain had begun to fall and it had turned quite cool outside, and inside, for all that. This was a fine manor home, make no mistake, but as was true of others of its ilk, when cold weather broke outdoors, it became extra cool and drafty indoors. And, thus far today, no fresh coal had been brought in for our fire, although I rather expected a cheery one burned down, or rather *up,* the hall in the Sedgwick suite.

In only minutes my wished for lie-down was interrupted by yet another insistent rap at our door.

As neither my mistress nor Mrs. Collins had yet returned from luncheon, I rose from my bed to answer the summons and found that a chambermaid, whose name I did not know, was *not* bringing in a scuttle full of coal as I had hoped, but that she had instead been sent up to fetch me. Again.

The girl bobbed a curtsy. "Mrs. Fullerton says all the lady's maids is to return to the servant's hall straightaway, miss."

Because I had already removed my cap, I hurriedly fetched it and reattached it to my head before following the girl below-stairs and straight back down to the dining hall where all the maids, including Lady Morland's tall, elderly maid Temple, who had not been present for luncheon, were now assembled. I noted a good many of the chambermaids also in the room, including Nancy Jane. We lady's maids, being a notch above the below-stairs staff were each accorded chairs upon which to sit around the table, while those lesser personages in the serving hierarchy were obliged to stand or lean against the wall along the fringes of the room. The questioning looks upon everyone's faces told me that no one had any notion what this hastily called meeting was about.

In only moments, Constable Wainwright advanced into the room. Because his dark blue coat and trousers were rumpled and his cheeks and chin were shadowed with stubble, I surmised the man had not taken time away from his ongoing investigation to tend to his own appearance. If he had slept at all the previous night, it had been whilst wearing his clothes. The man looked a fright, which is not to say he looked a great deal better when he was fresh. Without preamble, or taking a seat, the now rather fatigued, and no doubt, disgruntled, man began at once to speak.

"Just so's ye' know, not a single person in this house has yet been cleared of the dastardly crime that was perpetrated upon the Morland family here last night."

At those words, my heart sank. Was the constable starting all over again? How could I bear even *more* questions flung at me?

"Since last evening, the medical exam'ner has determined that the deceased, whilst he was alive, stood several inches over six feet tall and that whoever stabbed him in the back would have to be of a certain height to have drove in the knife in the precise spot that kilt the gentleman. The weapon was thrust into his back at such an angle that a person of lesser height would have had to bring along a stool to stand upon . . . or . . ." his voice trailed off as he turned to put down the sheaf of papers that he seemed to always carry on his person.

Following the constable's description of the sordid details regarding the murder, we all exchanged horrified grimaces with one another, it being the first we'd heard as to the manner in which the heir had been dispatched.

"Now then, folks." The constable glanced back up. "I've asked the medical exam'ner to assist me this afternoon . . . ah . . . here he is now." He turned as another gentleman, this one of middling height and with a full head of red hair and side-whiskers stepped into the room. "Folks, this is Doctor Morgan," the constable said. "Some of you might already be acquainted with the good doctor. Doctor? I'll leave it to you to explain what we's a-doin' this afternoon."

Doctor Morgan cleared his throat and in a pleasant-enough tone began to speak. "Neither the constable nor I wish to alarm you, but for this afternoon, I have engaged the tallest footman in the household, fellow by the name of Timothy, to pose as the heir and one by one, I will call each of you into the hallway and by conducting a . . . shall we say, re-enactment of the crime, we shall determine who amongst you could, or could not, be the guilty party."

Mine was not the only mouth that fell open! And yet, for the first time in a dozen or more hours, I relaxed. Truly, I did. I, Juliette Abbott, was not nearly tall enough to have stabbed anyone, male or female, in the back; anyone who stood more than a few inches taller than myself, or my cousin Nancy Jane, that is, who stood no higher than me. Drawing in a deep breath, I settled back in my chair, folded my arms across my very relieved chest, and watched as, one by one, the tallest amongst us were led into the hallway and handed a wooden spoon, which evidently was this afternoon's weapon of choice.

I knew that inordinately tall footmen were a premium in elegant households such as this one, and that Morland Manor boasted at least five or six of the giants, therefore the burden of guilt for the dreadful crime was not likely to land on anyone of us female servants. With the possible exception of Lady Morland's maid Temple, who stood quite tall, indeed.

By the end of the afternoon's demonstration, two women amongst us had received a nod from Doctor Morgan and Constable Wainwright, one of them giving me a ripple of perverse pleasure as she had been especially nasty to me the previous evening: Mrs. Fullerton. The other quite tall female was indeed Lady Morland's personal maid Temple, who reportedly dissolved into tears when asked to pretend to stab in the back with the long-handled wooden spoon the very tall Timothy, who carried the prestigious title in the Morland household of First Footman. Exchanging curious looks with one another we lady's maids listened to the woman's cries and even a scream or two as the good doctor told her over and over again what he wanted her to do. Eventually, Lady Morland herself had to be sent for to come and rescue her overwrought maid. But, once she had taken away the sobbing Temple, we all knew nothing would come of it, since it was obvious poor Temple was simply overset by the whole distasteful business, being on such close terms as she was to her ladyship.

I heard one of the chambermaids standing behind me say, "Temple knowed the Morland heir since he was in leading strings. To be sure, his death has come as a mighty blow to her."

When the ghoulish experiment was over and done with, even Mrs. Fullerton was excused, although it was said she did a credible job of the spoon stabbing, even hitting the exact point between the First Footman's shoulder blades where the knife blade had sunk into the Morland heir's back. But, of all of us, Mrs. Fullerton probably had the most air-tight defense, seeing as how she'd been on hand in the kitchen the entire evening, except when she came up stairs to haul me down to the drawing room for questioning.

Poor Timothy didn't fare so well. Nor did the four other quite tall Morland footmen, although they could all probably vouch for one another's whereabouts all evening, having stayed busy serving champagne and then supper and wine to all the guests. For now, however, they every last one found themselves on Constable Wainwright's growing suspect list.

Before we were all excused, however, he informed us that he now intended to center his attention upon the matter of motive, as that generally nailed down *why* the guilty party committed the crime in the first place, unless, of course, it was a random killing with no clear-cut reason to explain it.

Feeling especially tired now, I slowly made my way back upstairs and finally did get a bit of nap, knowing that as the long afternoon wore on, the majority of those guests who'd also been eliminated as suspects by the constable were, no doubt, now making haste to leave the house, quite possibly never to return again following this afternoon's frightful entertainment.

At supper in the servant's quarters that night, I learned that earlier in the day, before the majority of the house guests had departed, Constable Wainwright and Doctor Morgan had also conducted their spoon-stabbing experiment in the stable with all the visiting grooms and stable hands, but all of them had also been excused as none were deemed of sufficient height to have committed the horrid crime. Following the family's dinner that night, my Miss Featherstone returned to our suite bearing the news that, despite his grief, Sir Morland had declared at dinner that he would be off for London at first light the next morning.

"He means now to consult with Bow Street regarding the heir's murder," Caroline Featherstone told me as I, still feeling rather weary myself, assisted her to prepare for bed.

"You mean he's going to call in the Runners?" I asked, unable to stifle a sleepy yawn.

She nodded. "Apparently he and the constable have questioned everyone here who could have done it, unless the murderer was a footpad, or a gypsy, who it very well could have been, since there were several items taken from the heir's . . . hmm . . . person, that I understand were of considerable value. Anyhow, if it was a footpad or gypsy, Sir Morland is of the opinion that they would be long gone from the area by now, and therefore very likely never run to ground."

This was the first I'd heard that anything of value had been taken from the heir, but if the killer were a gypsy or footpad that would certainly constitute a motive for murder, as those types were generally always in need of the ready. Still, if that were the case, the culprit would indeed likely never be caught or prosecuted for the crime.

"Sir Morland intends to consult with the authorities in London," Mrs. Collins took up the narrative, "in the hope that they will dispatch a Runner to track down friends of the heir and make inquiries as to their whereabouts the past week, or perhaps determine if any gentleman in the City might possess a long-standing grudge, or vendetta, against William Morland, or even the entire Morland family."

"Such a dreadful business," I murmured, moving mindlessly across the room to hang up Miss Featherstone's gown in the clothespress. Since neither Caroline, nor Alice, had said anything about me having been named a possible suspect in the heir's murder, I saw no need to tell them. So far as I was concerned, that anxiety-ridden episode was behind me, and I was quite happy to never visit it again. They had also not said a word about me hiding on the ledge high up above the ballroom floor, so perhaps word of that ill-conceived escapade had also not left the drawing room last night. I was quite happy to also keep that secret close to my chest.

However, I did ask, "Did the other young ladies say anything about whether or not they intend to stay here a bit longer, or return home to London?"

I was anxious to know the answer to that since if my Miss Featherstone and her sister had plans to leave, it would mean that I, too, would once again be set adrift and quite possibly once again without a character, considering what Lady Morland had said this morning. Consequently, I had decided late this afternoon that, even though my time with Miss Featherstone and her sister had been short, perhaps one of them might consent to provide me with a character reference. Who knows, Lady Morland might not even honor her promise to pay me, let alone double my wages. Especially if I did not fulfill my duties for the entire fortnight; it being cut short due to the murder.

"Oh, I meant to tell you," Caroline's voice revealed her excitement over some new turn. "Two Morland cousins have decided to stay, with Lady Morland's blessing, therefore the party shall go on! Perhaps indefinitely, Lady Morland said. Now that Autumn is upon us and winter coming soon, Town is fairly empty so Lady Morland said we might all stay as long as we like. I thought it quite generous of her, don't you agree? Sir Morland was quite against it, but Lady Morland said having young people about would serve to take her thoughts from her troubles, therefore in the drawing room following dinner, she declared that things would proceed as planned. So, now we've four gentlemen to choose from!"

I looked up from my task. "Four?"

"Indeed!" Caroline said. "Edward Morland, who, of course, is now the heir. Isn't *that* a marvelous turn?"

"Caroline!" Her sister cried.

"Well, it's true, he is! Anyhow, the two Morland cousins are also quite nice. Reginald Morland is exquisitely handsome; he is tall and blond with impeccable manners, and Henry Morland; though not nearly so handsome, actually he is a bit shy, but is nonetheless agreeable. And, Mr. Talbot. That's *four* gentlemen in search of a bride instead of the original two. One, really, since none of us ever really believed William Morland meant to choose a bride."

"Caroline," her sister scolded her once more. "That will be the last I hear of you maligning the late Morland heir. If you are not careful, the constable will be questioning you! I understand it is generally 'motive' that convicts a killer."

"Oh, pishaw. No one would believe I killed the heir. One may as well point the finger at his mother. After all, Lady Morland is tall enough to have stabbed her son in the back."

"Caroline! That will be quite enough! Now, get into bed and never let me hear another word said on that score! Lady Morland, indeed. Good night, Juliette."

"So, you will . . . not be leaving, then?" I asked.

"Not for a long while, Juliette," Caroline replied on a yawn. Then before crawling into bed, she grinned slyly at me. "And not *ever* if I have anything to say about it."

CHAPTER 15

Bowling on the Lawn

Monday, 23 October 1820

I was told that early this morning the heir was laid to rest in the small cemetery next to the little stone church in Thornbury with only his father, his brother Edward, Mr. Talbot, Constable Wainwright and Doctor Morgan in attendance. Immediately afterward Edward and Mr. Talbot returned home and Sir Morland set out for London to attend to the distressing business of altering his will and then, securing the services of Bow Street to look into the matter of his eldest son's gruesome murder.

An hour or so after the sun popped out this afternoon, an impromptu game of bowling on the lawn was got up and all the young people gaily trouped outdoors to play. To adhere to propriety in regard to the young ladies, we lady's maids were also included in the game, which did skew the numbers a bit, there now being ten females pitted against the four gentlemen.

During yesterday afternoon's mass exodus from Morland Manor, Lady Sophia and her mother had once again *not* taken themselves off (as many of us thought they might). However, the pair did elect to merely sit and watch this afternoon's activities from the terrace rather than participate in the game, a decision to which no one objected. Several others of the older chaperones, Mrs. Throckmorton and Lady Wentworth also chose to sit outdoors and occupy themselves with their needlework, leaving the other women to keep Lady Morland company in the drawing room.

Of late, even before the heir was killed, Lady Morland had begun to complain of a mysterious stomach ailment, which seemed to have worsened since the heir died, rendering her virtually unable now to eat or do much of anything. Although the regal woman professed to wish above all things to have the house party proceed as planned, a veil of pain, as well as grief, seemed now to dull her countenance. When a small smile did lift the corners of her lips, it was not of sufficient strength to remove the sorrow that rendered her eyes all but lifeless. Not a one of us could help feeling sorry for her, for her physical pain and the immense loss she had suffered.

Still, today I was delighted to be asked to join the ladies and gentlemen who were assembling to compete against one another in a gay diversion on the lawn, a couple of footmen having joined in to round out the gentleman's team. I threw myself wholeheartedly into the game. The sun felt glorious on my back and with no constable lurking about to prod for answers to incriminating questions and then twist my answers around to suit himself, it felt good to finally be free to laugh aloud and exchange teasing remarks with others of the players.

In the end Edward's team won two games in a row after which everyone declared themselves in dire want of refreshment, so we all adjourned to the terrace where several tables had been set up and three or four footmen were already setting down pots of steaming tea and platters of tasty-looking tarts and biscuits. Truth to tell, not a one of us (except perhaps Miss Durham) had noticed the absence of the heir. If one dared say it, having him no longer amongst us only served to lift everyone's spirits and increase the lighthearted gaiety. His presence had always brought along with it a pallor of gloom that detracted from, rather than added to, whatever pleasant diversion was in progress. If asked I was certain everyone would agree that in all ways the heir was a veritable down pin.

But, the circumstances surrounding his recent death were still fresh upon everyone's mind and therefore fodder ripe for discussion.

"Did the constable reveal to anyone exactly *what* was missing from the heir's person?" the Lady Sophia asked of no one in particular.

Reginald Morland, who appeared to have taken a liking to the pretty auburn-haired miss and now sat slouched in a chair at her side, drawled, "I was told his diamond stick pin, an absurdly enormous thing, went missing; as well as the famous Morland signet ring, also large and gaudy, one-of-a-kind you know, with a huge ruby stone inlaid with the Morland crest picked out in gold."

"I do recall seeing that ring on his finger," replied Lady Sophia. "It was indeed quite large. But, I thought it also quite beautiful and impressive due to its size if nothing more."

"My Uncle Morland presented it to William the day he reached his majority," Reginald said. "Cousin Will was instructed to wear it until the day he presented it to his own son and heir. Quite sad to have lost it, actually. Family heirloom and all."

"But, would not a signet ring, especially being one-of-a-kind, and displaying the Morland crest as you describe, not mark the present holder of it as the killer?" asked pretty, black-haired Miss Elizabeth Banes, who I noted had jockeyed to sit to the right of Reginald Morland. I recalled her maid saying that gentleman had stood up twice with her at the ball.

When his shoulders merely lifted and fell, I, seated at a nearby table, recalled Miss Banes' maid Rosie also declaring that her mistress had taken a liking to him and thought he entertained the same affection toward her. In truth, Reginald Morland was, indeed, quite a good looking fellow, tall, blond with classical features, a straight nose and strong jaw, but his long eyes perpetually held at half mast, added nothing in my estimation to his appeal, although it did contribute significantly to the air of boredom he seemed bent upon projecting. Whether he was truly jaded or merely disinterested in all that was going on around him remained unclear.

As he did not now deign to answer Miss Banes' question with anything beyond another shrug of his shoulders told me that he cared not a whit about either the topic being discussed or about appearing pleasant to Miss Banes, or any one of us, for all that. Apparently sensing the gentleman's disinterest, the pretty Miss Banes said nothing further and instead delicately reached toward the platter before her for another biscuit while Mr. Reginald Morland returned his attention to the lovely blonde, blue-eyed Lady Sophia, daughter of an earl, I reminded myself, wondering if that alone was sufficient reason for Mr. Reginald Morland to transfer his interest from the lovely Miss Banes to the equally lovely Lady Sophia.

Not knowing, or caring overmuch what the answer to that question was, I ceased listening to the idle talk at the adjacent table and instead turned my attention to enjoying the delicious refreshments set before we maids. The rich black tea tasted delightful and I had never eaten such tasty, sugary-coated biscuits before. The food served to the staff below-stairs was fine enough, but that served above-stairs to the privileged guests was finer still. I confess I ate more than my share of the tasty treats and did not suffer a bit of regret for having done so. It was not long however, before the talk at the adjacent table drew my notice again.

"Well, I thought it quite despicable that Constable Wainwright treated all of us as if *we* were suspects in the terrible crime!" exclaimed Miss Amelia Durham.

"Until the murderer is uncovered," Mr. Talbot, who sat with his back to me, said quietly, "I daresay we shall all remain under a veil of suspicion."

"But to ask everyone of a certain height to pretend to stab that poor fellow in the back with a spoon was quite ludicrous, you must agree!" complained Miss Durham.

"I cannot say as I was not asked to wield the spoon." I heard Mr. Talbot's droll reply, which caused me to smile.

To me, Mr. Talbot seemed like a tall man, but then, to me anyone over five feet five, or six, inches was tall. Both Mr. Talbot and Edward Morland were neither a great deal taller than five feet nine, or ten inches, at most. Sir Morland was not a tall man either, so it made sense that at least one of his sons would stand no higher than he.

"Well, I was asked to wield the spoon and I don't mind saying, I did not appreciate being made to feel as if I were a criminal and that my name suddenly sat atop the constable's suspect list!" Miss Durham cried, her tone now quite enraged. "Where do those men of law dredge up such absurd notions? I thought it all quite rude and vastly impertinent!"

Hmm, thought I, Miss Durham did appear *overly* overset about yesterday's proceedings. She was indeed quite tall. I had not been privy to whomever other women, beyond Mrs. Fullerton and poor Temple, had received nods from the constable yesterday. Apparently he had also asked Miss Durham to perform the charade. How did she fare when it came to motive, I wondered. Could she have perhaps been angry enough with William Morland for dancing with the lovely Lady Sophia to have secretly followed him into the garden and committed the evil deed? I did clearly recall her approaching him the night of the ball, when he stood alone near the opened double doors, and the pair of them falling into what appeared to be . . . a heated discussion, then she stalked off, her head held high. What might they have been speaking of, and could it have anything to do with what later transpired in the garden?

" . . . Doctor Morgan approved of the experiment as did Sir Morland," Mr. Talbot was saying.

"But, it turned up nothing of consequence unless one believes Lady Morland's maid Temple is the guilty party and what would possess a woman of her age and bearing to commit murder?" demanded the still outraged Miss Durham.

"What would possess anyone to commit murder?" replied Mr. Talbot.

"I assume you mean anyone of *us*," declared the persistent Miss Durham.

Oh, my. I had never before heard Miss Durham utter so many words on the same topic at any one time. Her knickers were definitely in a twist with the effect that all vestiges of gaiety from this afternoon's party were now all but vanished.

In no time, I noted Edward Morland push back his chair and move to stand behind my Miss Featherstone's chair, whereupon she gazed flirtatiously at him from beneath long lashes and nodded sweetly. Assuming he had asked if she would like to take a turn about the garden with him, I also rose to my feet, intent upon following them at a discrete distance, since as her abigail that duty did fall to me.

But, my maneuver was forestalled by the sudden motion of Mr. Talbot also rising to his feet and coming to rest behind my chair.

"Shall we join them?" he asked in a low tone. "I daresay I rather dislike the turn of conversation . . . here." A head jab indicated the other table.

Noting his lips begin to twitch, I replied, "A walk would indeed be far more pleasant, sir." Rising, I fell into step beside him.

Mr. Talbot looked handsome this afternoon in a bottle green jacket, beige knee breeches tucked into shiny brown top boots, his gleaming white cravat tied as meticulously as ever. I, of course, looked the same as I always did in my black frock, ruffled white pinafore and white cap atop my head, my hair today drawn back in a knot at the nape of my neck, although after running about on the lawn, I rather expect a good many tendrils were now dangling loose about my cheeks.

To my delight, once the four of us descended the rock steps and began to follow the stone path that led around the side of the house, we headed straight toward the knot garden that stretched across the rear of the large, rambling manor house.

"Oh, I have been wishing to lose myself in the knot garden!" I exclaimed, which caused Mr. Talbot to laugh aloud.

"You are a delight, Miss Abbott! Most everyone *fears* losing themselves within the confines of a knot garden and never being able to find their way out again."

"But, it is so pretty!" I exclaimed. "Just look at all the different shapes of the shrubbery and the bright colors of the late-blooming flowers. It is all so beautiful! Let us hurry within."

I let go of his elbow and fairly skipped on ahead, which caused him to hasten his step to keep up with me as I darted behind a high hedge shaped like a lion.

"Please, Miss Abbott, do wait up. I shouldn't wish to lose you . . . Miss Abbott?"

I watched him turn full around in a circle before I jumped from behind a bear-shaped shrub. Lifting my arms over my head, I growled. "Here I am! Come and catch me!" Off I darted again.

Of course, he soon caught up to me and reaching for my hand, quite firmly held it over the crook of his elbow. "I shall tolerate no more growling from you today, Miss Abbott, or running ahead of me."

"Yessir," I contritely replied. "But, isn't it delightful here? I have only ever seen it from the window at the end of the gallery on our floor." A half second later I said, "I wonder that one or more of the guests did not lose their way whilst walking here the night of the ball."

"Perhaps one did," my companion remarked lightly. "We shall never know. Perhaps the heir's slayer is still lost in the garden and we shall come upon him today." His tone had turned deliberately ominous. "What say you to that?"

"I would say you are teasing me, and given the dreadful topic you and Miss Durham were discussing, I must ask you to please leave off." I walked a few steps beside him in silence before saying, "With the heir now gone and thankfully, also the constable, I think it best if we abandoned that distasteful topic and henceforth, speak only of pleasant things, do you not agree, sir?"

"I do, indeed," Mr. Talbot said. "It's just that none of us, I am assuming, has ever been involved in a murder before and it is a rather novel turn. One, I suppose, that could be talked of at length. Although not in Lady Morland's presence."

"Oh, that dear woman appears to be suffering so very much and not only from grief. I wonder if we should not send for Doctor Morgan again."

"Edward and I were earlier discussing that very thing. He is quite worried about his mother and her stomach ailment. Of course, this nasty business regarding his brother's death is also still fresh on his mind."

"I confess I do find parts of the nasty business intriguing," I admitted. "I daresay the dogged manner in which the constable questioned *me* that night in the drawing room could not have escaped your notice. It was as if he believed he had nabbed the *real* killer! As if *I* might have a reason to kill William Morland!"

Mr. Talbot said nothing for a long moment, then surprised me by saying, "I rather expect if the truth were known, a good many of us might have a valid reason to wish the heir dead."

My head jerked up. "What a frightful thing to say, sir!"

At that instant, our discussion was interrupted by the late heir's brother Edward, who, alongside Miss Featherstone suddenly appeared from 'round a clipped hedge shaped like the king in a chess set. Engrossed with one another, the pair very nearly collided with us. "So, it appears you two are as lost as we are!" Edward exclaimed.

"Is this not a curious place?" asked Caroline.

"I was just telling Mr. Talbot that I find it delightful. He, of course, declared I was being quite silly!"

"I said no such thing, you little minx!"

We all laughed, then Edward suggested that we four walk a bit closer together lest we become hopelessly lost in the tangle of hedges, and all miss our dinner.

Amidst our lighthearted laughter, I asked, "Did not you and Mr. Talbot play here as boys? If so, I would think you would both know where all the twisty little paths lead."

Both gentlemen shook their heads.

"Mother only just installed the knot garden a fortnight or so before the house party. I had never set foot in it until the other night when she asked me to relight the torches." Edward pointed up ahead. "I see one there, although I cannot say if it is one I came upon that night, or not. I daresay I could probably never find them again if I had to."

For the remainder of our walk in the knot garden, we did manage to keep one another in our sights. Before turning around to pick our way out, I had to admit, if only to myself, to a morbid curiosity as to exactly *where* the attack upon the heir had occurred. As it turned out, I had no need to voice my question, for as we strolled 'round yet another bend in the path, we came up a small gold cross lying upon a flat stone a few feet ahead of us. Near it, and quite visible to the naked eye, was a large brown stain of dried blood that had spilled across the flat stones surrounding the relic.

"Oh!" Miss Featherstone exclaimed, a hand flying to her mouth. "This must be where . . ."

Glancing down at the relic, I, too, stopped in my tracks. "Oh, dear." Looking up at Mr. Talbot, I asked, "Who . . . who do you think . . .?"

"Lady Morland, I would imagine. She is quite distraught over the heir's death, as you know."

"Or perhaps Temple placed the cross here," Edward mused, pausing to intently gaze down upon the very spot where his older brother had been slain.

"Might we go in now, please?" begged Miss Featherstone.

When Edward did not seem to have heard his companion's plea, Mr. Talbot said, "Come away, Edward, the ladies wish to leave."

Even so, Edward Morland seemed reluctant to turn away. And I also must confess to a morbid curiosity of my own. Had I been here alone, I would have taken the opportunity to have a thorough look about. In my opinion, since the slaying took place at night, it was very likely the killer might have left behind a clue, which he, or she, was entirely unaware of and which I felt certain that on my own I could find.

For today, however, a thorough search of the area was not possible. But, rest assured, I did not entirely abandon the notion.

CHAPTER 16

A Dead Body On The Stairs

Tuesday, 24 October 1820

The following day Miss Durham and her aunt, Mrs. Throckmorton, left Morland Manor under what can only be described as mysterious circumstances. Caroline Featherstone and her sister Mrs. Collins told me that soon after breakfast (where by-the-by Miss Durham's maid Tilly revealed nothing of her mistress's plans to we lady's maids) at any rate, I was told Mrs. Throckmorton called for a carriage quite early and the three women trouped down the stairs without so much as a word to anyone, not even Lady Morland, which in my estimation was quite ill-mannered, even inexcusable, given that Lady Morland has been such a very gracious hostess.

"Very bad *ton*," is the way Mrs. Collins put it and both Caroline and I heartily agreed.

The discussion regarding the Durham party's hasty departure continued after luncheon.

"Miss Durham must have a bee in her bonnet about something," Caroline said. "Of course, Lady Morland said nothing against them, but by the expression on her face, one could tell she was quite shocked over Miss

Durham's disgraceful behavior." Continuing to mull over the girl's discourtesy, Caroline shook her head. "Lady Morland is a dear, sweet person, who has borne a terrible loss. The very least we can do is treat her in a respectful manner."

"Well, I am glad to hear you say that, Caroline," her sister declared from where she sat on the window seat, having picked up a ladies magazine and now idly thumbing through it.

"I take it Miss Durham was returning home to London?" I ventured.

Mrs. Collins nodded. "Griggs said the ladies availed themselves of a Morland carriage to take them as far as Thornbury where they meant to catch the mail coach to London."

Caroline was now primping before the mirror. "Her departure does rather leave the 'gentlemen to lady' quotient more evenly distributed: four gentlemen to four ladies now. Although . . ." she caught my eye in the mirror. ". . . I daresay, Mr. Talbot does seem to have taken a fancy to you, Miss Juliette."

Saying nothing, I ducked my head from where I stood folding and replacing Miss Featherstone's clean chemises on a shelf in the cupboard.

"How's that?" Mrs. Collins glanced up. "You have not set *your* cap at one of the gentlemen, have you Juliette?"

"No, ma'am, of course not."

"Even if she has," Caroline put in, "I can see nothing offensive in it. Juliette is very pretty. I can certainly see how a gentleman would find her charming."

"For the gentlemen to find your lady's maid charming is clearly not what our hostess Lady Morland intended as the purpose for this gathering." Mrs. Collins laid aside her magazine and rose to her feet. "The gentlemen were invited for the sake of her *guests*, not her guest's *lady's maids*." Mrs. Collins moved a few steps closer to me. "Juliette, you are not to accept another invitation to walk with, or even *speak* with, Mr. Talbot, do you understand?"

"Alice, you cannot mean that!"

"I do, indeed. Miss Banes' mother, Lady Wentworth, informed me only yesterday that her daughter Elizabeth feels quite drawn to Mr. Talbot. She said he stood up with Elizabeth twice, *twice,* at the ball; and that she finds him agreeable. Therefore, *you* will leave off dangling after the man, Juliette." Her lips pursed. "Why, I cannot credit the impudence." After a pause, she added in a still firmer tone, "If you fail to do as I ask, I shall have no choice but to bring your impertinent actions to the attention of Lady Morland. We do not want *that* now, do we?"

I exhaled the breath I had been holding. "No, ma'am. We do not want that."

"Very well, then. I had best not hear another word about it," she said with a sniff of displeasure.

Feeling thoroughly chastised, I completed my task; then, after demurely asking Caroline if she required anything else of me, I retreated to my windowless little room and sat down heavily upon the bed. The only bit of pleasure I had found since coming to Morland Manor was now being denied me. And I had no choice but to do the bidding of my mistress' sister. Otherwise, the much sought after, nay, sorely *needed*, character reference that I had hoped to receive from Lady Morland, and perhaps from Mrs. Collins, would surely be denied me.

I stewed alone in my room for very nearly the entire afternoon. Because it had begun again to rain, I assumed the guests were being forced to spend

the long afternoon clustered together in the drawing room; I not amongst
them for Mrs. Collins had made a point of saying that they did not need me
to accompany them below-stairs this afternoon.

After tea, Caroline and her sister returned to our suite and once
again I could not help eavesdropping upon their conversation. Upon
hearing Caroline speak Mr. Talbot's name, I edged further into my
mistress' bedchamber, curious as to what was being said about the now
much sought-after gentleman. Had he spent the afternoon, as I feared, in
Miss Banes' company?

" . . . Reginald and Henry, too, in fact all *four* of the gentlemen
whiled away the entire afternoon playing billiards!" Caroline wailed. "How
are we to make headway with them when they prefer to play games rather
than pass the time with us?"

"Now, Caroline; it is the way of things with gentlemen.
Remember, they are our *whole* world, but to them, we are but a part. It is
something all women must learn to accept. It is the way of the world and
cannot be changed."

"Well, I cannot *like* it!"

"Oh, my dearest girl." Alice crossed the room to drape a consoling
arm about her younger sister's shoulder. "You mustn't fret. Lady Morland
told the chaperones this very afternoon that she intends to keep the
gentlemen with us in the drawing room after dinner tonight for the *entire*
evening. Certainly you will have an opportunity to sit with Edward, or
perhaps you might offer to play a piece on the pianoforte. Lady Wentworth
declared that her lovely daughter Elizabeth wishes to sing for her Mr.
Talbot. She insists her daughter possess a remarkable singing voice."

My heart sank. Miss Banes was so very pretty, how could *my* Mr. Talbot not be captivated by her beauty, and her charm? Especially if she also sang like a bird.

Some time later, seated at the supper table in the servant's dining hall below-stairs with the other lady's maids, I only half-heartedly listened as they gossiped about their mistresses, and also about each other, talk of the unfortunate murder having now all but been abandoned. I noted that Temple was not amongst us again this evening, which meant that conversation among the maids would be less restricted. More often than not, Temple did not take her meals with us, preferring to have a tray sent up, or, as I had learned from Nancy Jane, she very often dined with Mrs. Fullerton in that woman's private parlour, the two women being of an age, meaning a great deal older than we maids. By contrast, I rather expect they thought us quite silly.

Lucy began to go on about how handsome and attentive Mr. Reginald Morland was now being toward the Lady Sophia. Which came as news to me as I was in the Sedgwick suite twice every day and not once had I heard the Lady Sophia go on about any one of the gentlemen, except in the beginning to say how she had taken a strong dislike of the heir.

"And her mum, Lady Sedgwick, says she don't mind at all that he don't have a title," Lucy added.

"The heir didn't have a *proper* title either," Rosie reminded her. "He was the son of a Baronet, which ain't even a real peer. Mr. Talbot don't have a title neither, but Miss Elizabeth says she don't mind. Mr. Talbot is the kindest, most thoughtful man she has ever met and she hopes he'll declare himself to her quite soon."

I could not keep still a second longer, most especially since neither Temple nor Mrs. Collins were present to take note of my remarks. "I heard that Miss Banes' mother Lady Wentworth wishes her daughter to sing tonight . . . for *her* Mr. Talbot."

"Indeed, she does," Rosie said. "Miss Banes is quite the songbird, don't you know? Her mum is certain that will seal the deal with that gentleman."

"And what of Miss Grant?" To conceal my distress over what Rosie was saying, I turned to address my friend Meg. "Is she sweet on Mr. Henry Morland? He seems a bit shy to me, but then, so is she. I wonder what they find to talk about."

"Plenty," Meg replied. "You know how it is when you put two of a kind together, they somehow manage to draw one another out. Miss Grant quite likes Mr. Henry, she does; or perhaps I should say she *adores* him."

"As much as you like James, the footman?" Rosie queried, looking around Lucy at Meg.

Again, my head jerked up. "You have formed a *tendre* with one of the footmen?" My wide eyes held Meg's.

The little maid blushed to the roots of her hair. "I think him quite nice."

I confess I had not noticed any such attachments forming between the maids and those of the male household staff; but it shouldn't come as a surprise; such attachments were not uncommon when young ladies and gentlemen worked alongside one another for any length.

"Is his name actually James?" I asked. "My cousin said Lady Morland calls all her footmen James, except perhaps Timothy, who, as we all know, is First Footman."

Rosie laughed. "I believe for Meg, *James* is First Footman, ain't that right Meg?"

Everyone laughed.

I could not help wondering when, and how, Meg found the time, or place, in which to meet up with her James? And, would I ever find a way, or be *allowed*, to meet up again with *my* Mr. Talbot? If he were, indeed, *my* Mr. Talbot.

Fortunately, I had not long to wonder.

In mere minutes, Griggs stepped into the dining hall and informed we lady's maids that our presence was requested for the remainder of the evening above-stairs in the drawing room.

My heart leap to my throat as I scooted back my chair, sorely wishing I had time to at least brush my hair, but it was not to be.

Entering the drawing room, I noted that all the ladies and their chaperones were seated here and there at one end of the spacious chamber. Two of the four gentlemen were standing together near the fireplace; Mr. Reginald Morland leaning against it, one foot lounging on the fender as he lazily twirled brandy around the bottom of a plump goblet. Edward Morland and Mr. Talbot were both standing near the sofa upon which Miss Featherstone and her sister perched, their backs straight in deference to Lady Morland, although being the wife of a mere baronet, she was not *really* a bona fide peeress as Rosie had only just pointed out. Still, she was a lady and deserved everyone's respect.

When we were in the drawing room, we maids knew that we were meant to squeeze onto a pair of sofas at the far opposite end of the room, and rather than converse amongst ourselves, were instead to remain ever vigilant and alert to the goings-on in the room, most especially in regard to our respective mistresses. Were a gentleman to approach our young lady and most certainly, were he to actually slide onto a sofa or settee where our young lady sat, we were to quietly walk that way and remain standing behind them at a discrete distance, whilst carefully taking in whatever transpired.

Apparently shy Miss Hester Grant had only just been asked, or had volunteered, to play a piece upon the pianoforte, for at the moment, she was gliding toward that instrument which was tucked into the far most corner of the room, beyond the bank of floor-to-ceiling windows. Miss Grant looked fetching tonight in a gray silk gown demurely trimmed with lace as she slipped onto the bench before the pianoforte and began to sort through a folio of music, apparently deciding upon which piece to play.

Before she began to play, however, shy Mr. Henry Morland, an uncertain smile upon his plain face, boldly moved from his position before the fireplace to stand behind her. Miss Grant looked up, smiled with pleasure, then the lovebirds exchanged a few words, and after setting the pages of music she had chosen upon the rack before her, Mr. Henry Morland moved a step closer in order to more easily reach over her shoulder to turn the pages for her.

When Miss Grant began to play, everyone in the cavernous room ceased to talk and simply enjoyed the melodious harmonies drifting up from the square fruitwood instrument. All shyness from Miss Grant seemed to vanish as her fingers expertly flew over the keyboard. The final chord of the song was followed by near riotous applause, delighted smiles and appreciative nods all around.

"That was splendid, Miss Grant!" exclaimed Lady Morland, from where she sat upon a red silk sofa. "Do play another for us, dear." The smile upon Lady Morland's handsome face was serene. So serene, in fact, that it very nearly drew a tear to the eyes of all those who looked upon her. Because the poor woman had scarcely smiled since the night of the ball, to see one at last soften her features seemed a minor miracle.

"Yes, do; please play another . . . my dear," said Mr. Henry Morland, the uncertain grin on his face stretching from one pink ear to the other. In an eager fashion, he leaned forward to carefully place the fresh pages Miss Grant had chosen upon the rack before her.

When Miss Grant's second selection was completed, and rewarded with as effusive a show of admiration as the first, I fully expected Mr. Henry Morland to fall to his knees then and there on the carpet and openly declare himself to the sweet-tempered Miss Hester Grant. Apparently the girl's mother, Lady Stanhope, believed the same as the ear-to-ear grin now fixed upon her face clearly declared her emotional response to both the music and the pair of lovebirds gazing so sweetly upon one another. I even noticed Meg, Miss Grant's maid, seated near me, swiping at the droplet of moisture that had sprung to her eyes.

It took several seconds for everyone in the room to recompose themselves, whereupon Lady Morland, whose voice as the evening wore on was becoming noticeably weaker, next asked Miss Elizabeth Banes to please honor us with a song.

The beautiful, black-haired Miss Banes all but sprang to her feet and holding her head high, glided toward the now abandoned instrument. But instead of taking a seat upon the bench, she turned and said, "Mother, will you accompany me, please?"

Lady Wentworth did spring to her feet and hasten to take up a position of readiness before the pianoforte, her hands poised over the keyboard. At a signal from her daughter she struck up the first chord and the lovely Miss Banes dutifully lifted her voice in song. The sound that came forth, however, was not . . . unpleasant, but ready for the stage, Miss Elizabeth Banes was most definitely not. Evidently Lady Wentworth so worshipped her lovely daughter that in regard to her, the older woman had been rendered completely tone deaf, a condition that unfortunately her daughter had also inherited. With no unkindness intended, I will venture to say that it is a very good thing Miss Banes is inordinately beautiful.

Before the last sour note grated upon everyone's ears, I caught from the corner of my eye the quiet tip-toeing movements of my Miss Featherstone and Mr. Edward Morland as they silently slipped through the double doors of the drawing room into the corridor. I also caught the nearly imperceptible head-jab of Mrs. Collins, whose stern gaze was now directed at me, her speaking look clearly saying that I should forgo my enjoyment of Miss Banes' performance and do my duty by my mistress.

In seconds, I, too, had escaped into the corridor in time to see Mr. Edward Morland tipping up the heavy porcelain vase that guarded the door to the solarium and Caroline kneeling to retrieve the hidden key to the door. Wearing a sheepish grin, Edward glanced over her head at me and gave a little shrug, but being a gentleman through and through, he politely stepped aside to allow both Miss Featherstone and myself to enter the darkened room ahead of him.

After he had crossed the room to draw open the draperies, as Mr. Talbot had done for me a few nights ago, I walked straight to the French doors and stood with my back to the room, a position I hoped would afford my mistress and her companion a degree of privacy. Drifting toward us from the drawing room I could still hear the muffled strains of Miss Banes' voice raised in song, or rather . . . noise. Attempting to tune out the vexing sound, I instead focused my attention upon the shadows cast by the moonlight as bright shafts of it dappled the terrace. Looking out over the peaceful scene, the deep rumble of a masculine voice coming from near my shoulder quite startled me.

"I thought I'd find you here."

"Oh!" I cast a surprised gaze upward. "And I thought you would be in the drawing room enjoying Miss Banes' . . . extraordinary recital."

Mr. Talbot's brows drew together, but feeling as comfortable as the two of us did in regard to expressing our true feelings with one another, I did not miss the slight twitch at the corners of his lips. "Pray, why would you think that, Miss Abbott?"

"I was informed that Miss Banes' mother, Lady Wentworth, expects you to offer for her daughter tonight," I blurted out. "But . . . perhaps I should not have said that."

I noted both the sudden look of shock that appeared on his face and that he had drawn back in alarm. "I daresay I wish you hadn't," he said. "Is that what . . . *everyone* expects? Or just . . . the girl's mother?"

I shrugged. On the one hand, I wanted to curtly demand *why* he was trifling with me while at the same time, paying court to *her*? Instead, I managed to tamp down my irritation. "I could not say for certain." To keep from looking into his warm brown eyes, I looked down. "She is . . . very beautiful."

Seemingly recovered from my startling disclosure, he took a step closer to me. "You are far *more* beautiful, Juliette."

"But *I* have been forbidden to speak with you, Mr. Talbot."

Again, he drew back with alarm. "By whom? And, *why?*"

"By Miss Featherstone's chaperone, Mrs. Collins."

"Why would Mrs. Collins care a fig to whom you speak?"

"Because she and Miss Banes' mother, Lady Wentworth have become fast friends, and Lady Wentworth wishes to see you wed to her daughter."

He blinked and shook his head in apparent bewilderment. "I fear Lady Wentworth, and perhaps Miss Banes if she is of the same mind, are both to be disappointed. I confess that to declare myself to that young lady has not once crossed my mind."

Although my heart took flight over his candid reply, I remained calm. "Still, I think you should not have left the drawing room while she is still singing. The song was meant especially for you."

"Well, I . . . I am honored, indeed, but . . ."

I placed both hands upon his chest as if to give him a little shove toward the drawing room. "If you hurry, there is still time before she . . ."

Instead, he caught both my hands in his, flung my arms up around his neck, and dropping his to my waist, drew me to him and in the same swift motion, settled his lips on mine. As the kiss deepened, I melted hungrily into his arms. His lips not leaving mine, I kissed him back; our mouths pressed together as heat and longing stirred within me. When his hands began to move up my back, I wantonly pressed myself closer still, the desire inside me growing stronger. At last, my senses returned and I drew away.

"I must go, Mr. Talbot," I breathed. Blinking myself to full awareness, I looked beyond him and upon not spotting Miss Featherstone or Edward anywhere in the room, a squeak of alarm escaped me. "Oh! Mr. Talbot, we are alone! I truly *must* go!"

"But, why, Juliette?" He attempted to clasp my wrists to forestall my leaving. "Something is troubling you. Do tell me what it is, please."

"I cannot." Pulling from his grasp I scampered from the room but with my thoughts and emotions in such a terrible tangle, I knew I could not return to the drawing room, instead, I wished only to seek out . . . a friend; meaning my cousin Nancy Jane. She would know what to say to comfort me. I hurried toward the back stairwell, intent on rushing below-stairs to find Nancy Jane and pour out my sorrow upon her sympathetic shoulder.

Oh, dear, me, what had I done? Where had Caroline and Edward got off to so quickly? Had they returned to the ballroom and me clearly not with them? What would happen once Mrs. Collins learned that I had been sequestered alone with Mr. Talbot in the solarium so soon after she demanded I never speak to him? When Lady Morland found out, would she send me away with no money and no character? What would I do then? Where would I go?

Without a candle, the narrow stairwell upon which I was running down was quite dimly lit. I could scarcely see where I was going and with my thoughts in such turmoil I was not in full command of my feet or where I was stepping. Upon reaching the small half-landing, of a sudden, I stumbled and felt myself lurch forward a few steps. Pulling myself upright, in the dim light I could see that I had tripped over . . . *something*, a pile of . . . something *large*, larger than a spilled basket of soiled laundry, which is what I first thought the mound to be. Instead, upon regaining my footing, and looking closer, and closer still, I realized that . . . it was not soiled laundry at all. It was . . . a body.

CHAPTER 17

The Missing Signet Ring

Upon closer examination, I saw that the person lying in my path on the landing was Lady Morland's maid Temple!

Oh, dear God in Heaven! The poor woman had fallen to her death on the stairs! What must I do?

Thinking first that I should fetch Mrs. Fullerton, I ran down a few steps, then stopped. *No!* I must get Lady Morland! I carefully stepped over poor Temple again and ran back up several steps, then thinking better of that plan, turned and ran back down again towards the servant's quarters.

Griggs! I must find Griggs! He must send for Doctor Morgan at once! It might not be too late. The poor woman might still be alive and just . . . unconscious.

Pushing through the swinging door at the bottom of the stairs, I began to scream for help!

"Come quick! Somebody, come quick!"

Mrs. Fullerton's head appeared 'round her parlour door, her brows knit together. "What are you shouting about, Miss Abbott? I declare you'll wake the dead!"

Oh, if only it were that easy!

"Wish me to carry on, your ladyship," the doctor concluded, then turning toward Mrs. Fullerton, he said, "If you will be so good as to assist me, madam."

Refusing to be put off, Lady Morland advanced another step into the musty-smelling room filled with wooden buckets, tin tubs and various utensils used for scrubbing pots and pans, several mounds of soiled linens scattered here and there on the floor.

Drawing herself up, she said, "I must *insist* that you leave off at once, doctor. I do not wish my dear friend, for Temple was that and more to me . . . " She sniffed before continuing. "I do not wish to see my dear friend defiled in such a disrespectful fashion. Miss Abbott has declared that she found my maid lying unconscious on the landing. It is clearly evident that Temple fell to her death and there is nothing more to be said." Elevating her chin, she added, "In truth, there was no need for anyone to have sent for you tonight, sir. I shall see to having Temple's body carried to the village church on the morrow. In the meantime, you are excused, Doctor Morgan. Good night, sir."

Not a sound could be heard in the room, beyond a slight rustling noise from one corner, which now that I think on it was quite possibly a frightened mouse scurrying for cover. We all stood quite still, waiting to see what would happen next.

"Lady Morland," the doctor said, his tone now one of patient longsuffering, "with all due respect to your . . . er . . . position, your ladyship, I am still the Official Coroner in this County and it is my duty to make a Determination of Death, most especially when said death was *unattended*, meaning that no other person was present when the victim was carried away. Based upon the testimony of Miss Abbott here, and upon the fact that no one has stepped forward to dispute Miss Abbott's remarks, I must perform at least a cursory inspection of the body in order to determine the actual Cause of Death. For the Record," he said again. "You are welcome to watch, or you may leave the examination in my quite capable hands. Your choice, my lady." He did not wait for a response, but turned at once to Mrs. Fullerton. "I shall need rags and a pan of hot water, if you please, ma'am."

Mrs. Fullerton seemed torn, casting a confused gaze at her employer and then back at the doctor, then without a word, she exited the room to make her way to the kitchen, where I heard her issuing orders to one of the chambermaids who had not yet been dismissed for the night to set to and boil a pan of water.

Lady Morland whirled about and saying nothing further also quitted the room. Griggs remained in place and because the doctor had not yet excused me, I, too, stayed rooted where I stood, beside a very large wooden tub that I wasn't quite certain what was used for. Perhaps to bathe a footman.

While Doctor Morgan performed his examination, Mrs. Fullerton held up a sheet to preserve the dignity of the deceased from the curious stares of those who looked on, who in this case, had dwindled to only myself and Griggs. But when the jangling sound of a bell on the Bell Board startled everyone, Griggs promptly took himself off to see to it. Seconds later, he returned and announced to Mrs. Fullerton that the summons was from Lady Morland. As she was now holding up a large piece of fabric in order to shield poor Temple's naked body from view, she turned to me.

"Go and see what her ladyship wants, Miss Abbott."

Glad of a task to perform, I hurried out, but in an instant, returned to stand hesitantly in the doorway, reluctant to interrupt the murmurings of

Doctor Morgan. By then, Griggs was nowhere to be seen or I would have asked him.

"Well, what is it now, Miss Abbott?"

"I-I do not know where Lady Morland's chamber is, ma'am."

The woman's eyes rolled. "The Morland suite is located directly over the drawing room and down a bit, on the third floor. Now hurry up, or she'll be ringing a peal over my head!"

I scurried away and once I had gained the back stairs attempted to take them two at a time, then recalling Temple's recent accident, slowed my pace and merely walked up as quickly as I could on the narrow, but still quite dimly-lit, stairs. Upon locating Lady Morland's suite on the third floor, found only because it was the only chamber in that wing of the house with a small sliver of light visible beneath the closed door, I rapped upon it.

"Enter," came a weak response.

Furtively, I stepped inside, but I do admit to being unprepared for the elegance and grandeur that met my wide-eyed gaze once I gained the large chamber. Because the room was so very large, I did not know from where within it her ladyship sat. It was only when she demanded to know where Mrs. Fullerton was that I looked the direction from whence the voice came. And bobbed a quick curtsy.

"She is still assisting Doctor Morgan, my lady. She asked me to see what you . . . require, madam."

The tall woman had risen from the chaise upon which she had been reclining and moved slowly to her dressing table, a wide affair, made of polished mahogany and featuring a tall, three-fold mirror, much like, but far taller and wider than the one in the Sedgwick suite. The bench upon which she settled herself was draped in a matching blue silk curtain and padded with a darker blue silk cushion. The walls of the entire chamber, I noted, were lavishly covered with blue silk, as were the bed hangings, the top of the actual bed covered with a high arched canopy held in place by carved wooden pillars at all four corners.

"I would like a pot of tea and a hot buttered muffin, Juliette," Lady Morland said, without turning to face me. "It is what I sent Temple to the kitchen to fetch for me when she . . . when she . . ."

"I will attend to it at once, my lady." Again, I curtsied and had already turned to go when she spoke once more.

"When you return, I would like you to braid my hair and assist me into bed. Without Temple here to help me, I . . ."

"I will be most happy to assist you, my lady."

I hurried off to fetch the tea. Whilst on my way to do her ladyship's bidding, I wondered if I ought to pause to alert *my* mistress of my whereabouts, and also tell her what had transpired? It would only take a moment. Knowing Miss Featherstone as I did, I knew she would wonder what had become of me. The last time she saw me, I was in the solarium with Mr. Talbot, a fact I sincerely hoped she did not disclose to her sister.

On the other hand, since Lady Morland had been waiting quite a spell for her tea and muffin, perhaps I should at least relay that message to Mrs. Fullerton before I detoured to my mistress' bedchamber.

Upon re-entering the scullery, I noted Mrs. Fullerton had laid aside the sheet and that both she and Doctor Morgan now stood with their heads bent over . . . something.

"Oh, dear me," Mrs. Fullerton murmured. "This is perfectly dreadful, doctor."

"It is, indeed, quite alarming. I daresay, we might ought to send for the constable."

Wondering what the trouble was now, I decided to announce my presence with a little cough, which caused Mrs. Fullerton to glance up, although Doctor Morgan paid me no mind.

"What is it now, Juliette?"

I had noticed that when the woman was irritated with me, she addressed me by my given name; at other times, she used Miss Abbott. So, depending on the manner in which she addressed me, I could more easily determine her frame of mind.

To show my deference, I curtsied to her. "Her ladyship would like a pot of tea and a hot buttered muffin, ma'am."

"Well, put on the kettle! Oh, never mind. I'll do it myself." She dropped what she had been looking at and crossed the room to brush past me. "Where has Griggs got off to?" she asked of no one in particular.

As I did not know where the butler was, I paid her question no mind. Instead, curious to know what she and the good doctor had been so intently studying, and which had prompted him to remark that perhaps the constable might ought to be sent for, I saw that he had now laid aside the article, which from this distance appeared to be only a slip of paper. I edged that direction and picking it up while the doctor was distracted replacing his long-handled metal instruments back into his bag, I quickly read the contents of the note.

Grasping the message at once, I sucked in my breath. At that instant, the doctor whirled toward me, his bushy brows pulled together in a frown. "Give that to me at once," he commanded. He snatched the scrap of paper from me. "I do not recall granting you permission to read it. But since you have, you are to say nothing of its contents to anyone. Do you understand?" He paused, and I waited, but he had nothing to fear, I was already too frightened to say a word. Even to him. "I shall send for the constable as soon as possible and . . . and allow him to render a decision. You may go now, Miss . . . Miss What-ever-your-name is." Raising a hand, he brusquely waved me away.

Hurrying into the kitchen, I fairly collided with Mrs. Fullerton on her way out. "Juliette, I need you to take the tray up to Lady Morland. Griggs is . . . indisposed. Old man's bones aren't accustomed to climbing those stairs so many times in one day," she grumbled. "I've put several dabs of butter on the muffin the way she likes it; there's also cream and sugar on the tray. Off you go now."

She brushed past me before I had time to bob yet another curtsy. On the way up the stairs, balancing the heavy tray in my hands, my thoughts were again in a muddle as I thought about what I'd read scrawled upon the slip of paper the doctor had snatched from me and demanded I say nothing about. I could clearly see why both he and Mrs. Fullerton were troubled by the note's contents. But, all things considered . . . it did make sense. Still, I wondered if Lady Morland did not have a right to know. But, even if she did, it was certainly not my place to tell her. Therefore, I would honor the doctor's wishes and say nothing about the note to anyone, but, in all honesty, I *yearned* to! How long could I keep *that* under my cap?

Finally, inside Lady Morland's bedchamber, I admit to feeling a bit out of breath, what with lugging the heavy tea tray all the way up those steep narrow stairs. I was practically at the top before I realized it would have been far easier to carry the cumbersome thing up the front stairs. At least I wouldn't have worried about banging the contents of the tray against the wall on either side of me, or scraping my knuckles against the rough stonewall.

When Lady Morland pointed to a pretty pie-crust tea table I, at last, set down the bulky tray, trying hard to do so gently so as not to jiggle the empty cup and saucer, which would have set them to rattling.

"Well?" she raised herself to a sitting position from the chaise upon which she was again reclining. "Are you going to pour, or must I come over there and do it myself?"

I turned at once to do as she bid, wondering as I poured if she would tell me if she preferred cream or sugar, or a bit of both; or should I ask, and what would happen if I got any part of this delicate procedure wrong? When she said nothing, I turned to find her gaze boring into my backside.

"Do you read minds, Miss Abbott? Or do you intend to ask me how I take my tea?"

"I was just about to inquire, my lady."

"*Inquire,* were you? I would think it more the thing if a mere lady's maid were to *ask*, but I forget, you are *more* than a mere lady's maid, are you not? You were previously a *companion* to a fine London lady. A companion, who I was led to believe was *French*. Tell the truth. You purposely misled me, did you not, Miss Abbott?"

I felt the heat rise to my cheeks, but rather than bumble my way through a reply, or an apology, I said nothing.

"A dollop of cream and two sugars. And bring it all to me on the tray. Which means you must remove the pot, and the cream and sugar, before bringing me my cup and what I hope will be, a *hot* buttered muffin. If it is not hot, you will return to the kitchen for a fresh one, a fresh *hot* one." Her lips compressed into a thin line. "It is quite plain to me that while you might have some knowledge about how to dress a young lady's hair, you have *no* expertise whatever as a maid."

"None at all your ladyship."

"What was that insolent remark you just made?"

Because I had only then completed adding the cream and sugar to her tea and was about to head her direction carrying the far lighter tray, now that it contained only the one cup and a small plate with the muffin upon it, I smiled before saying, "I said I have no experience at all as a serving maid, my lady. Please accept my sincerest apologizes for my lack of training in that quarter."

"You are an impudent little thing, aren't you?"

Again, I said nothing. To my astonishment, as I drew nearer to her, I spotted about one corner of her lips a slight twitch and as I bent to place the tray before her, she looked up at me with the veriest hint of a smile, which went a long way in soothing my now quite jangled nerves.

"Will there be anything else, your ladyship?"

After taking a small sip of tea, and then reaching to pick up the muffin, which before leaving the kitchen, I had had the foresight to cover in an effort to keep the muffin warm, her eyes cut 'round.

"Have you forgot that I also wish you to braid my hair and assist me into bed before you leave?"

"I beg your pardon, my lady. I confess I did forget." After a pause, in which my thoughts turned to my obligations to my own mistress, I said, "I wonder if while you drink your tea, I might be excused to inform Miss Featherstone of my whereabouts? She will also be needing me to assist her into bed this evening."

"Miss Featherstone can wait."

I dropped my gaze. "As you wish, my lady."

"What you can do is return below-stairs and ask Doctor Morgan to send up a vial of laudanum. My stomach is quite upset again and I am certain I shall be unable to sleep tonight without help. Do hurry, and come back straightaway." As if to punctuate her complaint, she pressed a hand to her middle and grimaced.

Glad of a reason to vacate the room, I hurried to do her bidding, but once I reached the kitchen, I found no one about. Only one lone candle burned in the kitchen and no light at all shone from the scullery. Had everyone gone and left poor dead Temple in there all alone? I hastened back into the corridor and rapped at Mrs. Fullerton's door, which she answered with a scowl of annoyance on her face. "And what is it now, Juliette?"

"Lady Morland wished me to ask Doctor Morgan to send up a vial of laudanum for her. She said her stomach is ailing her and she is certain she will be unable to sleep."

"Well, as you can see, Doctor Morgan is gone." With an irritable eye roll, she swung open the door. "Come in. I have something here that will help her ladyship sleep." She crossed the room to a little wooden cupboard attached to the wall and opening it, withdrew a small green, corked bottle. "This is tincture of Lemon Balm. Tell her to put three drops in her tea and get into bed at once as it will make her drowsy in a very few moments." Handing it to me, she added, "I trust you will not bother me again tonight."

I curtsied. "Thank you, Mrs. Fullerton." I wanted to add that I truly hoped I would not bother her again tonight, but I refrained and instead, scurried off and this time, I did fairly run back up the stairs in my hurry to reach Lady Morland's bedchamber.

Only to find that woman also scowling. "What took you so long? My tea cup is empty. If I learn that you went by way of Miss Featherstone's chamber, I will . . . did you get it?"

Apparently me holding up the green bottle served to forestall further threats from her. "Doctor Morgan has already gone, but Mrs. Fullerton sent this up. She said to put three drops in your tea, and get into bed at once as it will make you drowsy in a few moments." In an effort to hasten her getting-into-bed ritual, I asked, "Shall I turn back the bedcovers?"

"Very well. You will find my nightdress in the cupboard. On the top shelf."

I set the bottle of Lemon Balm on the piecrust tea table and hurried to do her bidding. But, once I was standing alongside the huge bed, I hesitated, unsure if I were to completely remove the top cover pane, or merely fold it back to lie draped across the foot of the bed? And what of the pillows? Did she sleep on *these* pillows, which were also covered in blue silk, or should I remove the silk pillowslips and replace them with . . . what?

"I see you also have little to no experience as a chamber maid." Once again, Lady Morland lips had thinned with displeasure.

"I was wondering how you preferred to sleep, my lady. Upon the blue silk pillows, or should I replace the coverings with . . .?"

In clipped tones, she supplied directions and to the best of my limited ability, I did as instructed. As quickly as possible as it was already patently clear to me that I was unsuited to the tiresome tasks required of a chamber maid, or a serving wench. Still, the experience did give me a new respect for all that was required of Nancy Jane.

And, speaking of Nancy Jane, I had no sooner completed readying Lady Morland's bed to her specifications when a rap sounded at the door. Without being told, I crossed the room to open it and in walked my cousin, the small girl wrestling with a heavy scuttle filled to the brim with chunks of black coal. How she had managed to lug *that* up the narrow back stairs I hadn't a clue.

"Oh! Juliette!" she murmured then turned to bob a curtsy the direction of Lady Morland. "I come to lay out the fire, my lady and to prepare your bed for . . ." When her gaze alighted upon the bed, she stopped. "T-The bed has already been . . ."

"You may lay out the fire, girl. As you can see Juliette has already taken care of my bed. Do come and remove this tray. I am ready to have my hair braided now."

Assuming she was summoning me to remove the tray on her lap, I did so, and waited for her to take a seat at the dressing table while across the room, Nancy Jane scooped the messy chunks of coal into the fire and stoked it up 'til the bright orange flames sputtered to life and the whole affair began to crackle.

When I had finished brushing and braiding Lady Morland's long, gray-flecked hair, she stood and turned her back to me in order for me to unfasten the row of tiny hooks running down the back of her gown. The woman was so very tall that even standing on tip-toe, I could barely reach the top hook, but at length, she was out of her dress, which Nancy Jane obligingly hung up in the clothes press before she left the room while I helped her ladyship into her nightrail and then into bed.

Leaning upon a pillow, but still half-sitting up, she reached to pull the bedclothes up to her waist. I asked if I should ready her tea with the Lemon Balm.

"Indeed, but only half a cup with the drops." Then, before I had a chance to do so, she said, "In your haste to help me, Miss Abbott, you forgot to remove these." I watched as she twisted off the two heavy rings she wore, one upon each hand. "Put them inside the box on my dressing table; the gold one with the tassels on the lid. Then bring my tea."

I curtsied. "Yes, my lady."

I hastened to do as she instructed. But, when I opened the lid to Lady Morland's gold jewel box, my gaze fell at once to an object that I would never have expected to find there. Amongst her many sparkling jewels and brooches, I spotted a quite large, gold gentleman's signet ring with the Morland crest prominently displayed in the center of the bright ruby red stone. At once, I recognized it as being the very ring Mr. Reginald Morland had described as having been stolen from the heir's body upon his death . . . and that he had declared it to be one-of-a-kind.

How had the heir's missing signet ring come to be in Lady Morland's jewel box?

CHAPTER 18

What The Note Revealed . . .

Once I had delivered Lady Morland's tea to her and blown out the candle, I emitted a great sigh of relief as I stepped into the corridor only to find Nancy Jane waiting for me to emerge from Lady Morland's bedchamber. As I was now in quite a rush to reach Miss Featherstone's suite, Nancy Jane fell into step beside me as I hurried toward the stairs, questions tumbling from her lips as she struggled to keep the empty coal shuttle from hitting her shins as we walked.

"Why was you in Lady Morland's bedchamber? Why did you turn back the bed? I'm the one 'spose to turn back the bed, I'm the chambermaid. I heard it was you what found Temple on the stairs. Gor' Blimey! What a nasty turn; and how sad for Lady Morland. Is that why you was helping her? I'm 'spose to turn back the bed," she said again.

"I only did what she told me to do, Nancy Jane," I flung the explanation for my odd behaviour over my shoulder as I hurried away. "I wish I could talk to you now but I must tend to Miss Featherstone. She hasn't a clue where I've got off to."

Even before I reached the wing of the house where the ladies'
bedchambers were located, I had already drawn the conclusion that the
heir's signet ring now being in Lady Morland's possession was very likely
why Temple had flung herself down the back stairs, *why* she had taken her
own life. No doubt, Lady Morland found the ring, and perhaps also the
diamond stick pin, in Temple's room and confronted her, thereby forcing
Temple to confess that *she* had been the one who stabbed the heir in the
back and stolen the stick pin and the ruby signet ring, that most precious
family heirloom. It also explained why Temple went into hysterics the day
the constable instructed every person of a height to re-enact the crime. Poor
woman probably hadn't had a decent night's sleep since due to a guilty
conscience. Which might explain why Lady Morland needed the
laudanum; perhaps Temple had also lifted her ladyship's supply of that,
too.

I truly did want to tell Nancy Jane all I had only just learned about
the crime tonight, and also about everything else, meaning the part about
Mr. Talbot and me. But I knew I was already in the suds for being alone
with him this evening; plus Lady Morland had certainly not treated me in a
kindly fashion just now, so unless I wanted to be given the boot tonight
and sent on my way without a character, I'd best do as the doctor said and
keep the contents of Temple's suicide note to myself.

Still, I could hardly believe it. In the note, Temple had not offered
any sort of *reason* for killing the heir, she had simply confessed to the
crime, begged Lady Morland's forgiveness and ended her admission of
guilt with her signature, first name only. I don't know where the note was
found, probably in her apron pocket.

It truly was a nasty business. Made me wonder if there wasn't a mad man loose in Morland Manor and if the killing spree would never end?

When I entered our suite, Mrs. Collins barely glanced up from removing her shoes as she prepared for bed. It was Caroline who looked up and spoke to me.

"Oh, I heard the dreadful news about Temple and that you were the one who found her, is it true? You were there?"

"Indeed." I nodded as I crossed the room as if nothing were amiss. "Consequently I was obliged to wait until Doctor Morgan arrived and relay what I had seen to him and after that, Mrs. Fullerton sent me up to Lady Morland's suite with a tea tray. And then, her ladyship wanted laudanum. It was all very distressing."

"You poor dear," Caroline commiserated. "Would you mind terribly helping me with . . .?"

"I will be glad to help you, Caroline." I reached to begin undoing the hooks that marched down the back of her dress. Because she stood nearer my own height meant to help her posed no problem. "I am so sorry I could not get here sooner."

"How is Lady Morland bearing up?" Mrs. Collins asked in a dull tone.

"Still complaining of her stomach ailment," I replied. "And, of course, she is quite overset over Temple's death." Suddenly, it struck me that beyond sniffing into her handkerchief as she hovered in the doorway of the scullery, Lady Morland did not seem *one bit* overset regarding Temple's death. But, then . . . the dead woman did confess to killing her son.

"The entertainment in the drawing room tonight has quite jangled my nerves," Mrs. Collins was saying. "I daresay Lady Wentworth rather overstated her daughter's talent as a songstress." Directing a speaking look at her younger sister, Mrs. Collins added, "It did not escape my notice that you and Edward Morland, and Juliette, ducked out before the caterwauling drew to an end. If I had had the courage, I would have done the same."

By this time, Mrs. Collins had already donned her nightdress and was crawling into bed. "Good night, girls, I confess I am fagged to death."

Given the manner in which the older woman had indicated that the three of us, myself, Caroline and Edward, had ducked out of the drawing room made me wonder if she did *not* know that I had been left alone in the solarium with Mr. Talbot?

A few minutes later, after I had helped Caroline into her nightdress, she took a seat on the bench before the dressing table and I began to unpin her hair. Catching my eye in the mirror, she put a finger to her lips, and turning to face me, whispered, "Let us go into your bedchamber, where we might talk freely."

The hairbrush in my hand and a candle in Caroline's, we slipped through the dressing room and into my little room where, after she carefully pulled the door to, we both sat down upon the bed, Caroline with her back toward me so I could continue brushing her hair. As I was quite curious to learn why Mrs. Collins had not chastised me about not returning to the drawing room that evening, I asked in a low tone, "What did you tell your sister regarding my whereabouts tonight?"

"I told her I sent you below-stairs to inquire if my blue plaid afternoon gown had been pressed."

"Oh. I would never have thought of that. Thank you for not telling her the truth about me being with Mr. Talbot."

Caroline aimed a smile over one shoulder. "We are friends, Juliette. I do not wish to have you snatched from me. To say truth . . ." she turned full around, her hazel eyes sparkling, "if Edward offers for me, I wish you to stay on as my lady's maid! Will you consent to do so?"

"Oh!" I sucked in a breath. Her offer had caught me off guard. "Thank you, indeed, Caroline. You are very kind. I had hoped that you, or your sister, would provide me with a character when the fortnight is over. B-Beyond that, I cannot say for certain what my plans are."

Caroline's face fell. "Perhaps you do not wish to remain a lady's maid. I understand that before coming here you were a companion. Perhaps you would rather stay on as *my* companion, that is if . . . if Edward and I are to be wed."

"Is Edward close to declaring himself then?"

"Quite close, I believe." With a smile and a nod, she resumed her position before me on the bed and I returned to brushing her hair. "I shall tell you all that happened between us tonight. After I saw you and Mr. Talbot together in the solarium, Edward took me upstairs to a lovely picture gallery where we were deliciously alone. Not another soul was about. Arm-in-arm, we strolled up and down the gallery as he pointed out various portraits of his ancestors and told me about each one of them."

"That sounds delightful. I am so happy you had the opportunity to be alone with him."

"Well, if Mr. Talbot had not arrived in the solarium and begun to kiss you . . ." again she turned to grin at me, "it never would have happened."

I yearned to ask if Edward had yet kissed her, but didn't dare. I was pleased that she felt comfortable enough to confide her innermost thoughts with me, but I did not wish to pry. She soon turned full around and taking the brush from my hand, we both scooted back to lean against the wall at the side of my bed and continued to whisper secrets to one another like schoolmates.

"Did you know there is not a single female cousin still living amongst the entire Morland family?" Caroline marveled. "Which is why Lady Morland wished to see the heir wed, so that he might begin to fill up his nursery, hopefully with little girls, and of course, another heir."

I did know there were no living female cousins as Mr. Talbot had told me so, but for the nonce, I let Caroline go on uninterrupted.

"Edward showed me a portrait of the first Lady Morland, the heir's mother . . ."

"The first Lady Morland, the heir's *mother*?" I exclaimed. "Are you saying that Lady Morland, the *present* Lady Morland, is *not* the heir's mother?" The news quite astonished me.

Caroline nodded. "The present Lady Morland is Sir Morland's *second* wife. The first Lady Morland died of childbed fever soon after giving birth to a baby daughter. I find that terribly sad. Sir Morland then married *this* Lady Morland, and they had Edward. But, because William was still a tot when she and Sir Morland married, I rather think she considers herself mother to them both. Wouldn't you agree?"

What I thought was that this rather put things in a completely different light. Earlier I had wondered what could possibly be Temple Bradley's motive for killing the heir, now it appeared that the person who stood to gain the most from William Morland's death was *Edward Morland*! But, since I did not believe *he* murdered his older brother, I now wondered if another member of the Morland family might have done so *for* him, in order that *he* might inherit the entire Morland estate?

Much, much later, after Caroline had sought her bed and I was lying in mine, I began to wonder if that same member of the Morland family might have had a hand in Temple's death? A hard shove at the older woman's back would be sufficient to send her tumbling down the stairs. Then, all one would have to do was walk down to the landing where the dead woman lay and slip a scrap of paper into her apron pocket, turn around and retreat back up the stairs, no one the wiser. Even if he, or she, met a footman or chamber maid upon the stairs, a bit of play-acting would likely convince the innocent party that one was going in search of aid for the fallen maid, and not that she, or he, had had a hand in causing her to fall.

The signet ring now in Lady Morland's jewel box did rather raise disturbing questions. Or, perhaps not. Perhaps it just confirmed that Temple Bradley did commit the crime. Lady Morland discovered the heir's ring in her maid's possession, confronted her about it and Temple confessed to killing him. But, why? Why would Temple kill a young man she reportedly doted on?

Wednesday, 25 October 1820
By morning, I ached to talk things over with Mr. Talbot, but knew I would require Caroline's help in arranging that.

While we maids were seated at the servant's dining table for breakfast, Constable Wainwright arrived below-stairs to inspect the body still laid out in the scullery and make the final determination as to the cause of the woman's death, suicide; or another murder. Of course, the maids were all wide-eyed over the news about Temple's tumble last night, all of us speaking in hushed tones and at this point everyone (save me) still believing the elderly maid had simply fallen down the stairs. Of course, as

I fully expected, it wasn't too very long before I was called away to speak with the constable.

"So . . . you again, Miss Abbott," was his friendly greeting. He had apparently just concluded his cursory examination of the body and sent a scullery maid to fetch me before he left the premises in order to file his official report. "Understand it was you what found the body lying dead on the landin' last night on the stairs. What was you doin' there at that time of night?"

Feeling as if I were once again at an official inquest and being interrogated for a crime I did not commit, I said, "Generally speaking, sir, all the maids are *required* to use the back stairs both day and night. As it happened last evening, my mistress had sent me down to inquire if one of her frocks had been pressed. I assume she wished to wear it today."

"And, had it been pressed?"

A pang pierced me. "I-I do not know, sir. Once I came upon Temple lying on the landing, I forgot my errand at once and ran for help. After that, everything fell into a jumble of confusion. I-I never did ask about the dress."

"And did your mistress not ask you about it?"

"Sir, I have told you all that I know regarding Temple Bradley's death. The stairwell is quite dimly-lit at night. Truth is, it is *always* dimly-lit, anyhow, I stumbled over the . . . the body thinking it was perhaps a mound of soiled laundry, then when I saw that it was . . . not laundry, I panicked and ran to get Mrs. Fullerton."

"You did not first go in search of Lady Morland? I understand the dead woman is, rather, *was* her lady's maid."

"I started to go for her, then I turned and ran back down to ask Griggs to send for Doctor Morgan, and also to get Mrs. Fullerton."

"So, are you saying you fell over the body a *second* time on your way down the stairs again?"

"I did not *fall* over her, sir, I *stepped* over her. Once I had alerted Mrs. Fullerton, I never went back up the stairs again. I remained in the kitchen awaiting the arrival of Doctor Morgan. When he came, I told him exactly what had happened . . . just as I am attempting now to tell you, sir." The man's manner of twisting my answers around to where it sounded as if I were hiding something was quite annoying.

"Is there anything else you would like to add to your statement?"

"No sir, I have told you everything I know," I said again.

"Very well. That will be all, Miss Abbott." He turned to jot down something in the small notebook he always carried with him. "Try to stay out of trouble."

The constable's parting remark made me wish it had been *his* lifeless body I had found lying on the stairs instead of poor Temple.

If I had not been so off-put by the constable's reprehensible manner toward me, I would have asked if he, or Doctor Morgan, might have noticed a bruise on Temple's back, such as might be got from a hard shove, but I dared not. The man would probably decide then and there that *I* had pushed Temple down the stairs in a fit of anger, or something equally as ridiculous, and was now attempting to fob off my guilt onto someone else. Best to keep my thoughts on that score to myself. Still, I did notice that he said nothing about the suicide note, or the fact that the heir's murder had now been solved. Perhaps, for some unknown reason, he was electing to keep that new turn-up under wraps.

For my part, I did not truly believe the mystery surrounding the heir's murder had been solved. The uneasy feeling that had gripped me last night about both Temple *and* the heir's deaths still gnawed at me today.

Something was simply not right and I desperately needed to talk over my feelings with someone possessed of rational thought and an unsuspicious mind. Meaning unsuspicious in regard to me. I resolved once again to find a way to speak with Mr. Talbot as soon as possible.

Soon after luncheon, I, along with the other lady's maids, and the pair of Morland cousins, gathered in the drawing room, along with most of the young girl's chaperones, all of us talking quietly amongst ourselves. Henry Morland was boldly seated alongside Miss Hester Grant and her mother, Lady Stanhope, on a sofa, the three of them appearing to share a congenial discussion about something, quite possibly Miss Grant and Henry Morland's plans to marry.

Reginald Morland casually lounged against the mantelpiece, one leg drawn up before him, his boot resting behind him on the stone façade of the fireplace. As usual, he was wearing a bored look on his face as he directed a gaze up and over everyone's heads and through one of the floor-to-ceiling windows, as though something of interest on the lawn was garnering his rapt attention.

Miss Featherstone's chaperone Mrs. Collins was seated beside her friend, Lady Wentworth and that woman's beautiful daughter, Miss Banes, all three sorting through and commenting upon loose sheets of music, perhaps deciding upon which melody Miss Banes should next attempt to sing. More's the pity.

I lowered myself to a seat beside Miss Featherstone wishing to quietly alert her as to what I had earlier said to the constable in regard to why I was on the stairs late last evening, just in case he decided to question her by way of challenging my statement.

"You have nothing to worry about, Juliette. That is precisely what I told Alice regarding your absence last evening; it is what I will tell him, or anyone else who might ask." She inhaled a long breath. "I do wonder what is keeping Lady Morland today? I have also not seen Edward since last night. Neither he nor his mother were at breakfast or luncheon. Both of them being absent on the same day is most peculiar."

"Indeed," I murmured. Part of me fervently hoped that Lady Morland was not still abed and did not suddenly send for *me* and demand that *I* wait upon her today as she had last night. So far as I was concerned, to become Lady Morland's personal maid would bring my career at Morland Manor to an abrupt end. Yes, I would consider, and be very grateful for, Caroline's kind offer to become *her* lady's maid, or better still, her companion, in the event she and Edward Morland were to wed, but I would *never* accept such an offer from Lady Morland, not even if I had no where else in the world to go and less than a penny in my pocket, which was very nearly the case just now.

A quarter hour later, it appeared that Miss Banes and her mother were coming quite close to entertaining us yet again with another splendid rendition of another popular song of the day, made all but unrecognizable coming from her lips when both Mr. Edward Morland accompanied by Mr. Talbot entered the drawing room.

"If I might have everyone's attention, please," Edward Morland began, taking up a position before the polished mahogany table in the center of the room upon which afternoon tea was often laid out. "I have an announcement to make, and also a message from my mother, Lady Morland."

A bit of shuffling ensued, Lady Wentworth and Miss Banes returned to their seats from the pianoforte; Mr. Reginald Morland straightened up, both feet now on the floor, although his arms remained folded across his chest, and the expression on his handsome face remained as disinterested as ever.

Edward cleared his throat. "Firstly, my mother sends her regrets. She is not feeling well today and will not be joining us. I have taken the liberty of sending for Doctor Morgan to attend to her." Concern for his mother's health was evident upon the young man's face. He sucked in a breath before continuing. "As I am sure most of you know by now, mother's beloved personal maid of many years, Temple, passed away last night."

A collective murmur of sympathy arose from those of us seated in the room.

"Thank you, ladies. And gentlemen." Edward cast a long look across the room at one cousin, then his gaze searched out the other. "What many of you may not know is that, this morning, Constable Wainwright has determined from a . . . um . . . note found in Temple Bradley's apron pocket that . . . she took her own life."

"Oh-h!"

Following that disclosure, everyone's eyes widened as they all, save me, exchanged astonished looks. When the cries of alarm had died away, Edward continued to speak. "In her note, Temple also explained that the reason for taking her own life was because she . . . with her own hand . . . murdered my brother, William Morland."

A sharp chorus of horror followed this pronouncement.

"According to my mother," the young man went on raising his voice a bit in order to be heard, "there had been a long standing feud between Temple and my brother, which evidently escalated the night of the ball, or perhaps before. At any rate, in her note, Temple admitted to having committed the awful crime and then, rather than be hauled off to gaol and brought up on charges, she flung herself down the stairs, where she was found . . . last night."

"How perfectly dreadful!" Caroline exclaimed. "Did you know?" She turned to me, her eyes wide.

My lips tightened. "I was instructed to say nothing to anyone regarding the contents off the note until the constable was consulted this morning."

"How very, *very* shocking!" cried Mrs. Collins, at that moment lowering herself to the sofa beside us. "On the other hand, it is comforting to know the truth at last."

"I am going to sing now." Most of us were startled as we glanced up to watch Miss Banes once again charge toward the pianoforte, her mother fast upon her heels.

"I shall attempt to stop her." Mrs. Collins bolted up again to rejoin her friend Lady Wentworth and Miss Banes who seemed intent upon lightening the gloom that had engulfed the room.

The rest of us fell again to murmuring about Temple's untimely death. Below-stairs earlier that morning, a plan had been got up between we maids to wear a black ribbon tied about our arms in our fallen comrade's honor, but even then, I thought it a rather silly notion since our frocks are black and no one would notice a black ribbon tied about our arms; now, I rather expected that following Edward's announcement revealing the reason for Temple's death, the plan to *honor* her would never be brought up again.

My musings were interrupted when both Mr. Edward Morland and Mr. Talbot approached Caroline and myself. "Afternoon, ladies," Edward said. "I daresay now would be a good time to head for the garden." A gaze slid toward the pianoforte as he stretched forth a hand to Caroline.

His lips twitching, Mr. Talbot addressed me. "Will you join us, Miss Abbott?"

As if seeking permission I looked toward Caroline, but finding her gaze fixed upon Edward, I rose to my feet. "Indeed, sir. I will. Thank you."

At long last, I thought as Caroline and I both hurried up the wide sweep of stairs to fetch our bonnets, I was about to be accorded the opportunity to speak privately with Mr. Talbot.

In no time, we four had vacated the manor house and were following the stone path around the side to the rear, but this time rather than enter the knot garden, Edward headed off down the hill toward a lovely meadow, the far end of which dissolved into a thick copse of trees, their leaves now splashed with brilliant hues of Autumn orange and gold. Morland Manor was surrounded on all sides by picturesque scenes, the tranquility of which now seemed at odds with the turmoil and anxiety marring the interior of the beautiful manor home.

Almost at once, Mr. Talbot and I lagged far behind Edward and Caroline, who were walking at a swift clip and were already a good distance ahead of us, deeply engrossed in one another. At length, I gazed up at my handsome companion, who was today wearing a chocolate brown coat atop his buff-colored breeches, only to find him earnestly studying me.

"Last evening you declared that Miss Featherstone's chaperone had forbidden you to speak with me. Has the ban now been lifted?"

A nervous giggle escaped me. "I am uncertain what Mrs. Collins will say today. Such a great deal has happened since you and I last saw one another . . . in the solarium," I finished softly. Remembering the gentleman's sweet kiss, I felt a blush creep to my cheeks and quickly looked down. "It seems as if a full sen'night has passed rather than a single night." In an effort to compose myself, I lifted my chin and inhaled a deep breath of the crisp October air.

"So, what do you make of the events of last night? I refer to Lady Morland's maid confessing to the crime."

I worked to bring my thoughts around to the topic I had so ardently wished to discuss with him, rather than the ardent topic *of* him, which my heart keenly wished to linger upon. "To say truth," I tested my voice, "it all seems a bit troubling to me. When the constable was here on Sunday last to stage the reenactment of the crime, Temple could scarcely go through with it. As the rest of us sat around the table in the servant's quarters listening to her reluctant cries coming from the corridor, I clearly recall one of the housemaids saying that Temple had doted on the heir, that she had known him since he was in leading strings. If that is the case, it seems unlikely to me that she would be the one to . . . hasten his departure from this earth."

Nodding, Mr. Talbot glanced down at me. "Both Edward and I are of the same mind. Edward is deeply troubled by the news, despite his mother professing that Temple's confession is true and genuine. However, living as close as Lady Morland has all these years with the woman, I expect she knew her maid far better than the rest of us. But because Lady Morland is . . . not well, no one wishes to draw her into an . . . unpleasant discussion."

"I am so sorry she is still not feeling well," I murmured with genuine feeling. "I took tea up to her last night. She complained then of stomach pains."

"Edward is quite alarmed regarding his mother's health. So much so that he sent word to his father asking him to return home as quickly as possible."

"Oh, my, is it so very bad, then?"

Again, Mr. Talbot nodded. "Has been coming on a good many years. The doctor declared her stomach ailment is becoming progressively worse."

"Oh dear, and now all this dreadful business with William and now Temple. It's no wonder her ladyship has taken to her bed."

"Let us hope there will be no more . . ." His words trailed off. "Given Temple's suicide note and what Constable Wainwright declared this morning, I daresay, the case is now settled and done with. No need for further investigation or an official inquest before a magistrate or judge."

I could not help thinking that Mr. Talbot did not seem convinced, nor was I, for all that, but how to tell him of my feelings? In an attempt to prolong the topic begin discussed, I said, "Well, if what Temple said *is* true, I can understand why she would rather end her own life than suffer the embarrassment of being arrested, and locked up in a cell, then brought before the Assizes next Quarter."

"I quite agree." Mr. Talbot nodded. "A quick tumble down the stairs would indeed be preferable to the prolonged agony of a trial, one that is certain to end with a noose about one's neck."

I gazed up at him. "What does Edward say about it?"

"Not a great deal he can say. He is torn. He was also fond of Temple, but I believe he is reserving final judgment until his father returns from London. See if he turned up anything there. William Morland had a good many enemies in Town, you know. Everyone agrees the heir was a scoundrel. Fellow had a nasty way of alienating folks, men and women alike. "

I hesitated before revealing what I knew of Kenneth Grimes, then decided to forge ahead with that, as well. "Did you know about him . . . ruining Kenneth Grimes' sister? And, about the babe?"

He turned an astonished gaze on me. "How did you learn of that?"

"My cousin Nancy Jane told me. She's a chambermaid up at the manor house. It's because of Nancy Jane that I'm at Morland Manor. When I arrived here from London, she told me Lady Morland was looking to put on a new lady's maid for a fortnight, just for the duration of the house party. I hadn't anything else to do since my mistress, Lady Carstairs in Town had just passed on, so . . . I thought surely I could bear residing in the country for that length." My head shook with wonderment. "Given all that's occurred, it seems I've been here far longer than that already."

"Does seem that way." Mr. Talbot reached to pick up a stick and began to beat back the taller grass we had come upon. "Appears we've walked as far as the goats have eaten."

We both grinned. It also appeared we had exhausted the topic under discussion, but because there was still a great deal about *him* I wished to know, I said, "Tell me about your family, Mr. Talbot."

"I will if you'll call me Philip, at least when we're alone together. Mr. Talbot sounds far too formal between friends."

I smiled up at him. "Very well. Tell me about your family, Philip. Do you have brothers and sisters?"

"My family, or what's left of it, is a bit scattered, which I suppose explains why when I met Edward at Eton, he and I fell in together and after that, I rather finished growing up here at Morland Manor. I do have an older sister who is still living. Emma resides in Bath. Our parents are both dead, passed on due to what was then called the wasting fever by the old folks. My parents died soon after Edward and I became friends. An uncle

took in Emma and continued to pay my tuition so I might remain in
school."

"Has your sister married? Does she have children?"

He shook his head, one hand still waving the long stick back and
forth as we walked. Up ahead I could see that Caroline and Edward had
stepped onto a small arched stone bridge that spanned the width of a
narrow stream. At present, they had stopped in the middle of the bridge
and were standing with their elbows resting upon the railing as they gazed
out over the placid water. And, at each other.

"Emma is . . . unwell. An invalid, actually."

"Oh, I'm so sorry," I murmured.

He looked down at me. "She is a kind person, like you. You
remind me a great deal of her actually."

"Do I?"

"She also likes to read. The day you came upon Edward and me
playing billiards and you asked about the library, you put me in mind of
my sister. When she was a child, her hair was the same color as yours."

By then, we had reached the bridge and in seconds had caught up
to Caroline and Edward. The four of us talked quietly a bit, all leaning
against the somewhat rough wall of the bridge, enjoying the peaceful
sound of the water gurgling around the jagged rocks and pebbles beneath
us.

"Talbot and I used to come here as boys," Edward said with a grin,
"and see who could toss a stone the farthest."

"We angled here, too," put in Mr. Talbot.

Edward laughed. "Until father informed us that the fish we were
using as bait were larger than any we might catch in the stream."

We all laughed. Recalling that the heir had wanted to go angling in the lake the day we all set out to visit the ruins, I asked, "Did you also go angling in the lake down by the road, where we all walked the day of the picnic?"

Both Edward and Mr. Talbot nodded.

"Caught a good many fish there, too," Edward said. "We'd bring them back up to the house and sit in the kitchen and anxiously watch and wait while Cook prepared them for us to eat."

"We'd eat them right then, too." Mr. Talbot laughed.

I smiled up at the handsome man at my side. "When I was a very small child, my uncle Abbott, Nancy Jane's father, allowed the two of us to tag along with the boys when they went angling. I always enjoyed the fresh taste of the fish that we, or rather, the boys caught. I don't believe I ever caught one."

"I have certainly never caught a fish," Caroline said.

Edward gave her hand a squeeze. "I shall have to take you angling, my dear. Would you like that?"

"I would enjoy doing anything with you, Edward."

At that moment, we all heard the deep rumble of thunder overhead. Mr. Talbot hurried to the opposite end of the bridge, from where he could look up and clearly see a patch of darkening sky through the thick canopy of trees overhanging the bridge where we stood.

"Unless we want to get drenched, I'd suggest we all head back up to the house! The sooner, the better!"

A hard rain began to fall mere seconds after we entered the marble tiled foyer of the manor house. When Edward spotted Doctor Morgan only just descending the wide front stairs, he hastened toward him. Our escorts bid us a hasty good day and the three men advanced to the small chamber adjacent to the drawing room while Caroline and I slowly ascended the stairs to our suite. Coming from the drawing room, we could still hear the muted sounds of both male and female voices and assumed some of the ladies and perhaps both the Morland cousins were still sequestered within.

Reaching our suite, we found Mrs. Collins seated on the cushion before the bay window watching the rain pour in torrents, the cold, wet droplets making wavy rivulets down the windowpane. She turned as we entered the room. Spotting me, her lips pursed.

"Thanks to you, Miss Abbott, Lady Wentworth and Miss Banes are at this very moment preparing to *leave* Morland Manor. Dear Miss Banes is mortified over the fact that Mr. Talbot prefers the company of a mere lady's maid to her."

Caroline came at once to my defense. "Juliette is not a *mere* lady's maid, Alice, she is a *companion.* As you well know, there is a great deal of difference between the two."

"Nonetheless, her status at Morland Manor is that of a lady's maid and nothing more." Mrs. Collins fastened a disdainful gaze upon me.

Not knowing how to defend myself, I turned a helpless look upon Caroline.

"For your information, Alice, I have asked Juliette to become *my* companion."

Her sister snorted. "Have you now? And, how do you propose to compensate your new companion? Or will she work for nothing, since that is all you can afford to pay her."

Because Caroline had now removed her bonnet, I did the same whilst breathlessly awaiting her reply.

A stubborn gleam appeared in Caroline's eyes. "Once I become Edward Morland's wife, I shall have the means to afford anything I like."

"Very well, then, if and when Edward Morland *does* ask you to become his wife, I will concede defeat, and allow you to employ anyone you like as your companion." Mrs. Collins' tone said she was skeptical that anything of the sort would ever come about.

Wearing a very self-satisfied expression now Caroline turned toward me. "Juliette, my dear, I would like it above all things if you would consent to become my companion."

Mrs. Collins blinked. "Caroline, does this mean . . . has he?"

"Yes, Alice, he has!" Caroline squealed. Both women ran toward one another and Caroline flung her arms about her older sister as both began to dance joyfully about the room.

"How wonderful, my dearest, child! Father will be beside himself with joy!"

Though I felt equally as pleased for Caroline, I quietly looked on rather than say anything to interrupt the sisterly exultation.

"When did he ask you?"

"Just now! We came upon a pretty little arched bridge and as we were standing there, looking out over the water, my sweet Edward began to tell me of his deep feelings for me and then, he asked if I could be happy living at Morland Manor . . . as his wife!"

Certainly, I was thrilled beyond words for my mistress, but the bald truth was, *I* could never be happy living at Morland Manor either as Edward Morland's wife, *or* as his new wife's companion. But again, I did not wish to dampen the joyous moment by expressing my feelings on the matter just now.

"I was not going to say anything to you just yet, Alice, but I confess I did agree to become Edward's wife without the least bit of hesitation!"

"Oh, my dear!" As the two sisters exclaimed again and again over their immense good fortune, I stole quietly from the room.

Even if I wanted to stay on as Caroline's paid companion, I could, and would, not do so, not so long as Lady Morland lived. For reasons unknown to me, I was convinced the woman had taken a strong dislike of me and that given the opportunity she would do all in her power to make my life miserable.

Much, much later that evening, as Caroline and I once again sat upon my little bed in my windowless room after her sister had already fallen into a contented sleep, Caroline whispered to me that following Doctor Morgan's attendance on Lady Morland today, Edward now feared that his beloved mother was not long for this world.

CHAPTER 19

An Unwelcome Summons

Thursday, 26 October 1820

"Unfortunately, my darling child," Lady Sedgwick addressed her daughter the following morning as I was dressing the Lady Sophia's hair, "Reginald Morland's pockets are entirely to let. Despite his ardent declaration of love for you, I forbid you to *ever* become his wife."

The disappointed Lady Sophia looked inclined to argue the point. I was not certain how the news had got out, since my Miss Featherstone had declared that neither she nor Edward yet wished to reveal word of their engagement, but truth was, both the Lady Sophia and her high-ranking mother the Countess Sedgwick both knew of it. Perhaps Mrs. Collins had said something last night at dinner to her friend Lady Wentworth and that alone set off sparks in the ever-present chain of gossip. At any rate, both Lady Sedgwick and her daughter knew about my Miss Featherstone and Edward Morland becoming affianced. While the Lady Sophia and her mother continued to discuss the disadvantages of an alliance between her and the handsome Morland cousin, I continued with my work this morning on the Lady Sophia's hair.

"The boy is quite handsome, I can brook no objection there, but his way of living first with one Morland relative and then fobbing himself off on another, due entirely to his possessing no ready funds, would soon tamp down whatever ardent passion might have ignited between the pair of you."

"You know nothing of it, Mother, or of his expectations!"

"I know that he is the sort who spends his days progressing from one idle amusement to another with no thought to the future. Plus I now know that his side of the Morland family is penniless and that he has no prospects or hope for relief, unless, of course, he changes his stripes, which does not seem at all likely."

Lady Sophia's lips firmed.

"Your father may be an earl, my dear, but as you well know, we haven't the necessary funds to bring you 'out'. Still, I expect you to make a brilliant match. We came to Morland Manor with one goal in mind, that your beauty and accomplishments would be sufficient to snag the Morland heir. Instead, you have arrested the notice of a nobody, a man of far less consequence than can even be considered. Even with no dowry to recommend you, my dear, you can still look higher than the cousin of the second son of a mere baronet. It simply will not do, and there's an end to it."

Lady Sedgwick moved to stand near her daughter and to continue to speak as if I were not in the room listening to their every word. I do admit to having slowed my progress on the Lady Sophia's coiffure to little more than a crawl as I did not want to miss a single syllable of this heated debate. After all, I enjoy hearing tidbits of gossip as much as the next young lady.

"You may not be seeing things clearly now, my dear child, but I can assure you, I am. I was young once. I daresay when I was your age I had a good many suitors dangling after me, but thankfully I chose to listen to the clear-headed counsel of my mother and . . ."

"And look where it landed you!" her daughter cried.

Lady Sedgwick flung both arms into the air. "How was I to know that an earl with a sizeable fortune would eventually prefer the joys of a gaming table to that of hearth and home?"

"For your information, mother, Reginald has assured me that he cares nothing at all for gaming and that he wants nothing more than to make a home for me and our children."

"Children?" Lady Sedgwick's eyes widened. "Oh, my dear!" She hurried back to her daughter's side. "Tell me that nothing of *that* sort has hap . . ."

"No, no, no, mother. How could anything of *that* sort have happened? Either you or Lucy is sitting in my pocket at every turn. Reginald has done no more than kiss my fingertips." The pretty girl's bright blue eyes caught mine in the mirror. "Unlike Miss Featherstone, *or* her maid; I have not been accorded a single moment alone with my gentleman admirer."

Emitting a great sigh of relief, Lady Sedgwick turned away, at which point, Lady Sophia turned to whisper to me, *"However do you manage it?"*

I grinned a bit secretively and managed to smother a giggle.

"Nonetheless," the girl's mother continued from across the room, "I see nothing for it but to remove you from all temptation. You cannot and *will not* marry Reginald Morland and there is no more to be said."

Recognizing that she was defeated, the Lady Sophia sniffed and her eyes filled with tears.

"We leave at once," the older woman declared as she flung open the doors to the wardrobe. "Lucy!" she called for their maid. "Pack up everything at once. We are to leave Morland Manor straightaway."

By mid-morning of that day, which also dawned dark and gloomy and again appeared close on to rain, Lady Sedgwick and her daughter, the pretty blonde, blue-eyed Lady Sophia, indeed departed Morland Manor, along with a assortment of footmen, grooms and Lady Sophia's maid, Lucy. Their departure came none too soon since by mid-afternoon, a pelting rain began to fall, and in the midst of it, Sir Morland returned home. The thuds of his booted feet upon the stairs as he hurried up to his wife's sickbed alerted the remaining houseguests gathered in the drawing room of his presence.

At once, Edward Morland sprang from his place beside Miss Featherstone upon the sofa. Even Mr. Talbot, seated nearby on an overstuffed chair as he and I conversed quietly together, sat up a bit straighter as he watched the progress of his friend cross the room.

At the far end of the spacious chamber, a three-handed card game had been got up between Reginald Morland, Mrs. Collins and Lady Wentworth, who had not yet made good on her word to vacate the premises along with her beautiful daughter, Miss Elizabeth Banes. The girl was not present in the drawing room this afternoon, which for the rest of us was no great loss. I can safely say that not a one of us missed hearing her voice raised in song.

Miss Hester Grant, and Henry Morland were leaning into one another as they sat a bit too close together upon a sofa, while her mother relaxed in a comfortable chair nearby, lazily leafing through one of Lady Morland's magazines. I was the only one of the lady's maids in the room this afternoon, and I daresay I did not look one bit like a lady's maid today as I had abandoned my black frock and frilly white pinafore and cap and was wearing one of my finer gowns, a blue damask long-sleeved, high-waisted dress trimmed in black braid.

Late last night, as Caroline and I whispered together in my little windowless room, she had suggested that for this afternoon, at least, I wear one of the garments I'd brought along with me.

"When you become my companion, I will wish you to look your best at all times, Juliette. You look very pretty in black; but you would look far prettier in something less severe."

"Have you apprised Edward of your wish to employ me as your companion?" I asked, a bit wary of her bold suggestion that I abandon my maid's uniform and dress like a regular person.

"Indeed, I have. And he most heartily approves. Living here in the country for the bulk of the year, he wishes to provide me with as many pleasures and diversions as possible. He finds your company as agreeable as I do and since the notion of you remaining my lady's maid is *un*acceptable to you, companion it must be, therefore he and I both wish you to dress accordingly."

When I drew out my pretty blue-damask frock, the gown I had worn to services on Sunday last in the hope that Mr. Talbot might remark on how lovely I looked, but as it turned out, he was not even in attendance, Caroline declared it was just the thing and that I should wear it today. Other than a look of surprise on Mrs. Collins' face over my impudence, the older woman said nothing when Caroline and I boldly stepped into the drawing room this afternoon.

But the look of delight upon Mr. Talbot's face when he saw me was all the reassurance I needed that I had made the right choice. I'm certain an answering smile of confidence and pleasure lit up my face and, so long as I was in his company, it remained there still.

Now, with Edward gone from the drawing room, Caroline rose to join her sister at the gaming table and Mr. Talbot moved to take a seat beside me on the sofa.

"May I say again how lovely you look this afternoon, Juliette?" His low tone reached my ears only. "I hope to never again see your beauty hidden behind that dowdy black frock."

"Thank you, indeed, sir." I smiled up into his dark eyes. "I daresay I do feel much more like myself today than I have since arriving at Morland Manor."

"If you and I were alone in the solarium now, I would be unable to refrain from drawing you into my arms and kissing your sweet lips." He paused. "Were we at a ball, I would want to dance every dance with you." He cast a long glance beyond the window, and noting the rain still pelting the windowpanes, he frowned. "I was going to say if we were to take a walk in the garden . . . but since it is far too wet to walk anywhere but up and down the corridor, I daresay all I am allowed to do here is . . ."

At that instant, the Morland butler Griggs advanced into the room, walked the length of it and came to an abrupt standstill before myself and Mr. Talbot.

"Her ladyship requests your presence in her chamber, Miss Abbott."

My heart plunged to my feet, then the sudden pounding in my ears grew to such severity that I could scarcely draw breath. Had her ladyship somehow received word of my mutinous decision to abandon my black frock and now meant to sack me? Without thinking, I reached for my companion's hand. "Do come with me, please, Philip."

Mr. Talbot at once rose to his feet, as did I.

"I will be glad to accompany you, unless, of course, it is raining on the upper floor of the house." He paused to see whether or not his small jest had brought a smile to my lips. Ascertaining that my expression was as anxious as ever, he added, "I am curious, as well, to know how Lady Morland fares; and to learn what, if anything, Sir Morland has uncovered in London."

Grateful to have my dear friend by my side, Mr. Talbot and I quit the drawing room hand-in-hand, and with my heart still hammering in my ears, we climbed, a bit hesitantly on my part, up the wide sweep of stairs to . . . I knew not what.

Approaching Lady Morland's bedchamber, we spotted Edward and his father deep in conversation with Doctor Morgan, the three men standing a few feet beyond the entrance to her ladyship's suite.

Edward looked up. "Ah, Talbot. I was just about to send for you. Miss Abbott, if you will please go in, mother wishes to speak with you."

Inhaling a deep breath of courage, I stepped through the door that Edward Morland politely held ajar for me. That he was smiling provided me a measure of relief.

Inside, I found her ladyship exactly as I had left her the night of Temple's death, lying in her bed, shored up by a fortress of pillows and plump coverlets. Her skin, now devoid of color, was paler than ever I had seen it. So pale, in fact, that I confess, I grew at once alarmed.

I was about to inquire after her heath, but before the question that had formed in my mind could leave my lips, her sharp gaze raked over me.

"I see you have put off your black frock and . . . are now parading as one of my young house guests . . . in a gown designed to draw attention to yourself. I daresay your . . . reckless French heritage will one day be your downfall, Miss Abbott."

I did not know what to say. *'Oui, Madame'* nearly slipped from my tongue, but I caught it in time. Not knowing if Edward had yet told his mother of his impending marriage to Miss Featherstone, I did not wish to spoil the surprise by revealing that his future bride had asked me to serve as her companion, which is why I was dressed as I was.

"You have nothing . . . to say for yourself?"

I noted the grimace of pain that crossed her face and beneath the bedclothes, a hand move to clutch her middle. It had also not escaped my notice that her words were falling from her lips in a halting fashion, which caused my concern for her health to increase. Something was terribly wrong.

"I can see you are not feeling well, your ladyship. Might I get you something?"

Her eyes squeezed shut. "I could do with a draught of strong brandy."

I bobbed a curtsy. "Of course, your ladyship." Unwittingly I had fallen back into the role of lady's maid and turned at once to do her bidding.

Her voice halted me. "It will do no good to ask . . . Doctor Morgan refuses to allow me any such . . . fortification. Draw up a chair. I wish to speak with you."

I did as she directed and was soon seated near the bed, a part of me feeling less uneasy than I did when I first came into the room, another part of me still anxious to know what was afoot, and how it concerned me.

When Lady Morland appeared to be straining to pull herself to a sitting position, I rose to help by placing a firm cushion at her back. After drawing in several deep breaths, but before plunging in to tell me whatever it was she intended to tell me, she weakly asked for a bit of water, which I readily poured from a pitcher sitting on the small table beside her bed. I then held the glass while she slowly sipped from it. Even as she was now, in a semi-sitting position, the handsome woman appeared far older than her years and looked as if she were half her usual size, her vitality and strength fast ebbing away. I could not help wondering what sort of ailment was suddenly robbing this once proud woman of her life?

She wet her dry lips with her tongue before a small smile tugged at the corners of her mouth. "My son, the Morland heir, tells me he has asked . . . Miss Featherstone to become his bride." The hint of a pleased smile flickered about her lips. "Edward intends now to . . . escort his betrothed and her sister up to London to speak with . . . the girl's father." She paused in order to summon the breath to continue on.

I waited, my anxious gaze not leaving her face.

"Edward has also informed me that . . . Miss Featherstone wishes you to stay on . . . after they wed . . . as her companion."

At this point, I glanced down, perhaps from humility, perhaps from a sense of duplicity, as I knew very well that when all was said and done, I would *not* be staying on as Caroline's companion.

When I glanced back up, I found her gaze still fixed on me. "I surmise from your . . . present manner of dress that . . . this arrangement is . . . acceptable with you?"

I did not wish to lie, but I could certainly . . . hedge. "For the nonce, it is acceptable," I replied in a small voice.

Her ladyship's eyes fluttered shut, then a few seconds later, the lids flew open again. "Edward says that . . . he intends to procure a special license in Town so that he and his ladylove might . . . exchange their vows, and then return straightaway . . . to Morland Manor."

Caroline had not yet apprised me of their plans. Perhaps Edward had not yet told her what he meant to do. My spirits lifted as I wondered if, perhaps, I was now to accompany her up to London?

But, Lady Morland's next remark dashed my hopes to the ground. "While the pair are away, Miss Abbott, you will . . . remain here as . . . *my* companion."

For the second time in less than an hour, my heart plunged to my feet. Everything inside me screamed *No! I cannot! I will not!*

Lady Morland seemed to sense my hesitation. "Mr. Talbot will also . . . remain here," she added as if that incentive might help persuade me to do her bidding. "My husband intends to offer both boys, I should say . . . both young *men,* positions in his manufactories. It is time for my son, the Morland heir, to take his rightful place . . . on the estate."

While that was most welcome news in regard to Mr. Talbot; on the other hand, I truly did not wish to spend my days here at Morland Manor groveling before Lady Morland, and most certainly not at her beck and call every hour of every day. However, if Mr. Talbot were to also remain at Morland Manor while Edward and Caroline were in London, surely I could manage to steal away from my duties in order to spend a few stolen moments with him. I truly was not ready to leave Morland Manor for good and all if it meant I could never see *him* again. Because Lady Morland's once haughty manner had measurably dissolved, I decided to bargain with her for the remainder of what I wanted.

Drawing in a deep breath of courage, I said, "I will accept your offer on one condition, madam."

A flash of her former haughty demeanor returned to her face, but before I could say anything further, it melted away. "Very well," she murmured, as if all the fight had gone out of her.

"I have not yet told you what the condition is, my lady."

The weak flutter of one long-fingered hand, devoid of rings, I noted, seemed to say that whatever I wished would be granted.

Nonetheless I lifted my chin and proceeded, "I will *not* wear black and I will *not* serve as your lady's maid. You must employ another, larger woman to wait upon you hand and foot." My voice grew stronger as I went on. "Your new lady's maid will be the *only* one called upon to help you in and out of bed at those times when to do so is necessary. I am not nearly large enough or strong enough to perform such duties for a woman of your size." I waited and when she said nothing, I pressed on. "I will also *not* sleep here in your apartment. I will continue to occupy the suite of rooms that the Featherstone party is vacating, although I shall occupy the main bedchamber, rather than the tiny windowless room where I have been sleeping. During the daylight hours, I will sit with you, I will read to you, I will brush your hair and put it up for you, if you like, but if you wish to leave your bedchamber, your lady's maid must be summoned to help you dress. I will serve *only* as your companion, my lady, and nothing more."

Again, I noted the hint of a weary smile tug at her lips. "That appears to be . . . several conditions, Miss Abbott."

I held her gaze. "So, it is." Suddenly, another condition sprang to mind. "And, if Mr. Talbot should ask it of me, I also wish to be free to spend a bit of time with him, perhaps of an evening in the drawing room, or to take a turn about the garden. I quite enjoy the out-of-doors."

Her eyelids seemed near to closing. "Is that the end of it?"

Wondering if perhaps I had not asked too much, I rather haltingly nodded.

"Very well. I agree to all of your conditions with . . . one exception . . ."

At that moment, the door to her ladyship's bedchamber sprang open and three of the four gentlemen who had been assembled in the corridor when I arrived, entered the room. I rose from my chair and stepped aside as Sir Morland advanced straight to his wife's bedside and scooped up one frail hand.

"My dear, the doctor believes it is time for another draught of your medication."

He turned expectantly toward Doctor Morgan, who had walked to the dressing table where he had earlier placed his black bag bulging with ointments and tinctures. Withdrawing a bottle of brown liquid, he handed it to Sir Morland.

"See that she is given four drops of this three times a day. It can be taken in tea or placed under the tongue and washed down with water. It is most important that not a single dose be missed." He next spoke directly to Lady Morland. "It will help greatly to ease the pain, my lady."

"Mother," Edward said, stepping closer to the bed. "With your permission, I shall be leaving with Miss Featherstone for London at first light tomorrow. I shall not wake you to say goodbye. When I return, I will bring with me a precious wife and loving helpmeet." Having taken her hand, he raised it to his cheek and kissed the palm.

It was then I noticed that Edward Morland was now wearing the large, red ruby signet ring upon his middle finger, it being too large I assumed to be worn upon his little finger where his late brother William had worn it.

Edward next turned to me and with a speaking look, indicated that he and I should leave his parents alone with Doctor Morgan. "Be well, mother," he said before he and I stepped into the corridor and he pulled the door to his mother's bedchamber shut.

I looked about for Mr. Talbot, but did not see him in the corridor. Because Edward had begun to walk toward the staircase that led back down to the drawing room, I fell into step beside him.

His tone was low when he began to speak. "Caroline has requested that you accompany us to London, but I felt that having you stay here with mother would better serve. She is bereft since her beloved maid Temple passed away. Of course, the circumstances surrounding her maid's death are making it a great deal more difficult to bear; although I daresay Temple's death has affected mother more deeply than did my brother's. At any rate, it will only be for a few days, a sen'night at most. You do not mind, do you, Miss Abbott?"

"No, indeed, sir; I am glad to be of help to you and Caroline. She has become very dear to me."

"Mother is fond of you, as well."

I realized that Edward had mistaken my meaning. He thought I meant his *mother* had become very dear to me, when instead I was speaking of Miss Featherstone. If it were not for her, I would still be a lady's maid, doomed to dress in black and curtsy to all and sundry, including the housekeeper and butler, something which I was not accustomed to doing. While living in London and serving as Lady Carstairs' companion, I had been treated as one of the family, dining with my mistress and curtseying to no one, not even her. As things now stood here, I had succeeded in bargaining at least for the right to dress as a proper young lady and would also have my own suite of rooms within this lovely manor home. I could hardly wait to tell Nancy Jane of my elevated status.

When I went below-stairs for dinner that evening, a bit early as I was no longer obliged to dress the Lady Sophia's hair, I was met by a stern-faced Mrs. Fullerton before I even had time to draw up a chair to the table in the servant's dining hall.

"Miss Abbott." A crooked finger motioned me back into the corridor. Once there, the tight-lipped woman seemed reluctant to speak, which seemed odd since she was the one who had beckoned me to join her. At length, she said, "Her ladyship has sent word that from here on out you are to take your meals above-stairs."

"You mean . . . I am not . . .?"

"I mean you are no longer to eat with the servants. Your place is above-stairs with the Morland family and the . . . Morland family guests. You will be so good as to leave us now, Miss Abbott."

Fully grasping the woman's meaning, I managed to remember my now superior rank and to refrain from bobbing a curtsy to her as I joyfully turned and headed toward the front stairs that led up to the ground floor of the huge manor house. My status had, indeed, been elevated.

CHAPTER 20

In Which Things Are Sorted Out

Still, it was with some trepidation that I ascended the wide sweep of stairs leading to where the family dining chamber was located. Fortunately before entering that room, I met up with the handful of guests who remained still at Morland Manor as they were going through to dinner. Only, instead of heading toward the large formal dining room which I was about to enter, I ascertained that due to their diminished number, apparently dinner tonight had been laid out in a smaller chamber. And felt a stab of irritation toward Mrs. Fullerton, who had not seen fit to alert me.

"Juliette!" Caroline Featherstone hailed me. "I am so happy you are joining us. Edward told me you would be dining with us from now on. Do, come and sit beside me."

Once seated at the cozy oblong table, I quickly scanned the faces of those gathered here in search of Mr. Talbot, or Edward, but saw neither. Sir Morland was also not here. At the table tonight were only Caroline and her sister, Mrs. Collins; Miss Grant and her mother, Lady Stanhope; and Miss Banes and her mother, Lady Wentworth, plus the two Morland cousins. Henry seemed pleased to be accorded a seat beside Miss Grant, while Reginald Morland seemed pleased to have a plateful of food set before him. Focusing his full attention upon it, he began to consume everything upon his plate with relish.

I, too, thoroughly enjoyed what seemed to me to be a feast! The delicious meal began with a hot, tasty soup, followed by roasted fish *and* chicken, an assortment of vegetable compotes, peas and carrots, creamed asparagus and mushrooms, chopped beets and onions, all topped with rich, savory sauces. Several platters of soft, spongy bread sat here and there on the table, and for dessert, the footmen brought in cherry tarts and some sort of thick pudding, which I found far too sweet for my taste, but ate anyway. The meal was washed down with either ale or wine, and later in the drawing room, we were served coffee and tea and for those who desired even more food, there were additional tarts and small sugary cakes. I noted that even though he had eaten his fill at the table, Reginald Morland desired a plate heaped full of the after-dinner treats.

A bit after our tea and cakes were served, both Edward and Mr. Talbot arrived and promptly joined those of us scattered about the room, talking quietly among ourselves. Except for Miss Banes, who, with no persuading from anyone, was already lustily performing a medley of tunes upon the pianoforte for our dubious pleasure.

"Ah, Miss Abbott," Mr. Talbot greeted me with a pleased smile. Casting a glance at the corner of the room from which the music emanated, he murmured, "I had hoped I might arrive too late for tonight's concert, but, alas, it appears I have arrived too early."

My lips twitched. "Perhaps it will please you to know that tonight is, indeed, Miss Banes' farewell engagement. I learned at dinner that she and her mother will be leaving for London on the morrow."

"Ah, to depart for London tomorrow was also Edward's plan but his father has persuaded him to linger another day and night at Morland

Manor before he and Miss Featherstone, and her sister, journey up to Town."

"I take it you had your dinner with the Morland family this evening, perhaps in Lady Morland's chamber?" I ventured.

Mr. Talbot nodded. "Sir Morland is loath to leave his wife's bedside at present and requested that Edward and I take our dinner with them in order to discuss *his* plans for *our* future." A pleased smile creased Mr. Talbot's handsome features.

My expression conveyed my interest in what the fine gentlemen was saying. He looked especially grand tonight, his dark blue superfine coat topping beige breeches and gleaming black boots.

"As it turns out," he went on, "Sir Morland intends that both Edward and I take up positions with the Morland family enterprises. He wants the pair of us to accompany him tomorrow as he inspects his various concerns; I think, perhaps, for us to determine which of the businesses will best suit."

"That is wonderful news," I enthused. "So, I take it that very soon you will cease to be a gentleman of leisure."

"Indeed." His dark eyes twinkled. "I shall be obliged to work for my bread. I have also been offered accommodations here at Morland Manor for as long as I like. Certainly you have noticed this house is mammoth. Both Edward and his father fear that Lady Morland will . . . not be with us a great deal longer, so in the interests of keeping the house occupied, Sir Morland insists that I stay on. He declares he has witnessed far too many country estates fall into rack and ruin due to abandonment and neglect and does not wish that to become the fate of this grand house." He winked at me. "And, I am pleased to learn that you will also be staying on."

I looked down.

"What is it, my dear? You will be staying on, will you not?"

I did not answer at once. Lifting my gaze, I said softly, "I have agreed to serve as Lady Morland's companion, yes. And Caroline has asked me to become her companion after she and Edward are wed."

"Ah. The heir mentioned something to that effect."

His easy reference to Edward as the heir struck me. Just as it had earlier struck me that the term had quite easily slipped from Lady Morland's tongue. Several times, in fact. As if things were, at long last, now as they should be.

A few moments later, in the hope of finding a quieter place in which to talk, the four of us slipped from the drawing room and walked across the hall to the solarium.

Edward called for a footman to light the candles in the sconces along the back wall and we four took seats on a pair of sofas overlooking the terrace and the moonlit garden beyond. It was a peaceful setting and we all enjoyed the stillness and the easy camaraderie that always existed between us.

During a lull in the conversation, I addressed Edward. "Did your father learn anything new in Town regarding your brother's death?"

"Indeed, he did," Edward said. "Unfortunately, what he uncovered inadvertently solves one mystery, but rather throws the other one, the one we all thought had been solved, again into the shadowy unknown."

His answer quite intrigued me. "Do tell," I urged. "If you are free to do so."

"Quite free, actually. The Bow Street Detective assigned to the case was acquainted with my brother, not as a friend, but he had . . . heard things. Following a few inquiries amongst William's friends, names that I supplied Father before he left for London, the detective eventually arrived at the home of one David Durham."

"Durham? A relation of Miss Amelia Durham who was here at your mother's invitation?" I inquired.

"One and the same," Edward said.

"I do recall having seen from . . . where I was on the night of the ball, Miss Durham and the heir involved in what appeared to be a heated discussion. It was quite soon afterward that he retreated into the garden, and . . . was not seen again." My final words were delivered quietly.

"Turns out, Durham was so un-nerved by a man of law on his doorstep that he confessed at once to having killed Kenneth Grimes, the fellow we all thought had been done in by a gypsy or a footpad prior to my . . . brother's death."

"What brought Mr. Durham *here*?" Caroline asked.

Edward heaved a sigh. "Not entirely certain I should answer that, my dear. I fear the truth might prove a bit . . . sordid for your ears." Seated with one arm draped over her shoulder, he gave it a squeeze. Glancing around her at me, he added, "And you, as well, Miss Abbott."

"I rather expect Miss Abbott will not be shocked," put in Mr. Talbot. "Carry on, man. I admit I am most curious to hear the rest of the story. If you recall, your father left off at precisely this juncture when he was relaying the tale to your mother."

"Very well, then. I shall reveal all the foul details and leave nothing out. But, do not say I did not warn you." He paused to reach for Caroline's hand, which he lovingly clasped in his. "It appears there was a younger Durham sibling, a girl, about your age, Caroline. Quite young; quite innocent, at least, before she met my brother. When they did meet, the two were drawn to one another at once. Unfortunately, things between

them progressed . . . rather too rapidly . . . and the girl . . ." he paused
before stopping altogether.

"Spit it out, Morland," Talbot said impatiently. "Juliette herself
told me the tale of Kenneth Grimes' sister."

Edward's head spun toward me. "How did you learn of that?"

Before I had a chance to reply, Mr. Talbot said, "Juliette's cousin
is a chambermaid here. Says the whole village knows of the child; it's the
spit and image of William."

"Oh, my." Edward shifted on the sofa.

"Juliette, why did you not tell me?" Caroline demanded.

"I . . . did not wish to shock you. Or your sister."

"Carry on, man."

"Yes, well, at any rate. The same thing happened with the younger
Durham girl. Only the babe died and now the girl's reputation is ruined
beyond repair. When the Durham household received an invitation to come
here for the house party . . . mother unaware of the linked past between the
younger Durham girl and William . . . apparently Miss *Amelia* Durham
accepted in her younger sister's stead, and her brother David accompanied
his older sister here. At any rate, and keep in mind that Bow Street freely
admits that this last part is purely conjecture, David Durham quite possibly
came along with the sole intent of seeking revenge upon William for
ruining his younger sister.

"After Durham confessed that he killed Grimes, he further claimed
that it was an accident, that he came upon the fellow down by the lake,
they fought, Grimes fell and hit his head on a rock, and instantly expired.
Durham insists that Grimes mistook *him* for the heir and attacked *him*, and
he had no choice but to defend himself. However . . . none of that can be
proven, or dis-proven, at this point, so it is quite possible that in the end,

Durham may go free. Nonetheless, here's where the tale gets muddy. Durham claims that he had nothing whatever to do with killing William. He does admit to stealing up to the house on the night of the ball, but insists that when he arrived, he found the heir already dead, a knife in his back."

The three of us who were listening all exclaimed with surprise over that disclosure.

"Still," Mr. Talbot said, "it does fit with the fact that Lady Morland's maid later confessed to having committed the crime."

Caroline and I both nodded in agreement.

"Where is Mr. Durham now?" I asked.

"Locked up in Newgate Prison. Awaiting an inquest and possible trial. In the interim, Constable Wainwright is attempting to uncover exactly where Durham stayed while he was in Thornbury and exactly *when* he left the village, or the surrounding environs if he did not put up at the inn in Thornbury. All in an attempt to corroborate whether or not Durham's claims are true, or purely fabrication."

I digested all that Edward told us. "And yet," I began, "the *real* motive for the heir's death has still not come to light. At least so far as Temple's confession is concerned. There was only a vague mention of some sort of grievance between her and the heir. Yet, I clearly heard one of the chambermaids say that she had known him since he was in leading strings and doted on him. What might you, or your father, say to that?" I asked.

"Since father knew nothing of Temple's death until he returned home today, he is satisfied that Temple did kill William and so far as I know, has not inquired about a motive. Plus, nothing else was turned up in London regarding a possible suspect in my brother's death. That David

Durham has been arrested for killing Kenneth Grimes whilst he was in this area is simply an adjunct to William's murder investigation. In other words, that particular murder is of no matter to Father. And, I can understand why." Edward paused. "He is consumed with worry now over mother's illness. At first he thought that a day or two of bed rest would set her to rights again. She has suffered from stomach pangs for some time now and has always recovered tolerably well.

"Today, however," he went on, "Doctor Morgan revealed that the tumor in her stomach has increased to the size of a melon. Clearly her pain has reached an *intolerable* level. Father has no concern over the death of a man like Kenneth Grimes, a man with no worth and nothing to recommend him. That Temple confessed to killing William and that she is also now dead wraps everything up in a tidy parcel. Father is satisfied. His only concern now is to see my mother well again, to lessen her suffering in the interim, and . . . put myself and Talbot to work!" he concluded on a laugh.

We all laughed and the talk soon turned to less disagreeable things.

Later that evening, after everyone had gone to bed, I lay there in the darkness thinking back over all that Edward had said. It made sense to me that Lady Morland might have invited the younger Durham girl to attend the house party; perhaps she had heard the heir speak of the young lady and knowing nothing of the outcome of their earlier courtship, thought to place the girl before the heir yet again. And, that her older sister came in her place did explain why Miss Amelia Durham seemed a fish-out-of-water amongst the other *younger* ladies here, and also her testy attitude and ill-mannered ways, and even why she departed without a kind word to anyone. She had come under false pretenses and perhaps, while here even meant to collude with her brother in killing the heir, only the deed was done by another before they got to it.

I lay there thinking further. For some reason, I still doubted the validity of the story being put forth that Temple killed the heir. It simply did not seem plausible to me. Even if the older woman did hold a grievance against William Morland, why would she even attempt to kill a man far younger and stronger than she? But if he were not killed by Lady Morland's maid; then by whom? And, why would the real killer blame Temple for the crime, and then, perhaps, also kill *her*?

I just did not believe that Temple Bradley threw herself down the stairs to her death. I truly believed the older woman was pushed. If Miss Durham had still been here at Morland Manor when Temple died, I would say *she* had pushed the woman to her death, perhaps to cover up her, or her brother's guilt, in killing the heir, which perhaps Temple had somehow got wind of, but . . . by then, Miss Durham, and also her brother, if he could be believed, was long gone. Of course, that all seemed rather convoluted, which alone might render that theory cast aside as being too far-fetched to be true.

Still, the questions burning in my mind loomed large. Despite the puzzle pieces fitting into a tidy package for Sir Morland, and perhaps even to Bow Street in London and Constable Wainwright here, to me, things did not fit at all properly.

Therefore, I vowed that tomorrow I would seek out Nancy Jane and ask her what she knew regarding a grievance between Temple and the heir. I had not seen my cousin since the night of Temple's death. Perhaps Nancy Jane would know if the older woman had a daughter, or a niece, whom the heir might have also ruined. If that were the case, then I could plainly see where Temple would have a motive for doing away with him.

Otherwise, *why* she would kill William was as much a mystery to me as the real identity of the person who actually did kill him.

With that decided, I attempted to put all thoughts of the murder from mind, but try as I might, a good hour later, I still had not drifted off to sleep so pulling myself upright, I decided to go in search of my cousin tonight. I knew that without a half day off in over a sen'night, she would be worn to a frazzle by now, yet, not knowing what tomorrow held for me, in regard to my new duties with Lady Morland, I decided to seek out Nancy Jane tonight.

CHAPTER 21

The Search for A Telling Clue

Once below-stairs, I went first to the kitchen, hoping against hope that I did not encounter Mrs. Fullerton, who would, no doubt, berate me for being where I clearly now had no business being. Not seeing my cousin in the kitchen, I soon spotted her seated on a stool in the little closet beyond the scullery where I had found her once before scrapping mud from the heir's boots. Tonight she was hard at work upon Sir Morland's boots, caked with mud and grime collected, no doubt, upon his hasty return trip from London today in the pouring rain.

"You look as if you could use some help, Nancy Jane," I said, slipping quietly into the closet and pulling the door shut behind me.

As I climbed onto a stool, she glanced up and smiled wearily. "Thank you, I could, indeed, use some help. Do you want to scrape the right boot, or the left one?"

"Either one will do." I reached for the boot that she had not yet touched. "Poor dear, you must be fagged to death."

As if to prove my point, she yawned widely. "Can't recall when I last slept. Thank goodness most of the guests is gone. Mrs. Fullerton says I might get my half-day off this week, 'course that's two days away. Probably won't even go home. Probably just spend the whole time in m' bed a-sleepin'." Sighing, she returned to her work. "I heard about you being invited above-stairs. You's far better suited to life up there than I am, an' that's a fact." She glanced up again. "Believe me, Juliette, I don't begrudge you one bit for making a go of it here. I'm right proud of ye'."

"Thank you, Nancy Jane, you are very kind. But, don't worry, I shall never forget you."

"Glad you come to see me now."

"I've missed you. I told you two night's ago that I had things to tell you. But for now . . . I have a few questions to put to you."

"Hope I have a few answers for ya'." She grinned.

"My first question concerns Lady Morland. I'm wondering who has been taking care of her since Temple's death?"

"Oh. Mrs. Fullerton, mostly. Although from time to time, she sends one o' us chambermaids up to look in on her. Mrs. Fullerton said this evening that Sir Morland meant to engage one of the stronger women up at the mill to come care for her ladyship until she can find herself a new lady's maid. Mrs. Fullerton said the temporary woman ought to arrive in the mornin'."

"I see." Her answer pleased me. "I told Lady Morland that I am simply not big enough, or strong enough, to help her in and out of bed. Her ladyship is a good head and shoulders taller than me!"

"Indeed, she is. Plus, you're a fine lady now and you shouldn't be a-doin' that sort of work. You's far finer than me or m' mum, an' that's a fact."

"I don't know if that's true or not, Nancy Jane, but thank you." Detecting no hint of spite in her tone, I knew my cousin was sincerely pleased over my new status. "My next question concerns Temple," I said.

Her head jerked up. "I been a-wonderin' how long it'd take afore somebody started to wonder about her."

Since it was already quite late, and I was as tired as my cousin was, I rushed to tell Nancy Jane all that Edward Morland had said tonight about Miss Durham's brother having confessed to killing Kenneth Grimes, and that after Sir Morland learned about Temple's confession, how he was now satisfied that the heir's murder had also been resolved.

"What I'm wondering now, Nancy Jane, is if you know anything at all regarding the grudge, or what sort of grievance, there might have been between Temple and the heir?"

"Wasn't no grievance at all," Nancy Jane stated flatly. "Temple loved him bettern' Lady Morland did, an' that's a fact. She barely loved him at all. Make no mistake, she's the one what wanted the heir dead, not Temple."

I chewed on my lower lip. "Are you saying that you think Lady Morland had a hand in killing the heir?"

"Ain't saying that." She shrugged. "Just saying that she didn't care a whit about him. 'Course, not many of us around here did; he being such a bad-tempered sort, mean-spirited and all. Why I could tell you stories . . . but," she yawned again. "I'm far too tired now. Jes' believe me when I say nobody liked him. I didn't like him." She paused, then added, "If'n ye' ask me, he got what was a-comin' to him. But, Temple? No." She shook her head. "I don't believe for a minute that she done it."

She and I both fell silent. I continued to think while I scraped dried mud from Sir Morland's fine leather boots. While I was glad to see my cousin again and also to help her with her work, to attempt to get these filthy boots clean seemed a useless pursuit.

"Appears to me Sir Morland ought to toss these into the rubbish bin and get himself a new pair," I muttered. "From all accounts, he could easily afford a new pair, or several new pairs if he wanted them."

At length, I finished the hateful task and set the boot back up on the table, realizing that while the boot was now clean, the questions that had been weighing heavily upon my mind when I came below-stairs in search of answers, were still weighing heavily upon my mind. Who killed William Morland, and who shoved Temple Bradley to her death in order to make it appear that the maid confessed to the crime *before* she took her own life? To my mind, there was not just the *one* unsolved murder to sort out; there were now *two*.

"I'm going up to bed now, Nancy Jane. I hope I helped you a bit."

She smiled up at me. "You helped me a great deal, Juliette. Sleep well. And good luck with Lady Morland tomorrow."

I was half way up the back stairs and had only just reached the landing where I'd discovered Temple's lifeless body lying dead when something else occurred to me. Since I was fairly certain Nancy Jane would know the answer to this question, I turned right around and headed back down to the little closet where I'd left her dabbing polish onto Sir Morland's now mud-free boots.

"Nancy Jane . . . I have one more question."

She looked up and grinned. "Hope I have one more answer."

I smiled. Even as tired as she was, she could still make light of a situation others would likely find intolerable. "Do you know where Temple's clothes are?"

Her brows drew together. "Her clothes?" Again, she shrugged. "Probably still a-hangin' on a peg in her room. Why?"

"Can you get them?"

Staring quizzically at me, Nancy Jane slid off the stool. "You mean . . . now?"

No . . . I hadn't meant now, but now that she mentioned it, *now* might be the perfect time to do so. "Do you think you could?"

"Are you a-comin' with me?"

"Of course. Leave the boots and we'll go up together."

I knew I was taking an awful chance, but it was important. With no lady's maid asleep now in Temple's bedchamber, now was indeed the perfect time to inspect the dead woman's clothes.

Nancy Jane scooped up a lit candle and once she and I gained the third floor of the house, which at this time of night was as silent as a tomb, we stole quietly down the corridor, her hand shielding the flickering flame as we walked.

Reaching Lady Morland's bedchamber door, we paused. Although I spotted no sliver of light coming from beneath the door, still, I pressed an ear to the heavy oak barrier to listen before we barged in.

"What do you think ye'll hear?" Nancy Jane asked in a low tone.

"I don't know." My shoulders lifted and fell. "Sir Morland snoring, perhaps?"

"He don't usually sleep here, but what are you goin' to say?"

"To whom?"

"To anyone who asks why *we're* here," she whispered back.

"I'll say I've come to check on Lady Morland and you've come to stoke up the fire."

"I already done that."

I smothered a giggle. "Well, you came to do it again."

"But I didn't bring the coal shuttle."

"Listen, Nancy Jane. When we get inside, you head straight for Temple's room and gather up all her black frocks, then, come straight back out. I'll stand guard at the foot of Lady Morland's bed. When you have her black dresses, and also her white caps if you see them, we'll hurry back down. Are you ready?"

"Why am I gettin' her uniforms?"

"We're going to wash them so they'll be ready for the new maid who's coming tomorrow morning."

"That's right thoughtful of you, Juliette."

My eyes rolled skyward. "Sometimes I can be right thoughtful. Are you ready?" I asked again.

Our plan went off without a hitch, despite the fact that we were surprised to find a chambermaid sound asleep in the chair next to Lady Morland's bed, her head dropped forward, her chin resting on her chest. In the huge bed, Lady Morland lay flat on her back also sleeping soundly, no doubt, due to a heavy dose of laudanum administered earlier that night. Sir Morland was nowhere to be seen. The fire in the hearth burned bright which made the room feel pleasantly warm.

Nancy Jane hurried through to the dressing room and returned in a few seconds carrying a wadded-up heap of black clothing with the ribbons from several frilly white caps dangling from her fingers. We both hurried from the room, the candle in my hand now, and back down the stairs to the closet where we'd left Sir Morland's boots sitting upright on the narrow table used exclusively for polishing the Morland family shoes. Because another pair of boots now rested on the stool that Nancy Jane had vacated, we knew someone other than ourselves was also up and about below-stairs; and had left yet another pair of boots here to be cleaned.

"Now, what?" Nancy Jane asked, dumping the pile of black garments onto the table, in the process knocking over one of Sir Morland's clean boots.

"W-Who's there?" came a frightened sounding female voice from the corridor.

My head jab told Nancy Jane to go see who was out there. She opened the door a crack and said, "It's me, Nancy Jane. I just knocked over a boot. Need to polish 'em now."

The housemaid drew closer. I knew that because the sound of her voice grew louder. "Them's the heir's boots I just brung down. Soon as I finish hangin' these clothes up to dry, I'm off to bed."

Nancy Jane glanced back at me, her eyes a question.

"Tell her you have a few more things that need washing," I said in a low tone. "No, never mind. You can take them in to her later."

By the time Nancy Jane shut the door and turned around, I was already busy sorting through the clothing.

"What are we lookin' for?"

"Blood," I said. "Temple was wearing her maid's uniform the night the heir was stabbed." I held up a garment and leaned in close to inspect the bodice. "If you recall Mrs. Fullerton had insisted we all look 'just so' while the house was full of guests. When I came below stairs later that night, all the lady's maids were gathered around the dining table and we were *all* wearing our black uniforms and white caps."

I laid one black frock aside and pulled a second one from the pile.

"So, why are ye' a-lookin' for blood on Temple's uniforms? Do ye' want me to inspect one?"

I tossed the last dress to her. "Look closely at the skirt and hem, too."

"I don't see anything; but why are we a-lookin' for blood anyhow?" she asked again.

"Because if Temple stabbed the heir, his blood would have splattered onto her dress. And if it didn't splatter, she'd likely have got it on her clothes when she rolled him over to take the diamond stick pin off his chest or pull the signet ring from his finger."

"But, how can we see blood on a black dress? Won't it all look black, or at least *dark*?"

"I thought of that. But, if she were standing close enough to the gentleman to stab him, there would surely be a few drops of blood on the white collar, and quite a bit more on the white cuff of a sleeve. She couldn't have pulled her arm away fast enough to avoid getting blood on the cuff of her sleeve," I insisted, then paused, remembering what I had seen in the knot garden the day Caroline and Edward and Mr. Talbot and I had come upon the very spot where the heir was killed.

"There was a great deal of blood spilled on the ground where he lay. When she kneeled down to remove the stickpin and his ring, the skirt of her dress would have very likely dragged in his blood; maybe even been soaked in it. If nothing else, it would have caused the fabric to pucker, or become sticky and wrinkled." My hand indicated the garments I'd just examined. "I don't see a single drop of blood on the bodice, or the sleeves, and none on the hem. These all appear as fresh and clean as if she hadn't even worn them."

"Hmm." Nancy Jane mused. "Lady's maids uniforms are generally washed on Friday evenings so they's fresh for the week. Heir was killed on Saturday. Temple fell down the stairs on Tuesday. Today's only Thursday. Well, it's probably Friday now. Her clothes ain't been washed yet this week, but it's very nearly time to do 'em."

"You are absolutely right, Nancy Jane. Temple's maid's uniforms have not been washed. But . . ." my mind whirled as I reached for every possibility. "Do you happen to know if the clothes she was wearing when she died were removed from her body *before* she was . . . buried?"

Already Nancy Jane was nodding. "Mrs. Fullerton brought down her Sunday best and put it on her afore she was taken away."

Again, I sighed as I sagged against the table that was now strewn with rumpled clothing. "We've no way of knowing *which* black frock she might have been wearing nearly a sen'night ago. And which uniform she was wearing when she died doesn't signify. If one of her black dresses did bear evidence of the crime, she probably washed it away herself; or even burned it, meaning that one of these black uniforms could, or could not be, what she had on that night." Heaving another weary breath, I said, "Well, at any rate, that today is Friday is the very reason why you brought Temple's clothes downstairs. Today is Friday and it's time to wash them."

"Shall I take them into the scullery now?"

"Might as well. Save putting them back in her room and then carting them back down here again . . . today. If anyone asks, you can tell them what you just told me. Today's Friday and it's time to wash the lady's maid's uniforms." I paused. "I should have brought mine down." I grinned. "Thank you for your help, Nancy Jane. I'm off to bed now. Don't you stay up too late; you need your sleep, too, you know."

On my way back upstairs to my suite, I realized that the idea to examine Temple's clothing had been quite silly; there were any number of ways in which she could have disposed of a soiled frock, the least troublesome being to simply wash it. My thoughts flitted to my own black dresses hanging limply on pegs in my little room. Realizing that it didn't really matter if *my* black frocks got washed today or not lifted my spirits for truth was, I would no longer be wearing black anymore at all now, would I?

CHAPTER 22

A Bit of Sleuthing

Friday, 27 October 1820

The next morning was the first time I took breakfast with the family. I chose to wear another of the gowns I had brought with me, a pretty lavender round gown that once belonged to Lady Carstairs' niece and which I was quite proud of as it was still almost the height of fashion in London. As the three of us, myself, Caroline and Mrs. Collins, descended the stairs and headed for the same small dining chamber on the ground floor where we had taken our evening meal the night before, I could not help smiling as I eagerly looked forward to seeing Mr. Talbot again. How lovely to exchange a few words with him of a morning.

My first surprise as I entered the dining chamber was to discover that breakfast at Morland Manor was not served up by footmen as were other meals of the day, but rather all the hot covered dishes were laid out upon the buffet along one side of the chamber, leaving each guest free to help themselves to whatever they liked. Footmen were present in the room, of course, to serve tea or coffee, and I discovered it was also entirely proper to ask one of them to bring a dish to the table so that one could enjoy a second serving of something they particularly liked.

My second surprise was noting the variety of foodstuffs laid out on the sideboard. Being accustomed to the sparse fare served for breakfast below-stairs, such as a simple bowl of oatmeal, or toast and marmalade, or on occasion, coddled eggs and a thin slice of ham, the tasty choices laid out for the Morland family and their guests seemed endless to me. On display were several types of meat, ham, sausages, slices of cold roast beef and chicken, and smoked kippers, as well as steaming platters of eggs done up in a variety of ways, buttered toast, scones, muffins, an assortment of cheeses and fruit compotes, and jellies and jams. The pots of hot coffee and tea sat at the end of the buffet. Next to them were several platters containing more of the dainty fruit tarts and cakes that had been served up last evening in the drawing room. Were a guest to go hungry after leaving the dining chamber of a morning would be their own fault, I concluded.

Upon slipping into a chair, held out for me by a footman, my eyes at once sought out the Morland men. Edward and his father, plus Mr. Talbot and Edward's cousin, Henry, were seated together near the top of the table, all distractedly engaged in discussing things of import to gentlemen while the female guests were scattered along the sides of the table, nibbling quietly at their food.

Miss Featherstone and her sister, and I, appeared to be the latecomers to the meal, and as we began to eat, I did notice that both Edward and Mr. Talbot managed to aim a guarded glance our way, but neither spoke. Sir Morland, however, continued uninterrupted with his lengthy monologue directed at the gentlemen as if no other party joining those at the table were worthy of any sort of acknowledgment from him, such as politely rising to his feet when a woman entered the room, or uttering a single word of greeting. I have to say it all seemed more than a trifle ill-mannered to me. But, perhaps things were done differently in the country, or perhaps good manners were tossed aside at the morning meal as if everyone were still too sleepy to bother with civility.

But, knowing as little as I did of Sir Morland's character, gathered from things Caroline and Mrs. Collins had said of him, perhaps this was normal behavior for that gentleman. Apparently for Sir Morland, a new day meant his undivided focus was centered on business and nothing, not even the dictates of Polite manners, would deter him from whatever task he had set for himself for that day. I was fast coming to realize that Sir Morland was not a man to be crossed and apparently not even interrupted by a pleasant "Good morning, sir" from anyone, least of all, a mere female. Consequently, a quarter hour later, when he, seated at the head of the table, concluded his meal by hurriedly gulping down the last drop of coffee in his cup, he abruptly rose to his feet, which to his son, and apparently also to Mr. Talbot and Henry Morland now was a signal to them that they had also finished their breakfast and it was now time to leave the manor and get on with the business of the day.

The four gentlemen rose in unison and without so much as a backward glance at the ladies, all four quitted the room *en masse*. Quite odd, I thought, but who was I to judge the peculiar ways of my betters? Despite Sir Morland having appeared solicitous, even tender, last evening toward his ill wife, to most all others he appeared distant and aloof and more apt to inspire fear within a feminine heart than invite frivolous solicitation. Not until he left the room this morning did the women seated around the table exhale the tight breaths they'd all been holding and relax enough even to speak to one another.

The collective exhale of breath within the room, some coming from the army of footmen posted here and there like statues, was actually audible. The first thing we ladies wished to know was how Lady Morland fared this morning? Had she slept well? Was she feeling better? I wondered if the new lady's maid Sir Morland had indicated he would employ had arrived? Who was looking after her ladyship this morning, and should I, perhaps, go up and check on her? All too obvious to me was that not a single woman present at breakfast this morning had dared inquire of Sir Morland, or in his presence, even of his son Edward (the new Morland heir) as to the well-being of Lady Morland.

"Well, perhaps Griggs, or Mrs. Fullerton will know how she fares," I ventured to remark, although I did not want to be the one to ask if the doing of that task could be avoided. In my estimation Mrs. Fullerton was cut from the same cold cloth as Sir Morland and was not a woman to be approached if it could be at all avoided.

Now that the gentlemen were gone from the dining chamber, pleasant talk among the ladies and even lighthearted laughter very soon dispelled the oppressive gloom that had filled the room when I entered it. I soon learned from Miss Hester Grant that Sir Morland had also presented the opportunity to Edward's cousin, Henry Morland, to join one of his business concerns, and that last evening, Henry had at last declared himself to Miss Grant. She, of course, had joyfully accepted the long-awaited proposal of marriage, although as Miss Grant did not speak of their plans following the exchange of their wedding vows, I did not learn whether or not the couple planned to also reside here at Morland Manor after they wed.

"We are to be married just as soon as a Special License can be obtained," she told us, a sweet smile of happiness bringing a blush of color to her pretty face.

"Edward means to obtain one for us, as well," Caroline put in. "Just as soon as he speaks with my father and all the arrangements have been agreed upon and set down in place."

I wasn't certain what sort of arrangements must be agreed upon or set down in place, but then this was the first marriage amongst Quality that I had had a small part in witnessing. For those of us who occupied the lower orders, a young man generally just informed a girl's papa that he wished to wed the man's daughter, and then, three weeks after the couple's banns were posted on the church house door, a lively country wedding took place in the village church, it attended by the bride and groom's entire families, young and old alike, and all their friends. In my seven and ten years of living, I had *heard* of a Special License before, I just wasn't certain what its function was and to whom one applied to issue the thing, or what exactly rendered it so very *special*. Perhaps I would ask Mr. Talbot to explain it to me tonight. I was also quite anxious to know which of Sir Morland's many business concerns my Mr. Talbot would be keen on joining, and therefore what sort of work would be filling his days?

Turning my thoughts back to the lively conversations taking place now around the breakfast table, Miss Grant's mother was mentioning that quite early this morning, Mr. Reginald Morland had hastily departed from the premises. Whether or not he had also been presented with an opportunity to work with his uncle, and had declined, no one seemed to know. I also learned that Miss Banes and her mother, Lady Wentworth, had at last made good on their word and had also departed for London at first light this morning.

"Miss Banes was quite disappointed that Mr. Talbot did not seem as taken with her as she was with him," Lady Stanhope said.

Though that woman cast a pointed look my way, I said nothing, and neither did Caroline, who was seated to my right. She and I merely exchanged a speaking look and continued to leisurely munch upon a hot buttered scone slathered with raspberry jam and to sip our delicious black tea.

We all remarked upon how delightful it was that the rain had at last let up and the sky above the English countryside today had dawned cheerful and cloudless. The beautiful day was deemed by all as a most pleasant one in which to travel.

"I do hope the weather holds until tomorrow when Edward and I shall be traveling up to London," Caroline said.

Despite the stilted beginning to the meal, I must admit that breakfast did turn out to be a pleasant albeit lengthy interlude.

Following the meal, Miss Featherstone and her sister and I returned above-stairs to begin packing up their belongings in preparation for their return trip to London early the next morning. I stayed busy alternately folding up various garments, or running up and down the back stairs to take something to the scullery to be laundered, or retrieve something that had already been laundered. Consequently, given how busy I was, I decided that at present, I would not excuse myself to go up and check on Lady Morland. If she wished to see me, she could send someone to fetch me. So long as Miss Featherstone lingered at Morland Manor, my first duty was to her. Besides, with her and her sister both in high alt over all that lay ahead of them, I knew I much preferred to remain in their company than in a dismal room cloaked in the gloom of illness.

"I cannot tell you, Caroline," Alice Collins addressed her younger sister, "how very proud and happy I am for you and Edward. Father will be elated when he hears the news of your betrothal. You have done very, *very* well for yourself, my dear."

Caroline's eyes actually misted over when she paused in her work. "I confess I love Edward so very much that even if he were penniless, I would still wish to marry him."

This brought such a burst of laughter from Alice that the unexpectedness of it caused both Caroline and myself to look up in surprise.

"Well, I would!" Caroline insisted.

"You silly girl. You know very well Father would not consent to such a match." Mrs. Collins turned back to her task of placing their shoes into little bags before settling them into the corners of a valise. "I daresay he might even have second thoughts regarding *this* match due to the former heir having been *murdered* on the estate grounds whilst we were here."

"O-oh, Alice, do you really think he will refuse?"

The older woman shrugged. "It is quite possible. For a certainty once Mother hears of it she will be far from pleased. It does rather make Morland Manor seem a dangerous place in which to live." With a sniff, Alice crossed the room to retrieve another pair of shoes.

I wondered why she was now being such a down-pin? It was almost as if she were displeased over Caroline's good fortune in snagging the present heir to the Morland estate. Casting a sympathetic look at the younger girl, I said, "I'd be willing to wager that your mother will be *quite* pleased, Caroline. So pleased, in fact, that she might even wish to return here with you and take up residence alongside you at the Manor. The house is plenty large enough for several families to live here in comfort."

"Oh! I had not thought of that! What do you think, Alice? Do you believe Mother and Father would want to give up their home in London and live here with me?"

Alice's lips pursed. "I daresay I could not hazard a guess on what our parents might wish to do. But, I rather expect not. As you are well aware, Mother is quite attached to Town living and all that it entails, taking tea with her many friends, and what not."

"Well, then what of *you* and Richard? And, the . . . babe, once it comes. I should think Morland Manor would be a delightful setting in which your child could grow up. Along with mine . . . of course, when Edward and I . . . start our family."

This remark brought a blush to Caroline's smooth cheeks. But, I noticed the suggestion rather brightened the older woman's countenance, for she actually smiled before replying.

"Why, thank you, indeed, Caroline. I will mention the idea to Richard and see what he thinks of it."

"Perhaps Richard would also want to take up a post within one of Sir Morland's business concerns!" Caroline enthused. "What say you to that? Shall I suggest the idea to Edward on your husband's behalf?"

"Why, how very thoughtful of you, indeed, sister! I can think of no reason at all why Richard would refuse such a kind offer. Our families will *both* be set. You are very thoughtful, Caroline."

I smiled inwardly. Quite obvious to me was that the older girl had been wrangling for that very thing but wanted the suggestion to come from Caroline rather than proposing such a wily scheme herself.

By luncheon of that day we all felt a bit fatigued and were eagerly looking forward to spending the entire afternoon seated on the terrace at the side of the house in order to soak up the warm sunshine and enjoy the pleasant air. Today was the first in the past several that the weather out of doors was not overly cool, damp or rainy.

Once outdoors, both Mrs. Collins and Miss Grant's mother, Lady Stanhope, settled down to the bit of needlework they had brought along to occupy themselves, whilst the younger girls, Miss Hester Grant and Caroline, both with sketchbooks and colored pencils in hand, debated on which aspect of the glorious scenery that stretched before them on the Morland Manor estate would be the most picturesque to capture on paper.

"Morland Manor is surely the most glorious spot in the whole of England," declared Caroline, high admiration in her tone as she, no doubt, happily envisioned herself residing here for the remainder of her days.

"I cannot disagree," lightly remarked Miss Grant. "I wonder if we might set up our chairs near that stand of chestnut trees, just there?" Pencil in hand, she pointed to a spot some distance from the terrace.

"That will not do at all, girls," Lady Stanhope remarked, not looking up from her needlework. "Best do your sketching from right here on the terrace where the ground is dry. We do not wish to soil your gowns by trailing them in the mud, or your slippers by treading upon wet grass."

"Indeed," Mrs. Collins chimed in, "I daresay the ground is still quite wet further afield. One has only to look in any direction from the aspect right here to find any number of pleasing settings, all of which will make lovely drawings."

"If your sketches are fine enough, or even if they are not," added Lady Stanhope, "we shall have them framed and you girls can present them to your future husbands as gifts. Your drawings will make for lovely remembrances for the gentlemen."

As I was not in possession of either a sketchbook or colored pencils, or even needlework, and Meg, who was my one true friend amongst the lady's maids but for whatever reason, had not accompanied Miss Grant outdoors, meant I had no one with whom to converse. Therefore, I soon grew restless and began to wander away from the others. Although I remained upon the flagged-stone terrace, which encircled the whole house, I knew exactly where I was headed once I descended the steps onto the stone path at the rear of the manor. Looking toward the knot garden, I headed that direction.

Last evening, after having thoroughly inspected Temple's clothing and not finding a speck of blood anywhere on them I was determined to go into the knot garden today and make my way to the very spot in which the killer had dispatched the Morland heir from this earth. I did not know precisely *what* I intended to search for; I just wanted to poke around and see what, if anything, I could find. The murder having taken place in the dead of night told me that the killer could have possibly left behind a clue that he was completely unaware of.

It made sense to me that anyone who had just committed a crime of such magnitude would not linger in the area simply to insure that he left nothing behind that might prove incriminating. The killer would instead be intent upon leaving the scene as quickly as possible. And because Constable Wainwright was so insistent upon questioning the entire Morland family and their guests, it occurred to me that perhaps he had not even come back into the garden to comb the area for clues. Therefore, it was quite possible that something had, indeed, been overlooked. And, I intended to find whatever might have been carelessly forgotten, or left behind by the guilty party. Today, with the gentlemen gone from the premises and the ladies busy on the terrace, seemed the perfect time in which to do a bit of sleuthing.

To find the area I was searching for within the tangled paths comprising the knot garden took far longer than I expected, but eventually I came upon the stained patch of ground, made easier to identify by the relic that someone had placed there to denote the exact spot where the heir had lost his life.

As if overtaken by a compulsion to show reverence for the living, breathing being whose life had been so violently taken, I knelt down. Although the heir had been disliked by all and sundry, he did not deserve to die in such a cruel fashion. In seconds, however, I composed myself and rising, brushed the bits of leaves and debris from my skirt as I turned away to look around and see what I could see. If anything.

Glancing about, I noticed that both sides of the path here were obscured by tall, unclipped hedges. Unlike other areas of the garden where the shrubbery had been neatly clipped and trained into identifiable shapes, this section, which lay very nearly at the center of the maze, was a twisted tangle of gnarled branches and intertwined limbs protruding from a variety of tall, leafy, untrimmed bushes, which suggested that this particular area of the garden might have been chosen specifically by the killer because it was so very wild and secluded. Had the killer laid in wait for his victim to join him in this exact spot? Or, did the killer somehow *lure* his victim to this specific area of the garden, his sinister motive uppermost in his mind? Poking here and there amongst the greenery, I wondered if this area had been left purposely wild and untamed, or had the workers simply not had sufficient time in which to trim it up? I recalled Edward saying his mother had put in the knot garden especially for the house party. Had the gardeners simply run out of time before they reached this area, I wondered?

I attempted to peer through the mass of shrubbery to the other side, and could see nothing but more tangled limbs and branches. It was as if I had stumbled into a thick forest that lay only yards away from the terrace and the huge house. If the heir had been purposely lured to this very spot, it would have to have been by someone familiar with the design of the garden, otherwise in the dark of night, one would be loath to venture this far into the tangled interior. I recalled Edward declaring that he was not at all familiar with the knot garden. And yet, *someone* was familiar enough with it to know their way around. But, who?

I turned slowly about. The path here had also narrowed from those that led up to it. Here, the dusty lane was wide enough for no more than three persons to stand abreast, whereas at the mouth of the garden, the paths were wider, more generous. If Edward was not familiar with the tangle of paths that comprised the garden, then neither was the heir, therefore it would have been easy for him to become confused if he wandered this far in or had, in fact, been lured, or pursued, by someone through these twisting footpaths. And yet, I reasoned, his killer had to have known the area *well*, otherwise, he would not have been able to so quickly make an escape once the deed was done.

And, what of the weapon? That night the sumptuous garden was alight with torches, which would make it unlikely that one could enter its paths unnoticed while at the same time carrying a long knife, unless the knife was concealed in some fashion. I looked about for the tall, round posts upon which the torches sat, unlit today, of course, and discovered that above the towering branches here, I could not spot a single pole. Apparently they lay closer to the mouth of the garden where the majority of the guests would have strolled and then upon reaching the darker, unlit interior, they would have been inclined to turn back to those illuminated paths upon which they could better see.

I trained my gaze more closely upon the foliage that lay nearer to where the body was found. As I had earlier thought when inspecting Temple's clothing, the killer would have had to drop to his, or her, knees to heft the bleeding body over in order to remove the diamond stick pin and pull the ruby ring from the heir's finger. In the dark. How might that action have been achieved while *not* getting a single drop of blood smeared upon one's clothing? Most especially when one could not clearly see what one was doing.

A man would indeed be the more likely culprit since to move a dead body the size of the heir, would take abundant strength. Therefore, assuming David Durham were the guilty party, he could have also more easily managed to emerge unnoticed from the garden, and the entire area, with his clothing completely covered in blood. The knife was conveniently left behind protruding from the victim's body. All Durham would have had to do is hide himself amidst the bushes here and wait until all the guests had vacated the garden to go into supper before he vacated the grounds and disappeared unseen into the night.

But, if a Morland guest killed the heir, and then thought to casually reenter the ballroom unnoticed, it would be impossible to do so without causing comment or raising horrified questions over the person's bloodied appearance. I recalled that it was a young lady that night and her companion who burst into the ballroom screaming that the heir had been found dead. Closing my eyes, I thought back. Mr. Talbot and I had been together at the time, high up above the ballroom floor when it happened. I remember I did not know the identity of either of the guests who ran screaming into the ballroom. Did Mr. Talbot mention their names? I could not remember, not that it mattered, I suppose, for they would have been questioned by the constable along with everyone else before being allowed to leave the house, either that night or the following day.

The killer had to have been someone who was *not* at the ball that night, or someone who *was*, and who knew their way around the grounds *and* who could have reentered the house unnoticed. That meant it had to be a servant, or a stable-hand. But . . . all of them had also been questioned. And, a servant had confessed to the crime a few days later. The confession discovered on the heels of her own death, but still, an admission of guilt.

I continued to look about, this time closer to the ground. Perhaps I would find some item that belonged to the killer, which would serve to identify him, or her. Perhaps a button from a coat, or if the pair had fought before the killer stabbed the heir, perhaps a lock of hair . . . or . . . what was that? Just there . . .

Dropping to my knees again, I bent closer to what had caught my eye, bright and fluttering a bit in the breeze. The sun glinting upon the small object had rendered it . . . shiny. I reached for what appeared to be a tiny scrap of cloth that had been snagged upon a twig near the ground. Carefully, I extricated the shiny cloth. Rubbing it between my finger and thumb, I recognized at once that it was . . . silk. The ragged scrap was no more that two inches in length. And, the color was . . . midnight blue.

My heart pounding in my chest, I lurched upward and turned to run in the direction I hoped lay the house.

After several false twists and turns, I, at last, emerged from the garden and bolted toward the huge manor house and entered it by way of the servant's entrance in back.

I had to find Nancy Jane at once.

Coming upon a chambermaid who was just then entering the scullery, I blurted out. "Do you know where I might find Nancy Jane?"

Before answering my question, the girl bobbed a curtsy, which I admit caught me off guard, but given my recent elevation in status, I suppose her action in regard to me should not have been surprising. It was just the first time it had happened. At any rate, the girl, whose name I did not know, said, "Your cousin went a-lookin' for you out on the terrace, Miss Abbott."

"Oh. Thank you, M-Mary," I stammered. Now, I knew why Lady Morland called all the chambermaids by the same name. I whirled around and had gained the front stairs when I bumped clean into my cousin rushing down them. Falling into step beside her, I breathlessly inquired if Lady Morland had sent for me and should I go up?

"No." Nancy Jane shook her head. "I come a-lookin' for ye' 'cause me Mum jes' come up to see her ladyship. Entire village knows she's ailing and most ever'one is worried about her." She reached into her apron pocket and withdrew a letter. "Mum said this arrived on the mail coach for ya'. She brung it up with her; said I was to give it to you straightaway."

"Oh, thank you." Not the least bit concerned about the letter, I stuffed it into my pocket without bothering to even see who it was from. "There's something I have to tell you, Nancy Jane. Can we go to your room?"

"Now?" Her eyes became a question.

"Yes, right now. It's important."

"I-I suppose it would be all right. Mrs. Fullerton is also with Lady Morland, so . . . she won't be a-needin' me."

We hurried toward the steep back steps that led to the lower floor, then meandered through a long winding corridor to a crowded labyrinth where the cluster of servant's bedchambers were located, males separated from females, of course. Most of the chambermaids and footmen were obliged to share with one another, but because Nancy Jane had been at Morland Manor quite a spell, she was lucky enough to have been accorded her own room.

"What's the matter?" she asked mere seconds after we entered the tiny chamber, which was furnished with only a narrow bed, a small cupboard with a porcelain pitcher and washbasin sitting on top, and a single straight-backed chair.

"Close the door, and latch it," I instructed.

She did and again turned wide eyes on me.

"Do you recall the night that the heir was found dead in the garden and I bumped into you on the stairs after the constable had questioned me? You were carrying Lady Morland's ball gown draped over your arm. You said she had soiled it and you helped her change into another gown that night. Do you remember?"

Nancy Jane was already nodding. "Yes, but, why . . .?"

"Do you still have the gown?"

She headed across the room. "I put it here in my cupboard for safekeeping."

"Did she tell you to . . . destroy it, perhaps?"

"No! She gave it to me! Lady Morland always gives her cast-off frocks away. She said I could have me Mum cut it down and make it over to fit me. She said there was enough fabric in the skirt to fashion a new bodice . . ." By now, Nancy Jane had withdrawn the folded up garment, made of midnight blue silk, and carefully laid it upon the bed. "Ain't it beautiful? So soft and all."

"It's very pretty, yes. But, tell me again exactly why she wished to change her gown that night?"

"She said she had spilled red wine on the bodice and perhaps on the skirt, too, and she . . . oh, Juliette! I know what ye're a-thinkin' and it can't be . . ." Nancy Jane's eyes grew even wider. One hand flew to cover her mouth as she sucked in a horrified breath. "Tell me it don't mean that Lady Morland . . . oh, it ain't true!"

Already I had unfolded the garment, but instead of studying the bodice, I was lifting the soft folds of the long skirt and examining the hem of the gown closely as I went. Upon spotting the rent on a panel in the back, near the bottom of the dress, I sat down heavily upon the bed before I'd even withdrawn the tiny piece of matching blue silk fabric from my pocket. Upon doing so, I carefully placed it upon the small hole that had been torn in the skirt of the gown.

The scrap fit perfectly.

Her eyes round, Nancy Jane leaned forward. "W-where did you get that?"

"I found it just now in the knot garden . . . in the exact same spot where the heir was killed."

She reached to touch it. "I mean, where was it . . . *exactly*? Where did you find it?"

"It was snagged upon a twig near the ground, as if it had caught there and was ripped from her skirt when she . . . knelt down to remove the heir's signet ring, or when she rose to her feet to . . . hurry away."

"But, it ain't proof that she done it, Juliette! How would she have got *out* of the ballroom carrying a knife? Oh, dear me, this is awful!"

"Perhaps she stashed the knife in the bushes earlier that day and . . . and, of course, after the deed was done, she left it right where she'd put it. In her stepson's back."

Already I was reaching to study the bodice. It had indeed been stained with something that had originally been wet and dark in color. Everyone knew that liquid always puckered silk, which was a fragile, delicate fabric. It was then I recalled that copious amounts of red wine had been served at *supper* that night. Mr. Talbot said he had consumed a good bit of it. But, during the hours the ball was in progress only amber-colored *champagne* had been served to the guests. I looked up and into the still horror-stricken face of my cousin.

"Do you recall what time it was when you helped Lady Morland change out of her ball gown?" Without waiting for an answer, I said, "It was sometime *before* supper, wasn't it Nancy Jane? And if she told you she spilled red wine on the bodice of her gown, you know as well as I do that red wine was *not* served . . . until *supper*. This stain was *not* made from red wine."

"Oh-h. It's his . . . blo-o-od," she breathed.

"And it got there when she stabbed him in the back and look, here's more blood on the skirt." I fingered another puckered area on yet another panel of the long skirt.

"But what about Temple? Why would Temple say *she* done it?"

Inhaling a long breath, I shook my head. "I suspect Temple must have found the heir's signet ring and confronted her ladyship about it . . . then a few days later, Lady Morland, fearful that Temple would say something to someone, *pushed* her to her death. Lady Morland stood at the top of the stairs and watched her maid tumble and fall, then, she made her way down the steps to place the handwritten confession that she, herself, had written into Temple's apron pocket, and left her there. Alone to die."

Stunned, Nancy Jane sank to the floor. At length, she looked up, tears streaming down her cheeks. "W-what are you goin' to do now, Juliette? Are you goin' to tell someone? Who? Who are you goin' to tell? What will happen to Lady Morland?"

I sorrowfully shook my head. "I don't know what I'm going to do. We have the proof of her guilt right here, but who would believe *she* committed such a horrendous crime? Who would believe Lady Morland killed *two* people? And, who's going to believe *me*?"

Nancy Jane scrambled to her feet. "We have to get rid of the dress, Juliette. We have to get rid of it at once! We can burn it! No one will ever know if we don't say anything about this!"

"No!" I snatched the gown from my cousin's grasp. "If she killed the heir, she must be . . . it is the duty of us all to bring about justice, Nancy Jane. We cannot destroy the only evidence in this crime that has yet been found. We *cannot*. It would not be right."

Nancy Jane took a step backward. "Mrs. Fullerton says her ladyship ain't goin' to make it this time. She says she's dyin'. That's why me Mum come up to see her. Mum ain't been up here in an age." Nancy Jane's eyes were wide as the words tumbled out. "Vengeance is mine saith the Lord. We know that's true, Juliette. The Lord's gonna' take vengeance on her. He will. We don't have to do nothin', Juliette. He's a-goin' do it for us. Ain't that right?"

"Yes, that's right, Nancy Jane. The Lord will extract vengeance upon Lady Morland for killing the heir, and also for killing Temple. In the meantime, we still mustn't destroy the dress. Promise me you will put it back in the cupboard, at least, for now. And, I promise I won't say anything to anyone . . . except for . . . Mr. Talbot."

"But why do you have to tell him?"

"Because he's my friend and he is also a friend of the Morland family. He'll know what must be done. And he'll know how to do it." I paused. "I definitely do *not* want to speak to the constable again, not *ever*, not in the whole of my life. That man will not believe anything I say. He accused *me* of killing the heir." I rose to my feet. "Put the dress back in the cupboard, Nancy Jane. And do not say a word about this to anyone. Not one word. For now, it shall be our secret."

Brushing the tears from her eyes, my cousin began to woodenly fold up the dress. "Even if me Mum did make the gown over for me, I wouldn't want to wear it," she muttered.

I stuffed the small scrap of blue silk back into my pocket and murmuring a few consoling words to my cousin, left her alone to compose herself before she headed back up to resume her duties.

It was then I remembered that she had given me a letter, and I had not yet read it.

CHAPTER 23

I Know Who Killed The Heir

Above-stairs, I advanced into my suite, which if everything went as planned on the morrow, would, indeed, be *my* suite. Once Miss Featherstone and her sister were gone, I would have three whole chambers to myself, a large clothes press, a dressing table, a wide, soft bed and a comfortable, cushioned window seat. Plus, a nice, long window to go with the window seat. How lovely to sit and look out upon the beautiful grounds of Morland Manor early of a morn, or late at night, or any hour inbetween. Never again would I be obliged at night to struggle to find a comfortable spot on a tiny cot that was scarcely wider than myself with a mattress no thicker than a thin rug lying flat on the floor. But . . . knowing all that I had learned today, the burning question now was, could I remain at Morland Manor? Could I truly relax and enjoy the sumptuous comforts of this beautiful house?

I did not know.

Inhaling a troubled breath, I sank down upon the window seat. I was alone in the room so who was to know I was seated upon a cushion where, for today, I shouldn't be? Thrusting that thought aside, I hastened to withdraw the letter I'd received from my pocket, broke the seal and unfolded the single sheet of paper. Something from within the missive fluttered to my lap. Picking it up, I saw that it was a ten-pound note: my inheritance left to me by Lady Carstairs. A small smile lifted the corners of my mouth. I was no longer penniless. Even if I left Morland Manor, never to return again, and Lady Morland refused to pay me for my fortnight of service here as Miss Featherstone's lady's maid, I still had something upon which to live, at least for as long as ten pounds would last.

Turning my gaze to the letter, I saw that it was, indeed, from Miss Cathleen Haworth, Lady Carstairs' niece in London. The lovely girl, a scant few months older than I, said she had been attempting to sort through her aunt's possessions on her own and found the task far too daunting to complete without help, her elderly mother being of no use whatever. Because I knew Miss Haworth's aunt Lady Carstairs nearly as well as she did, and I also knew the value of her many books and costly artifacts, Cathleen was writing to invite me to return to Town and help her sort through, and catalogue, her aunt's things. And, to stay with her family whilst there. Would I please consent to come and help her? She indicated that she would pay me for my services and afterward she and perhaps, also, her mother, if able, would assist me in finding a new situation.

I laid the letter aside and breathed a heartfelt prayer of thanksgiving. To return to London is precisely what I had wanted all along. On the other hand, I truly did not wish to desert Caroline whom I had also come to care a great deal for, but . . . again, I hesitated. How could I remain here at Morland Manor while Lady Morland still breathed?

I did not know.

And, what of my feelings for Mr. Talbot?

The answer to that question rather lay at his feet, didn't it? I did not know what his true feelings were towards me. He had never said anything beyond murmuring that he liked me and I had already cautioned myself to not refine too much on those sweet words. Or his sweet kisses.

For all I knew, I was no more to him than a pleasant diversion, a meaningless flirtation to pass the time whilst he was here in the country. We felt drawn to one another, yes; but . . . what did the involvement, if it could even be called that, *really* mean? In all honesty, I did not yet feel that I wished to throw caution to the wind, as both Caroline and Hester Grant were doing, and marry a man I had known for such a very short while.

Especially not if it meant I would also have to live *here* as that gentleman's wife. Here, alongside Lady Morland. And perhaps still serve as her personal companion. But, would Mr. Talbot consent to leave Morland Manor if he and I were to wed? Not likely, I feared. He was only now attempting to settle into his own seemingly bright future in one of Sir Morland's lucrative business concerns.

I shook my head as it to clear away the tangles that were tying my thoughts in knots. At present, no clear path was presenting itself to me. I simply must speak with Mr. Talbot and tell him what I had discovered this afternoon in the garden and hope that he could advise me regarding what was best to do with the terrible truth.

After that . . . I did not know. Would I return to London to help Miss Haworth, or would I travel to Bath and enroll myself in a finishing school for young ladies as I originally planned? However, at seven and ten, it was quite possible I had already attained an age far too advanced to return to the schoolroom. The only thing I *did* know at this juncture was that I was ill-suited for the life of a lady's maid. Beyond that, I knew nothing for certain.

Weary of mulling over my troubles so very long and hard, I leant my head against the warm windowpane and closed my eyes, and did not resist when I soon felt myself being lulled to sleep.

I slept through tea and was awakened only when Caroline and her sister returned to our suite much, much later in the day and found me sound asleep on the window seat, although I am embarrassed to say that I had slumped down and by then my head was resting on the cushion, my legs dangling limply to the floor.

"Juliette, are you unwell?" Caroline's voice held concern as she rushed toward me. "We had about despaired of you."

Blinking, I sat upright. "I am so sorry to have alarmed you," I murmured. "Do forgive me. I-I did not mean to fall asleep."

"We thought that perhaps Lady Morland had sent for you and you had gone up to sit with her," Caroline said, as she carefully laid her pencils and sketchbook down upon the dressing table.

I pulled myself to my feet, the action causing the letter and ten-pound note in my lap to flutter to the floor.

"Oh! You received a letter," Caroline glanced at me again. "I hope it did not bring bad news, no trouble, I mean."

I knelt to retrieve the pages. "No, no trouble; just a . . . summons." I looked up with a shaky smile. "My . . . former employer's niece in London has asked me to come up and help her catalogue her aunt's things."

"And you wish to go," Caroline said flatly, her gaze trained on me. "I can see the desire in your eyes and hear it in your voice. Oh, I do understand, truly I do. Have you decided then to go?"

"I-I would like to help her," I murmured.

"Caroline, do you wish to change your frock for dinner?" asked her sister from across the room. "The gentleman will be returning home soon and we'd best prepare to go down. I am certain Edward will have a great deal of import to tell you this evening. Which of his father's concerns he wishes to join, and what not."

"Yes; yes, of course; he will. Juliette, do you mind terribly rearranging my hair, please? Only moments before I completed my drawing, the wind whipped up and blew it all asunder. Oh, would you like to see my picture?" She reached for her sketchbook and flipped it open. "In any case, I would like your opinion. Lady Stanhope said we might have our sketches framed whilst we are in Town, and bring them back here to hang upon the wall. Edward will be so pleased. What do you think?" she asked me expectantly. "Do you like it? I had a bit of trouble capturing all the bright colors on display in the trees. Autumn is such a lovely time of year, don't you agree?"

I praised Caroline's work and once she had laid her sketchbook aside and sat down, I brushed out her baby fine hair. At length she and her sister were satisfied with the gowns they had chosen to wear to dinner, and with their coiffures. I had also obligingly redressed Alice's hair and secured a small wad of curls atop her head with a brooch and a feather headdress, which she herself had fashioned from a peacock feather she found fluttering upon the lawn.

I had no time to change my frock, which was just as well, for I had only one other gown to change into and it was not nearly so fine as the one I was wearing. I did, however, take time to brush out my hair that my impromptu nap had tousled. I left the long soft curls hanging loose about my shoulders in the same manner I had worn my hair the night of the ball. I recalled Mr. Talbot then remarking on how lovely he thought my hair looked that night.

My anxiety over seeing him again this evening as well as broaching the topic of conversation that was once again tying my stomach into knots brought heightened color to my cheeks. As I contemplated all that I wished to tell my friend tonight, and also considered the possibility that tonight could very well be the last time I might ever see him, my anxiety and unease rose.

Dinner was a rather stilted affair as was any meal, I was coming to realize, that was attended by Sir Morland. Without a doubt, that gruff gentleman was consumed by his business interests, and, throughout the long meal, kept up a running commentary with Edward and Henry Morland, and also Mr. Talbot, about all that had transpired that day, and the future prospects of this mill and that manufactory. We ladies hardly said a word and were every last one greatly relieved when the tedious meal concluded and we were finally set free to adjourn to the drawing room where we might speak openly, if only to one another.

I slipped onto a sofa next to Caroline, and moments later, was pleased when both Edward and Mr. Talbot joined us. Alice was seated some distance away next to Lady Stanhope, the pair of them apparently now fast friends, based, no doubt, upon the fact that they both now looked forward to bright futures connected by marriage to the wealthy Morland family. Henry Morland claimed a seat next to Miss Grant and they were already carrying on an intimate, whispered conversation. That Sir Morland did not accompany the gentlemen into the room told me that he had elected to spend the remainder of the evening in his wife's company above-stairs. I daresay his decision did not disappoint me in the least, nor any of the rest of us, for all that.

I turned a small smile of greeting upon Mr. Talbot. "Good evening, sir."

"Miss Abbott." The expression on his face was pleasant. "You look lovely tonight. But, then, you always do."

I murmured a thank you as he sat down beside me.

Edward and Caroline had already begun to discuss the events of the day, and their shared future together.

Even as Mr. Talbot began to tell me all that had transpired, I found I only half-listened as a part of my mind raced ahead to how I might draw him away so that we might speak privately. He was animatedly telling me a bit of what had taken place while he and the other gentlemen were away from the manor house today in Sir Morland's company.

At length he said, "You seem distracted, Juliette, is something troubling you?"

Looking down, I inhaled a long breath, but said nothing.

"There is something wrong, my dear, what is it?"

Again, I sucked in a breath but the words would not come. How was I to reveal all that was on my mind when I was so very fearful of what it would mean to everyone in this room, or perhaps everyone in the entire household? I had no clue what would happen to Lady Morland once the awful truth came out. What would Sir Morland say when his ill wife was accused of murder, or worse, if she were taken away and locked up and later found guilty of killing his first-born son and her own maid? The horrible truth I had uncovered today would alter the entire Morland family from this day forward.

But . . . the truth had to come out. Didn't it? I could not keep it buried within myself forever. Nor, I realized of a sudden. . . could I remain here at Morland Manor. Everything had already changed for me and I could not stay here. Not now.

"Juliette, please."

I looked up and fastened my troubled gaze on the concerned countenance of my companion. "Might we . . . walk a bit?"

He reached to take my hand. "Of course, shall we adjourn to the solarium?"

My hand in his, we both rose. "If you don't mind, sir, I would rather we adjourn to the terrace."

He glanced over the top of my head toward the bank of windows marching along the outside wall. "I daresay it's a bit chilly outdoors this evening."

"I'll just get my shawl." I hurried past him and all but ran up the stairs to my suite, scooped up my shawl, and hurried back down. He stood waiting for me near the massive front door to the house and out we went together into the cool night air.

He headed straight for a stone bench recessed into a secluded alcove on the opposite side of the house from where the ladies and I had sat this afternoon. Shafts from the bright moon overhead dappled the stone walkway before us and also illuminated the cozy alcove. The hidden aspect of it meant that any breeze that might drift onto the terrace would likely skirt past us.

"It might be a bit warmer here," he said by way of explaining his choice.

Still, once seated, we snuggled close to one another, my woolen shawl wrapped tightly about my arms, his arm wrapped tightly about my shoulders. I leaned into his far larger and warmer body. Being so very near him felt heavenly, but I did not let my thoughts linger there for but a brief spell. The cool air circulating about us meant that I must not waste precious time, or words, in relaying to Mr. Talbot all that I had to tell him.

I began by saying that there were things about William Morland's death that had continued to trouble me, as well as, things about the death of Temple Bradley that also did not seem right.

"I simply do not, and cannot, believe that Lady Morland's maid murdered the heir," I stated emphatically. "Furthermore, I believe that the person who murdered William Morland *also* murdered Temple. I never did believe that she fell to her death. I believe she was *pushed*. Temple somehow learned the truth about who stabbed the heir, and the real killer silenced her and planted the confession note on her body, even as she lay dying on the stairs," I blurted out in a rush.

"Juliette, my dear, the investigation is over and done with." His tone was as gentle as if he were placating a child. "The Constable, Sir Morland, even Bow Street in London are satisfied with the conclusions drawn. Justice has, indeed, been served. It is time to put this nasty business behind us. Two deaths here at Morland Manor, the second one coming so soon after the first was unfortunate, but it has all been settled to the satisfaction of everyone concerned. Promise me you will not trouble yourself any longer over this."

"But I am certain Temple did *not* kill the heir, Philip! I know it. Not only do I know it, I can prove who *did* kill him. I found the indisputable proof today."

He shifted on the bench beside me. In the moonlight I saw his brows pull together as he continued to study my face. "What do you mean? Exactly *what* are you saying?"

"While the ladies were sketching this afternoon, I . . . took a solitary walk in the knot garden and I . . . I found something. Something near the spot where the heir was murdered. Something incriminating; and which clearly proves *who* committed the crime. *Why* that person did so, is . . . also obvious."

"What did you find?"

"I found a small piece of cloth."

I went on to tell him about the scrap of midnight blue silk I had found snagged on a twig, and how on the night of the ball, I met my cousin Nancy Jane on the back stairs carrying a blue silk dress draped over her arm and how today, we discovered that the tiny piece of blue silk perfectly fit the torn place near the hem of the skirt of that very gown. What I did *not* reveal, yet, is to whom the gown belonged.

"But, how does a torn gown prove anything? Anyone could have walked into the garden *since* the night the heir was killed, just as you did today and rent their gown."

"There's more."

I told him my theory about how the sudden impact of the knife being thrust into the heir's back would have caused the victim's blood to splatter from the wound onto the sleeve, and even the coat, or bodice, of the outer garment worn by the killer.

"Are you saying there was blood also on the bodice of the blue silk gown?" His tone revealed rising interest.

"A great deal of blood. The entire bodice of the gown was puckered from blood stains."

"And . . . *who* wore this gown? Where is it now? How did your cousin come to be in possession of it?"

For answer I replied, "Sir, I do not wish to ever speak with Constable Wainwright again. I would like to go straight to the Magistrate with the new information I have uncovered. It is my understanding that anyone can appeal to the Magistrate to issue a warrant for the arrest of a person who can be proven guilty of a crime, is that not true?"

"Well, I-I believe so, but as I have had no experience with this sort of thing, I cannot say for certain what the correct procedure is. You've not yet told me *who* was wearing the blue silk gown. If it were, perhaps, one of the guests at the ball that night, then, the person is no longer in the area and it would indeed be up to Constable Wainwright to run the party to ground and ascertain for himself if . . ."

"No." I shook my head. "It was *not* one of the guests. T-The person is right here . . . within Morland Manor. Right now."

Alarmed, Mr. Talbot lurched to his feet. "Then we must call the constable at once, Juliette, and let him apprehend the killer! You, or perhaps, your cousin could be in grave danger if the killer realizes you have uncovered evidence that can identify them as the . . ."

As I had not yet made a move to rise, he paused. "What is it?"

"You do not understand. I am not the least bit afraid of the . . . the killer. The guilty party does not know what I have uncovered, and unless you, or I, reveal what we know, they might never learn of it. Which is precisely why I wished to tell you alone, in private, so that you could advise me. I truly think it best if we consult with the Magistrate at this juncture and let *him* decide what is to be done now."

"Very well, then. Come along." Taking my hand, he again urged me to my feet. "We will go up at once."

"U-up?" I hesitantly arose.

"We shall consult with the Magistrate at once," he said again.

"W-who is the Magistrate?" Although now on my feet, I had still not taken a step forward.

"The Magistrate is Sir Morland. Morland is both Magistrate and Justice of the Peace in this district. He will know how best to handle things. I shall send Griggs up to fetch him at once."

"Oh-h-h." My heart sank as I slumped back down onto the bench. "There is . . . no point in telling *him* any of this."

Mr. Talbot also sat back down. "Why ever not? Morland is a fair man. No matter who the killer is, depend on it, he will insist upon extracting justice for the death of his son, and for that of his wife's maid. Now, tell me at once the name of the guilty party. Is it one of the remaining house guests, or perhaps, a servant . . .?"

My eyes squeezed shut as my head dropped forward. At length, I lifted a tortured gaze to his. "The killer is . . . Lady Morland."

CHAPTER 24

In Which a Decision is Reached

He blanched. "I see." His shoulders dropped. After a pause, he said, "This does rather put a different complexion on things."

"Now you understand why I wished to speak privately with you."

Slowly, he nodded. "Indeed." He continued to digest the shocking truth, then, at length, said, "Can you be certain of this, Juliette? How did your cousin get the dress? And, when? Could it have, perhaps been worn by someone else, such as Lady Morland's maid?"

"No. At the time of the heir's death, Temple was below-stairs with all the other maids. The blue silk gown is the *very* gown that Lady Morland wore to the ball. I saw it. I noticed what she was wearing from where I stood the night of the ball. She was already in her chamber changing into another gown, one of a similar color, *before* the heir's body was even discovered dead in the garden."

"You are certain of this?" he asked again.

"Yes, I am certain."

"Why did she not just burn the gown? She could have done it easily enough with no one the wiser and then . . ."

Shaking my head, I half-smiled. "Philip, no fine lady, no matter how enterprising she is, is capable of getting herself out of a ball gown, and into another one, without assistance. That my cousin was there to help her was mere happenstance. Nancy Jane had been dispatched above-stairs that night to help lay out the fires. She appeared in Lady Morland's bedchamber at precisely the same instant Lady Morland was attempting on her own to remove her gown. Nancy Jane said she seemed quite agitated and of course, offered to help. Lady Morland told my cousin she had spilled red wine upon the bodice." Shifting a bit on the bench, I looked intently at Mr. Talbot. "But, don't you see, at *that* time, red wine had *not yet* been served to the guests?"

Nodding thoughtfully, his brow wrinkled. "True. The red wine appeared only at supper. I recall because I had been wanting some, and was told by a footman that it would be served with supper."

I heaved a troubled sigh as he continued to think on all I had told him. I remained silent as I watched conflicting emotions chase one another across his face.

"But, why give the gown to a chambermaid? Why did she not keep it in her room and burn it later?"

"Nancy Jane said she gave *all* her cast-off clothing to the maids. To treat this gown as if it were somehow special would raise more suspicion than to toss it into the fire. Besides, the burnt remains would, no doubt, be discovered by a chambermaid; or even Temple, that evening or the following morning . . . and raise questions, causing someone to wonder, and even comment on the oddity of Lady Morland burning her ball gown."

Talbot inhaled another long breath. "The pieces of the puzzle do appear to fit. But, what about her maid, Temple? How, and why, did Lady Morland do away with her lady's maid?"

"I believe Temple discovered the heir's ruby signet ring in her ladyship's jewel box. I saw it there myself. The night Temple's body was found on the stairs, Mrs. Fullerton asked me to take a tray up to Lady Morland and when I helped her disrobe for bed, she pulled off her rings and told me where to put them. The heir's ring was right there in the box, which is when I grew suspicious about both the heir's death, and also Temple's death. Temple would have also seen the ring in Lady Morland's jewel box, and perhaps asked about it, or even demanded to know how her ladyship came to be in possession of it."

I proceeded to tell him that I believed that when Lady Morland realized that Temple knew the truth, she pushed her maid to her death on the stairs and planted the false confession and suicide note in her apron pocket.

"Well, it does appear you have rather cleverly sorted out the details of the mystery." He sucked in another ragged breath. "Let me think further on what should be done at this juncture. You are right that it would do no good to apprise Sir Morland of the facts. To say truth, I am uncertain he would even believe his wife capable of murder, and even if he did, I doubt he would go so far as to issue a warrant for her arrest. Which is quite possibly what she was counting upon. It is always easy in the country to blame what appears to be a random death upon a footpad, or a wandering gypsy. That sort is always in want of the ready," he mused.

"And, Temple is not the only servant who has lost her life from an unfortunate fall down a flight of poorly-lit stairs. I wonder that many more servants at Morland Manor have not taken a tumble down those stairs. They are so very narrow, I struggled to get up them carrying Lady Morland's tea tray."

Exhaling a long breath, he turned to scoop up my hand. "You've given me a great deal to think about, Juliette."

We rose and began to slowly make our way to the front door of the huge manor house on the hill, the house to which I had come fully expecting to pass a dull fortnight in the country.

Once at the door, my companion paused. "Does this mean you will not be staying on at Morland Manor?"

Gazing up at him, I shook my head. "I do not see how I can."

In a quick motion, he dropped my hand and clasping my shoulders, drew me into his arms. "I will miss you, Juliette. I was hoping we could . . ." He let the remainder of the sentence dangle unfinished.

Hot tears were already swimming in my eyes as I buried my head in his strong shoulder. "I will miss you, as well."

I felt him kiss the top of my head. "Perhaps we will see one another again some day."

The pent-up emotion within me rose to such a height I could scarcely speak. "I would like that," I murmured into his chest.

My heart was heavy as I lay in my bed that night, my thoughts still churning over the dilemma I found myself in. It went without saying that my faith in the goodness of mankind had been severely shaken. I wondered if I was legally bound to reveal what I knew about the murder at Morland Manor to the authorities here in Thornbury? Or might it serve equally well to pay a visit to Bow Street in London since they were also looking into the case? Or should I forget what I knew altogether and remain silent?

Thinking further, I realized that if Lady Morland were arrested, there would likely be long-reaching effects with disastrous results. Because Nancy Jane was in possession of the incriminating blue silk dress, to keep her out of the investigation was not possible. Then, when Sir Morland discovered the part she played in uncovering the true identity of the killer, what kind of revenge would he extract from the Abbott family? Would he toss the entire Abbott clan from the shabby little farmhouse in which they now lived, since in actuality it belonged to him and sat on his land? Uncle George would be left with no land to farm and Aunt Jane and all my cousins, including Nancy Jane, would no longer have a home. Furthermore, Nancy Jane would also be turned away with no character reference from the Morland family, meaning she could quite possibly never get another post. What then? Mr. Talbot said Sir Morland was a fair man, but from what I had seen of him . . . he was also a ruthless man. Did I dare take the risk of finding out how he would react if his beloved lady wife were accused of murder? Or convicted of *two* murders as she surely would be?

The mysteries might have been solved, that much was true, but if I said *nothing* to the authorities regarding what I knew, would justice *ever* be served? And since Sir Morland was the magistrate in this part of England, *could* it ever be served? Would he allow it?

The more I thought on it, the more I came to realize that Nancy Jane was right when she pointed out that it was up to God to extract revenge. In truth, I do believe there are two types of justice; that which is dispensed by law and the other, the more lasting sort, dispensed by God. Oddly enough, in this case, it appeared that both sentences carried the same punishment.

Clearly Lady Morland already lay upon her deathbed, which meant that God was already handing down justice for the two innocent lives she had taken. Her life was now being taken from her, and by all accounts, it was ebbing away quickly albeit in a slow, painful fashion. Perhaps this was a far worse sentence than that which would be dispensed by the law, a quick death by hanging. The further and also painful truth was, God's sentence would have been carried out even if I had not meddled with the matter. Even before I began poking around in the knot garden, His judgment had already been set in motion, and according to Scripture, it was, indeed, swift and sure.

By remaining silent and saying nothing about what I knew, I was leaving Lady Morland's sentence up to God, and at the same time, keeping my own family safe. Uncle George still had land to farm, and my aunt and cousins still had a home, and Nancy Jane, a post. I was the only one to be set adrift . . . again, but that was by my own choice. I *could* stay here, but in my heart, despite insisting that I could not stay here so long as Lady Morland lived, everything in me rebelled. I could *not* stay here. I had to leave and forget all that had happened during the short time I resided here at Morland Manor.

I had no choice.

My path was crystal clear to me now. I had to say nothing, but I also had to leave.

Saturday, 28 October 1820

By first light the next morning, I had packed up my few belongings and when a footman arrived to collect Miss Featherstone's and her sister's things, I asked Caroline if I might accompany them up to London. She joyously agreed. Apparently she had told Edward of my letter of the previous day and of the invitation it contained from Cathleen Haworth for me to come up to Town. A bit later, when we all gathered in the foyer, he did not seem at all surprised to see me.

Dawn was only then breaking on the horizon and as we waited for everyone's bags and valises to be secured atop the heavy closed carriage awaiting us on the gravel drive in front, Griggs stepped forward to announce that he had laid out coffee and scones on the sideboard in the drawing room. The four of us made our way into that chamber. I kept glancing to the double doors in the hope that Mr. Talbot might come down to say goodbye and God Speed, but he did not appear. Not even Sir Morland came down to see us off.

However, Mrs. Fullerton appeared in the drawing room and I heard her tell Edward not to worry about his mother, that she and Doctor Morgan would take good care of her.

Once we received word that all was in readiness with the carriage, we all began to head toward the foyer, and then onto the gravel drive. Suddenly, Nancy Jane scampered through the heavy front door and in the early morning mist, flung her arms around my neck with a cry.

"They said you was leavin', Juliette! I'll miss you terrible. But, don't worry none. Me Mum's a-goin' to help take care of Lady Morland. Everything will turn out right in the end, you'll see."

I hugged my little country cousin to me. "I'll miss you terrible, too, Nancy Jane. I'm glad you were here to look after me. You must write and let me know how you are getting on, and . . . and how things are . . . progressing."

"Oh, I will! I will."

"God bless you, Nancy Jane. Tell Aunt Jane I said thank you, and . . . goodbye."

Looking up, I saw that John Coachman was already seated on the bench, his long whip in hand. An outrider was mounting up while a pair of stable hands kept a strong grip on the harnesses of the lead horses, both pawing the ground in their eagerness to be off.

Once we were all comfortably settled inside the big black coach, and it jerked forward, Edward reached into his coat pocket and withdrew a small black pouch that jingled with coins. "Mother sent this down for you, Miss Abbott."

"I told her you were coming up to London with us," Caroline said. "She doesn't mind that you are going, truly she doesn't. She's a dear, sweet lady." Her gloved hand clutching the crook of her intended's elbow, she gave his arm an affectionate squeeze. "I am so looking forward to getting to know her even better after we are wed. I do hope she recovers . . . quite soon. Even before we return to Morland Manor."

Edward glanced down at Caroline. "Now, darling, I have told you what the doctor says. We must prepare ourselves."

Seated beside me, Mrs. Collins was gazing from the coach window, apparently lost in thought for she was contributing nothing to the conversation.

Before I placed the pouch Edward handed me into my reticule, I drew apart the strings and noticing there was a scrap of paper tucked inside, I withdrew it and quickly scanned the scrawled, handwritten words.

"I am aware that you took a walk in the garden, Miss Abbott. I daresay if you plan to blackmail me, you will not find me at all receptive to your demands. In the meantime, take a bit of advice from a dying woman: Watch your step, my dear. In future, you may find yourself far too clever for your own good."

"Oh, Juliette, did Lady Morland enclose a little note for you? How very sweet of her! What did I tell you, Edward, your mother is a dear. I love her almost as much as I love you!" She turned back to me. "What does she say?"

I forced a smile to my lips as I slipped the note and pouch into my reticule. "Her ladyship merely said . . . good bye. You are, indeed, a lucky young lady, Caroline. I wish you and Edward a happy, and *very* long life together."

With that, I turned and drew aside the leather curtain covering the coach window beside me in order to gaze from it into the misty countryside the heavy coach was now tooling past. For the remainder of the journey up to London, I endeavored to put all thoughts of Morland Manor from mind, and chose instead to think ahead to my own future. Whatever new adventure lay ahead of me, I hoped that at some point, it would also include seeing Mr. Talbot again . . . for he is the only part of Morland Manor that I would truly miss.

48493187R00162

Made in the USA
San Bernardino, CA
17 August 2019